T0013956

SOMETHING BETWEEN US

Visit us at www.boldstrokesbooks.com

SOMETHING BETWEEN US

by
Krystina Rivers

2022

CREDITS
EDITOR: BARBARA ANN WRIGHT
PRODUCTION DESIGN: STACIA SEAMAN
COVER DESIGN BY TAMMY SEIDICK

Acknowledgments

When I started writing this book at the beginning of the pandemic, I wasn't sure if it was going to amount to anything or if I'd even figure out how to finish it. Instead, I unleashed a passion that had long been simmering in me. Writing became a therapy of sorts to help me get through some of the difficulties we have all faced over the past two years and also something I cannot imagine living without.

Thank you to everyone at Bold Strokes Books and for accepting me onto your team. This process has gone easier than I could have hoped, and I'm grateful to everyone for your encouragement, guidance, and faith in my abilities. A huge thanks to Barbara Ann, editor extraordinaire. You made a scary process much less so and actually fun. This book is a lot better for the work we did together, so thank you for your patience with all of my rookie mistakes, occasional pushbacks, and general stubbornness.

Thank you to my entire family who was so encouraging on every step of this journey. Firstly, my ever-understanding wife, who let me bounce ideas off of her constantly, was my beta reader, and has been my biggest champion from the moment I said, "I think I'm going to try writing a book" two years ago—and the eighteen before that day as well. To Cheryl, who has been my writing friend and always sent me little encouragements at the moments I needed them most. You are without a doubt the best, and you're next. To my mom, who always helped me believe I could do anything that I put my mind to. To Mom Angel, who has been my own private marketing agent since she found out I was getting published. And to the rest of my family and friends, who have been so supportive. I love you all and couldn't have done this without you.

Finally, to those of you who honor me by picking this book up to read, I hope you enjoy reading it as much as I enjoyed writing it.

For Kerri, my champion, my rock, my love,
and the holder of my heart for the past twenty years—
and the next eighty or so.

CHAPTER ONE

Balancing four summer shandies, Kirby Davis threaded her way through a sea of undulating women to get back to her friends in the middle of the outdoor Pride concert. Kirby grumbled to herself as she stood on her toes, trying to catch a glimpse of them to verify she was on the right course. Topping out at only five four and three-quarters, she struggled to keep an eye on her group and get people to move out of her way as she passed. However, she also had the impressive talent to carry more beers than any of her friends, so she was almost always nominated to make beer runs. Since those same friends also always paid for her drinks, she generally decided to give in.

Kirby gritted her teeth as she bounced back and forth like an air hockey puck between sweaty, half-clothed women writhing under the hot June sun. Normally, she would have appreciated the view, but it was hot, and her fingers were beginning to ache from carrying the slippery beers for so long. To make matters worse, an incredibly tall woman on the left swung her elbow as she laughed. Kirby jumped to the right to avoid getting hit in the face and landed off-balance on a Converse-clad foot. Strong arms kept her from completely wiping out, and she said, "Oh my gosh, I am *so* sorry. I was trying to dodge an elbow to the nose and landed on…"

She looked up as she regained her balance and gazed into a pair of very familiar amber eyes that made her lose her balance all over again. "Oh shit…Quinn Prescott," she barely whispered as her stomach fluttered up into her throat, blocking her airway.

The feeling appeared to be mutual as Quinn stared, her eyes wide, lips slightly parted. God, those lips. That mouth. Kirby had a difficult time pulling her eyes away as Quinn moistened them with a quick flick of her tongue.

Quinn finally seemed to pull her words together—she had always been better at that than Kirby—and said, "Kirby Davis, as I live and breathe. What are you doing here?" She released her grip, and Kirby took a half step as she regained her physical balance. Her mental balance was something else entirely. Her skin tingled along the imprint left behind by Quinn's hands.

Kirby's head was still spinning as words started to fall out of her mouth of their own accord. "I live here. Well, clearly, not exactly here in this parking lot. River North, actually." It was like verbal diarrhea, and she couldn't stop her mouth from moving. "I've lived in Chicago since I got out of the Army. What are *you* doing here?"

Quinn ran her fingers through her hair, a nervous gesture Kirby recognized, causing her blond locks to cascade around her shoulders. Had it somehow gotten hotter out here? A bead of sweat trickled down Kirby's spine. "I retired a few months ago. From the Navy. I got my commission a year or so after…well, after, and I ended up finishing my career at Great Lakes. Now I'm taking a few weeks off before I start a new job downtown." She paused. "My God, what are the odds? It's been…"

Odds? She wanted to talk about odds? Quinn might be just as stunning as she'd been the last time she'd seen her, but Kirby remembered the cold heart that beat within her chest. "Yeah," Kirby interrupted. "Nine years, since, well, you know." Nine years was a long time, but when her heart had been broken into too many pieces to count, nine years wasn't nearly long enough to pretend that everything was fine.

"Yeah." Quinn replied.

"Yeah," Kirby parroted, her anger quick to rise, surging through her chest. "Well." She nodded to the beers. "I should get these back to my friends, and my girlfriend is waiting too." She inserted that last piece primarily out of spite. It was true that she was sort of seeing someone, in a very loose interpretation of the word. Marilyn was more of a friend she occasionally slept with versus an actual girlfriend. But Quinn definitely didn't need to know that.

"Oh yeah, of course, of course, your girlfriend. Of course." Quinn looked as flustered as Kirby felt. "Well, it was incredibly good seeing you, Kirby. Truly. Maybe we'll run into each other again sometime. I sincerely hope so." She touched Kirby gently on the elbow. She seemed genuine—too genuine—and Kirby had to get the hell out of there. Unwelcome nostalgia bubbling within her at Quinn's nearness was beginning to blunt the sharp edge of her anger. She feared she might do something stupid like stay and talk. Or start crying, and she couldn't let her shell crack right here in front of Quinn effing Prescott.

"Yeah, sure." Kirby said as she backed up and hightailed it the hell away at a near run. Or as near a run as she could manage given the packed crowd and the four perspiring plastic bottles she was trying to hold on to. She couldn't believe how nonchalant Quinn had seemed with seeing her.

Quinn had been the first—and only—woman to truly break her heart. The first and only one who had ever owned her heart, and she hadn't just broken Kirby's heart. She'd pulled it out of her chest, dropped it into dry ice, and then stabbed it with a jeweled Manolo pump until it had broken into so many pieces, it had taken Kirby years to put it back together. Unfortunately, as Kirby ran, that same traitorous heart was stuttering at how breathtaking Quinn was after all these years.

As Kirby walked back to her friends, the bass thrumming in her chest from the band morphed her from shellshocked to resentful. Of all the places in the world, Quinn had to settle in her adopted city. Regardless, she could process all of those feelings later. She was here to have fun and wasn't going to let Quinn Prescott ruin the day. She tried to calm her racing heart with every step she took closer to her group and hoped she'd gotten herself back under control enough so what had just happened wasn't telegraphed all over her face.

"Good God, Kirby what took you so long? Was the line for beer out the gate or something?" Her best friend, Emily, said, her gaze trained on the stage. As she looked up to reach for her beer, she stared. "Wait, are you okay? Why are you so pale? What's wrong with you? Did you throw up? Do you need to go home?"

Apparently, no such luck controlling her expression.

"Goodness, Emily, slow down," Kirby pleaded as she handed the remaining beers to their other friends, Liesel, and Marilyn.

"Thanks, lady, I was getting a little thirsty there," Liesel said, as oblivious as always. She took a sip of her beer and turned back to the stage.

"Thanks, babe." Marilyn said but also seemed to notice that something wasn't right. "Are you okay?"

"Yes, fine. Enjoy the music. I'm all good. I swear," Kirby replied with as much casualness as she could muster and smiled.

"You sure?"

Kirby's nod apparently sufficed as Marilyn gave her a wink and turned back around, watching the queer group's lead singer slink across the stage in her black leather bodysuit, singing a cover of an 80s queer anthem.

Emily took a discreet step back from Marilyn and Liesel and pulled Kirby with her. "Okay, I know you are not actually fine. Spill, woman."

"Okay, okay." Kirby needed more time to unpack everything that had transpired a few minutes ago before she attempted to talk about it, but she also knew Emily was not going to let this go unless she gave her something. She exhaled to prepare herself. "Do you remember the woman I told you about that one time you got me drunk on Red Bull and vodka? The one from the Navy? We were together for almost two years and then…" Kirby trailed off as she mimed an explosion and wiggled her fingers like debris floating everywhere.

"Of course. What was her name? Finn? Something weird. Anyway, what does she have to do with you looking like you've seen a ghost?"

"Quinn. And yeah, I feel like I saw a ghost. I almost fell on top of her when I was coming back with the beers."

"Holy mother. She's not from Chicago, is she? Why is she here? What did you say? What did she say?" Emily always talked like a machine gun when she'd had a few beers and was even worse when she was upset.

"She recently got out of the Navy and is staying here for good, starting a new job in a few weeks. What the frickety fuck? What did I do to deserve this?" Kirby groaned and took a sip of her beer, trying to wash away all the old hurt that was threatening to overtake her. Unfortunately, her throat was so tight that she had a hard time swallowing.

"Well, hey, this was a random run-in, but three million people live in this city. What are the odds of you ever running into her again? This is nothing more than a blip." Emily shook her shoulder slightly and smiled. "You are amazing, and you've moved on. This is a beautiful afternoon, we have warm sun above our heads, cold beers in our hands, and are watching a sexy bitch in a leather bodysuit strut her stuff onstage. It's a perfect afternoon, babes."

"You're right." Kirby looked back at the stage. "Damn, that woman does know how to wear leather." She could appreciate the singer and her curves, but she didn't pay much attention to the rest of the concert. Her mind had involuntarily floated back to a chilly early-December evening in 2008 in California. No matter how much Kirby wanted to deny it, there had always been chemistry between them. Her heart quickened as she remembered that first moment when their eyes had connected across the bar. Kirby scoffed at her naiveté back then.

❖

When Kirby walked away, Quinn leaned into her group of Navy acquaintances and made an excuse to get away. She needed space to breathe and think, and luckily, the lines at the porta-potties were so long, she would have time to walk and process before anyone got suspicious. Hell, they were all so drunk, she could probably disappear, and no one would notice.

As Quinn wandered away, her ears rang, and everything had a bit of a glow around it, as though a bomb had exploded nearby. She couldn't believe Kirby freaking Davis had literally fallen into her arms. And, wow, did she still look amazing. Those toned shoulders and arms exposed under that black racerback tank top looked better than the last time she'd seen them. She wished she could have held on longer after she'd saved Kirby from wiping out but without seeming creepy, but Kirby's eyes had clearly said no.

Not a day had gone by in the last nine years that she hadn't regretted how things had ended between them, and to randomly run into her in a city that neither of them had ever spoken of—but now apparently both called home—was surreal. She wished she had handled that interaction better or had at least asked for Kirby's number or email or something, anything, that she could use to contact Kirby again, but that was foolish. Kirby was so cold. Quinn didn't want to set herself up for the rejection she knew she deserved.

What she did have was the neighborhood Kirby lived in, which also happened to be where she hung her own hat these days. That was something. Quinn didn't delude herself into thinking that there was a chance for her and Kirby again, but there was so much unfinished business between the two of them. Now that they were in the same city, she could only hope that she might be able to finish some of that business. Somehow. After such an unexpected jolt, Quinn's mind drifted back to that early December night nine years ago.

CHAPTER TWO

Monterey, California, December 2008

Quinn sat at the bar, nursing her second beer and wondering why she was still sitting there. She'd always been something of an introvert, but after arriving in the city two months before, she'd felt more out of place than normal and more isolated than she had since enlisting in the Navy a decade ago. After living under the US military's anti-LGBTQ Don't Ask, Don't Tell policy for her entire adult life, Quinn was used to being very cautious about coming out to anyone new, but for the first time since basic training, she was stationed in a new city, and not a soul around her knew she was gay. Quinn smiled ruefully. As she was sitting at the bar in a gay pub, probably everyone around her assumed she was, but she didn't actually *know* any of them.

There was something about being in a new city and knowing it would likely be months before she was comfortable enough with anyone to tell them who she actually was that made her feel incredibly alone in the world. It was that deep-seated loneliness that drove her out to the only gay bar in town on this Friday night, but in all honesty, it wasn't helping her loneliness.

Quinn looked around the bar and wondered how many of the patrons were military. In a smallish town like this, where half of the population was transient military, odds were that a lot of them wore a uniform during the duty day. The men were easier to identify. They had a certain look: clean-shaven, short hair not touching the ears or collar, well-trimmed sideburns if any. The women were tougher based on appearance alone. Marine women tended to wear their hair rolled into buns in a particular way, even after-hours, and had a certain swagger that they carried at all times, but otherwise, it was almost impossible to tell. Unless they were still wearing their government-issue combat boots because they were so fresh out of basic training, Quinn thought with a snigger as one particularly baby-faced butch almost marched by in her GI boots.

Quinn had taken another swig of her beer when an entrancing laugh from the other side of the bar drew her attention. A group of six people crowded around two dartboards caught her eye. They were definitely more than two drinks in as they played a very boisterous game of darts. She thought she recognized an airman from her class, but in the dim light of the bar, it was hard to see from that distance. However, that wasn't what drew her attention: she was transfixed watching the most enchanting creature she'd ever seen in the middle of a hearty belly laugh at something the maybe-airman had said.

She was undeniably beautiful, with dark brown hair in a pixie cut that complemented piercing blue eyes that stood out even from across the bar, but there was something about her entire presence that resonated in Quinn's middle, drawing her in. The flutters in her low belly made her feel like she'd taken a shot of tequila but without the burn in her throat.

If she was braver, she'd walk over on the pretense of heading to the restroom down the corridor past the dartboards and strike up a conversation as she happened by. However, that was not at all Quinn's style—most assuredly not when the beautiful woman was surrounded by five other people—so she continued to watch as the woman lined up her next throw. There was something incredibly sexy about the way she confidently stepped up to the line. Quinn polished off her drink and ordered another one, riveted but trying not to stare.

❖

Kirby stepped her right foot up parallel to the oche and took a cleansing breath. She went through her pre-throw ritual of one slow, deep breath in through her nose and out through her mouth to clear her mind as she visualized the dart landing exactly where she needed it. At the bottom of her exhale, she fluttered her eyes open, lined up the dart, and let it fly. It sailed right into the double fourteen, ending the game. She spun around with a cocky grin and said to her best friend, Allie, "Boom, bitch, and that, my friend, is how it's done. Pay up."

Allie pouted. "Aw, come on, Kirbs, that's not even fair."

"What part isn't fair? The part where I spotted you a one-hundred-point handicap and still kicked your ass? Or ended the game on a twenty-eight-point throw? I'm not sure how much else I can do to level the playing field. Maybe I could try throwing with my left hand?" Kirby laughed back. She actually agreed with Allie that it wasn't fair, given her background, but what could she do? They insisted on playing against her for money.

"There's no reason to be an ass, you know," Allie said with a giggle that only someone who was somewhere past tipsy could achieve.

"Me? An ass? Never. Anyway, are you going to go get us another round or what? It would appear that both of our glasses are empty, and I think you owe me a drink, due to your embarrassing defeat."

"Okay, okay, but why don't you go get the drinks and put them on my tab while I hit the head? I broke the seal about an hour ago."

"You're ridiculous but sure. Malibu and pineapple?" Kirby asked with a grimace that she couldn't hide and didn't bother to try.

"Yep. And you're not going to shame me about it."

"I'm embarrassed to order such a froufrou drink, but since you're buying and all, I guess I can do it. However, I will definitely make sure Peter is aware that shit isn't for me," Kirby half laughed, half yelled as she walked to the bar.

Kirby was still laughing as she turned and noticed a sexy woman with gorgeous, long blond hair sitting on the far side of the bar. If her quick look into her beer was any indication, the blonde might just have been watching Kirby too. The next moment, she looked up again with a shy smile and made brief eye contact, sparking a tingle in Kirby all the way down in her toes. *Well, hello there.* That tingle, combined with the liquid courage already coursing through her veins, led her to make a game-time decision to walk to the other side of the bar and place her order right where there happened to be an empty seat. Serendipity.

Kirby slid onto the tall barstool and first looked to the bartender, who was chatting with someone else, and then to her right, at the woman who had captured her attention from the other side of the room. Kirby opened her mouth to introduce herself with the confidence that she only found when slightly inebriated, but no words came out as they again made eye contact. The most soulful pair of amber eyes stared into hers, and this time, Kirby felt that tingle through her entire body. She realized that she must look like a fish with her mouth open and a simple "Hi" caught on her tongue. She closed her mouth, smiled her most endearing smile, and tried again, starting with that simple, yet somehow elusive word: "Hi."

"Hi," the stranger answered, again with that shy smile that was somehow stunning despite being muted. Kirby wondered what it would take to see her full smile.

They continued to stare as if no one else was in the bar. Kirby knew it must seem as if her brain was no longer functioning, and she needed to say something, so she stammered out, "I…uh…haven't seen you here before. Are you new in town?"

As the words left her lips and her new not-quite friend started laughing, what she'd said sunk in, and, thank God, her brain finally kicked back in, though too little too late to keep her from making a fool of herself. "Shit," she said and started rambling, making it worse. "I cannot believe that trite, terrible, old pickup line just came out of my mouth and made me sound like an alcoholic. I generally have at least a little charm. Wow. Can't believe I just said that either. I must be drunker than I thought. I should probably walk away now before I embarrass myself any further." Kirby could feel the blush creeping up her neck and into her face and started to push off the barstool.

"Wait, don't leave yet." The woman lightly touched the back of Kirby's arm while unsuccessfully trying to suppress a snicker. "You haven't even ordered your drinks. I suspect your friend would be sad if you came back empty-handed. I'm Quinn, by the way." She stuck out her hand.

"Nice to meet you, Quinn. Kirby." She took Quinn's hand, certain her blush was full into her cheeks at this point. God, her hand was soft. Kirby had to remind herself to let go before she was any more awkward.

"Looked like you guys were having a pretty rousing game of darts." Quinn angled her head at where Kirby's friends were laughing.

Kirby liked the idea of Quinn watching her from across the bar. "Yeah, my friends and I like to come here on Friday nights to blow off a little steam, have a few drinks, play darts. Unfortunately for them, I've been playing since I was a little kid, and every week, they still think they're going to win. And every week, disappointment for them all." Kirby laughed at their futile attempts.

"That sounds like an…interesting…childhood. Why were you throwing darts as a kid?" Quinn ran her hand nervously through her hair, the sway of her long tresses mesmerizing Kirby.

"My parents owned a bar—still do, actually—so I spent a lot of time there after school growing up. You pick up a few things. I've always been *a bit* outgoing, so I had a lot of friends there. I've got a pretty good hand at pool, and I can make a mean old-fashioned amongst many other drinks, but that's my favorite." Kirby's childhood hadn't exactly been typical, but she'd been surrounded by so much love her entire life that she wouldn't change any of it.

"Schoolwork?" Quinn cocked her head to the side.

"That was always done first, of course, but after, I could work on whatever skill I wanted as long as it didn't require me to be of age to do it. I gravitated toward billiards, darts, a little shuffleboard, games of skill and coordination. And ones I could use in the future to generate a little cash flow." Kirby laughed, thinking of her ornery younger self.

"Wait, what?"

"That's a story for another day...once I know you a little better. And look, my friend, Peter the bartender, is here," Kirby said shifting her gaze away from Quinn and at Peter, grateful to change the subject before Quinn could press. There were some secrets that shouldn't be shared on the night she met someone. "Hey Peter, can I get—and I'm embarrassed to even say this—a Malibu and pineapple and a whiskey sour with Maker's Mark for me, easy on the simple syrup? And this should go on Allie's tab."

"Ha," Peter, the gorgeous—if a person went for that sort of thing—shirtless bartender, scoffed. "Did you school her in darts again? No surprise there, I suppose. And you think I don't know how you like your drinks, Kirbs? You insult."

"Of course. They never learn. I almost feel guilty taking her money, but she insists on betting. And sorry, I didn't mean to offend my second favorite mixologist. I know you take my drinks seriously."

"Thanks, sweetie. But second favorite?" He turned his head to the side and made pouty lips.

"My dad has to be my number one, of course. But you're a close second, and you are the only person I trust to make a whiskey sour at a bar, if it makes you feel better." Kirby laughed.

"So sweet, girl. Thank you." Peter winked and moved to make her drinks.

"Hold on a sec, Pete," she said, turning back to Quinn. "Can I get you another?"

Quinn looked into her nearly empty glass. "Sure, that'd be great."

"And another for my new friend, Quinn, please, Peter. You can put that one on my tab, though," Kirby said with her impish grin.

"Coming right up, ma'am," Peter said as he tipped an imaginary hat.

"You really do come here often, don't you?" Quinn asked Kirby with a wink as Peter retreated. "Are you actually an alcoholic despite your denials earlier?"

"Ha, no. But we do come here most Fridays, sometimes Saturdays if we're in town, depending on life and homework load, I suppose. It's so beautiful in this part of California. Sometimes I need to get out into nature on the weekends too." Kirby paused and gathered her courage. "If you're a nature person, there are some great hiking trails down in Big Sur. We could go together sometime, uh, if you're interested." For frick's sake, the stammering was back. Where had her confidence and suaveness gone? She thought she might fall down through a hole in the floor. It might be less embarrassing. Significantly less embarrassing.

Thankfully, Quinn put her out of her misery when she responded with another endearing smile and said, "That sounds nice. I'd like that."

Right then, Peter showed up with their drinks and said, "Cheers, ladies." He blew Kirby an air kiss before heading to the other end of the bar.

"Well, I should probably take this back over to the crew. I'm sure Allie is bemoaning how thirsty she is, but…" Kirby looked directly into Quinn's eyes and felt that jolt deep down again. This was definitely something *interesting*. "Would you want to come back over? Perhaps join a game of darts? They can be a bit rowdy but are a lot of fun."

Quinn hesitated as she mulled it over, and Kirby was wondering if she should run Allie's drink over and come back when Quinn spoke just loudly enough to be heard over the ambient bar sounds. "Okay, but maybe I'll just watch. I don't exactly have the best hand-eye coordination and would probably hit the wall with the wrong end of the dart."

Quinn's nervousness was endearing and, as luck would have it, gave Kirby a little more of her confidence back. "Well, I could probably be persuaded to give you a lesson if you were very nice to me. I can't give away all my secrets, but I could give you a few pointers." Kirby grinned.

Quinn laughed. "What is entailed in me being 'very nice'?"

"Nothing too arduous, I would think." Kirby slid the tip of her pinky finger along the side of Quinn's hand and looked through her eyelashes, thinking, please say yes, please say yes.

"With that type of an offer, how could I refuse?" Quinn smiled, and Kirby let out a long breath.

They slid off their barstools and walked to the back of the bar where her friends were waiting. Quinn lightly touched Kirby's back and made an after-you gesture with her other hand. Kirby could only wonder if Quinn felt the same heat building between them as the spot on her back almost burned from the touch, even through her sweater. Quinn's eyes bored into hers, so she thought the chances were good. She looked forward to confirming it.

As they walked up, Allie said, "It's about time, I'm thirsty, bitc… Oh, Petty Officer Prescott. Nice to see you this evening."

"Ah, Airman Reader," Quinn said with mild discomfort in her voice. "Nice to see you as well. While in a bar, however, please call me Quinn. For obvious reasons, of course, but also in a social setting, it's plain weird," she said with a smile.

"Of course. Of course. I'm Allie," she said with something of a gleeful grin. "I didn't know you were a…" Allie waggled her fingers as if trying to figure out what word to use.

"I am actually quite glad to hear that seeing me in class didn't scream 'I'm a lesbian' to you." Quinn laughed, and Kirby became even more enthralled.

"So you two already know each other, Quinn?" Kirby asked, looking at her and then Allie.

"Yes, we're actually in class together. Arabic, which I am sure you've already surmised." Quinn smiled. "You're also at the language institute?"

Speaking nearly inaudibly, Kirby said, "Yes. Army Specialist Kirby Davis, at your service." Discretion was imperative given the shadow of Don't Ask, Don't Tell that they all lived under, so she quietly introduced Quinn around. "Everyone, this is Quinn. We just met, but she's quite funny, and I invited her to toss a few darts with us."

Once they were all settled at the table, Kirby got another round of darts set up, this time playing against a few other acquaintances. Quinn stayed out of the game and ended up chatting with Allie when Kirby wasn't sitting. Their table was conveniently close to the boards, and Kirby eavesdropped unabashedly.

"Where are you from?" Allie asked.

"A small town in Oregon."

"That's pretty cool. It's gorgeous up there, isn't it?"

"Yes, though a bit conservative for me. I'm certain that the entire town voted for McCain last month." Quinn grimaced. "How about you?"

Allie laughed before she answered. "I'm an Army brat, so I grew up all over, but I graduated from high school in DC. My mom was stationed at the Pentagon for quite a few years."

"Oregon, huh?" Kirby said as she walked back to the table and slid onto her stool.

"Yeah, about two hours south of Portland, along the coast."

Kirby leaned in closer, nearly whispering she was so close to Quinn's ear. "Breathtaking?"

"Absolutely." Kirby could feel the warm heat of Quinn's mouth so close to her ear and missed it when she had to lean back. "I think I'll always be drawn to the ocean."

"We're near the ocean now, but do you get home often?"

Kirby didn't understand the blankness that came across Quinn's face as she answered with a flat, "No." There was more to the story, but Kirby wanted to change the subject as quickly as possible before the night was spoiled.

"I love to go down to the bay here at night and listen to the waves and the sea lions. It's so peaceful." She had never lived close to the ocean before, but Kirby found herself drawn to it and would often head down to the beach on weekend afternoons to study and relax by herself.

"I haven't done that before, but it does sound nice." Quinn hesitated for a moment and then shyly asked, "Maybe we could try that together sometime?"

"I'd like that." Had Kirby ever been so drawn to someone before?

Quinn and Kirby exchanged smiles before Kirby excused herself to play again, but the pattern continued. Quinn chatted with the group while Kirby was away, and Allie peppered her with questions that Kirby eavesdropped on. Every time Kirby came back to her seat, it seemed like she and Quinn gravitated closer and closer, until their thighs pressed against one another, and Kirby's forearm rested against the back of Quinn's stool.

When Allie went to the bar for another round, Kirby, buzzed from the bourbon she'd been drinking all night as well as the feel of Quinn's thigh against hers and the lingering looks they'd been sharing, leaned close and said, "Any interest in that lesson I promised you?"

The smoldering look Quinn sent her went straight to her crotch. "Yes." It was almost a growl. Kirby stood on less than steady legs and walked to the dartboard, bringing Quinn with her.

"Okay, this line here is called the 'oche' or toe line or throw line. Regardless, you line your foot up at or behind it for your throw. Are you right-handed?"

"Yes," Quinn answered, standing in front of Kirby.

"Perfect. I'll give you a little demo first and then walk you through the same thing, okay?" Quinn nodded. "So you stand here with your right foot parallel to the oche and your right shoulder pointing toward the dartboard. I like to stand a little to the left of the bull's-eye. I find it helps my alignment, but to each her own." Kirby had slipped into teacher mode, but as soon as she looked at Quinn for a breath, she felt that same heat hit her squarely in the stomach again. She smiled and tried to settle her stomach, realizing she probably shouldn't look at Quinn if she wanted to keep her wits about her.

She shook her head at herself and turned back to the dartboard. "Feel the balance between your front and back feet. Before you throw, you'll put about eighty percent of your weight on your front foot, but I like to shift my weight back and forth while I'm shaking out the kinks and getting loosened up." She exaggerated her rocking forward and back.

"Bring your elbow up in line with your shoulder and take a breath as you line up your target with the circle between your thumb and index finger. Lean to the front and make a few practice movements like this." Kirby looked at Quinn and loosely mimed the throwing motion. "Then release as you breathe out." Kirby looked back to the board and threw the dart perfectly into the triple twenty. "See? Easy. Ready to give it a try?"

"You make it look easy, but I suspect there's a lot more to it than that," Quinn replied dryly.

Kirby laughed and said, "Well, there's only one way to find out. Step over and I'll walk you through it."

After a moment's hesitation, Quinn moved into the spot that Kirby vacated and looked at the dart like it might bite her. She glanced over at Kirby and said, "Like this?"

"Sort of, but you look like the Tin Man." Kirby stepped behind Quinn and placed her hands on her hips, gently turning them slightly from side to side to loosen her up. "You've got to relax as you stand here." She couldn't help but move in a bit closer and press her hips against Quinn's, rocking them and taking a shaky breath as she tried to help Quinn relax. The feel of Quinn's hips against hers made it a bit difficult to take a full breath, so Kirby settled for shallow ones instead. "Feel the difference?" she asked.

"I think so," Quinn answered in an unsteady tone.

Relieved she was not the only one affected by their proximity,

Kirby pulled her hips a bit more firmly into Quinn's and breathed in the intoxicating scent of her hair, perhaps sweet pea but something else too.

"Okay, once you feel a bit more relaxed, raise your elbow in line with your shoulder, keeping your wrist over your elbow."

When Quinn lifted her arm, Kirby slid her right arm around to Quinn's stomach and said, "Now, pull your belly button in toward your spine and lean your weight on your right foot."

Quinn took in a sharp breath but did as instructed and whispered on a soft chuckle, "Now what?"

"Move your forearm forward and back a few times to get the feel of the dart, bringing the tail back until it barely grazes your chin." Seeing the tips of Quinn's fingers turning white, she brought her hand up to Quinn's, lightly grazing her fingers and added, "Loosen your grip. Imagine you're gripping a perfect feather, and you don't want to break it, but you also don't want to drop it. Very good. Now, line up the bull's-eye. Close your eyes and take a breath in through your nose and slowly out of your mouth while you visualize the dart flying right into the bull's-eye. Once you reach the bottom of your exhale, slowly open your eyes, verify your alignment, and let the dart fly."

"I'm not sure I'm going to be capable of throwing anything like this," Quinn whispered.

"I have faith in you," Kirby said, her mouth directly behind Quinn's ear as she stood on her tiptoes to even their heights, but she did take a small step back to give Quinn some breathing room.

Quinn followed all of Kirby's directions and threw the dart. Kirby watched it sail toward the board and land in the bottom half, slightly above the three.

"Nice." Kirby pulled Quinn into her arms before she realized what she was doing. "That was amazing for your first throw. You'll be a pro in no time."

Quinn chuckled. "I'm not sure how good of a throw it was, but it hit the board, so I'm going to take it as a win. And retire from my professional career."

As Quinn's chuckle turned into a laugh, Kirby realized how close they were. She could feel Quinn's breasts against her own. Feel the shuddering breath that Quinn let out. She looked into Quinn's eyes and saw the same desire she felt. She shifted her gaze to Quinn's mouth, then back up to her eyes. Her heart was beating so hard, she wondered if the entire bar could see her ribs pulsing.

Quinn leaned in, and Kirby was sure they were about to kiss, but instead, Quinn whispered, "Do you want to get out of here?"

Kirby slowly nodded. Quinn grabbed her hand and pulled her to the door, stopping briefly at the bar to close out their tabs.

Once outside, Kirby dropped Quinn's hand in unspoken agreement, in case anyone who knew them as military saw them walking together, though coming out of a gay bar with a blazing rainbow flag hanging over the door probably would give them away anyway. Sometimes, Kirby wondered at their boldness even going to a gay bar in a small military town. "Where's your car parked?" Kirby asked her quietly.

"I walked here," Quinn said. "You?"

"I rode with Allie. Shit, I should text her and let her know we left." When Kirby looked up from her phone, Quinn was looking at her with an intensity that made her instantly wet. "What?"

Quinn grabbed her hand and pulled her a few steps into an alley. Once they were off the street, Quinn spun her around, pushed her up against the side of the building, and crashed their lips together in a searing kiss. Kirby threaded her hands into Quinn's hair as she pressed her hips forward, tilting her pelvis ever so slightly. Quinn slid her tongue delicately along Kirby's lower lip, and Kirby opened, taking her in. Goose bumps broke out along Kirby's arms as Quinn deepened the kiss and moaned into her mouth. Kirby pushed off the wall, reversing their positions, and slid her hand along Quinn's side and under her sweater.

Quinn groaned and pulled back, her eyes unfocused. "Do you want to come back to my place? I'm only a few blocks from here."

"Definitely," Kirby breathed.

Kirby grabbed Quinn's hands and pulled her off the wall and out of the alley. "Let's make it a quick walk," she said with a smile.

They walked side by side on the sidewalk, intentionally not touching, though every few steps, the backs of their hands grazed. It seemed as though an unseen force was pushing them together over and over again. The air felt thick with anticipation. To lighten the mood, Kirby asked, "How long have you been in the Navy?"

"Nine years. This was my first training location back in 2000. I was here for 9/11."

"Wow, that must have been intense. I was a sophomore in high school, and I can't imagine what it would have been like to be serving at that time. Did you serve overseas?" September 11 felt like a lifetime ago, but their brothers and sisters in arms were still serving overseas in unending wars, and she hoped that nothing too tragic had befallen Quinn in her years of service.

"Yes, but on a ship only, never on the ground. Benefit of being in the Navy, I guess," she said with a slight chuckle.

The backs of their hands brushed again, and Quinn shivered. Kirby caught one of Quinn's fingers and intertwined their hands.

"Not worried about being seen?" Quinn asked, her voice strained. Her hand stiffened but didn't let go.

"Well, it's dark, this street is deserted now that we are off the main road, it's after midnight, and we're off base. The odds seem good no one we know will happen upon us. Plus, I can't seem to stop touching you." When Quinn's fingers relaxed, Kirby grabbed her by the shirt and pulled her in for another kiss. "You don't have any military neighbors, do you?" Kirby mumbled against her mouth.

"Good thing for both of us, I do not." Quinn pushed Kirby against a tree as she deepened the kiss. "Though we're literally a half block from my house, so…"

Kirby heard Quinn's words but was entirely too distracted by the feel of her mouth and the press of her body to be the one to break their kiss and pull them that last half block.

CHAPTER THREE

When they finally made it into Quinn's house, Quinn barely got the door closed and locked before Kirby spun her around and shoved her up against it. Her mind went blank as Kirby slid her hands under Quinn's sweater and up her back. Quinn heard someone moan as their mouths collided, but she wasn't sure if it was her or Kirby.

Kirby began kissing a trail up her jawline to her ear. When Kirby gently nipped her earlobe and licked a path along her ear, Quinn's knees went weak, and she tipped her head against the door with a thud.

The dull bite of pain brought Quinn's wits back, and she decided she was tired of being passive. She pushed Kirby's jacket off her shoulders and spun her around, quickly reversing their positions and pinning Kirby's arms over her head. She looked into Kirby's lust-filled eyes and dipped her head to bring their mouths together again. The electric connection was like nothing she had ever experienced. It was like a drug. She could stand there kissing Kirby for an eternity and not get tired of it. But she didn't want to *only* kiss her.

Quinn slid her thigh into Kirby's center and was rewarded with a deep gasp. When Kirby rolled her hips against Quinn, the pressure on Quinn's clit was almost too much, even through her jeans. She began grinding wantonly against Kirby but didn't care. She had no shame.

If she didn't get some of their clothes off soon, they would both spontaneously combust, so she released Kirby's hands and dragged her fingers down her arms to the hem of Kirby's sweater. But before she could lift, Kirby tugged Quinn's own top up. Quinn realized that it didn't matter who won this race, so she ceded to Kirby and allowed her sweater to be pulled over her head first. A shiver ran up her spine both from the slight chill and the yearning in Kirby's eyes as they raked over her nearly bare skin.

Quinn took the momentary pause to also relieve Kirby of her top. She gazed at the swell of Kirby's breasts above the edge of her lacy black bra, and her mouth begin to water. She ducked and pressed a kiss into that cleavage, savoring the soft swell of Kirby's breasts against her cheeks. She dropped to her knees and took a breast into her mouth through the lace and scraped her teeth along the rapidly hardening nipple. Kirby's moan of pleasure almost undid her as Kirby's back arched, pulling her in closer.

Quinn drew Kirby in tighter with one hand while she palmed the breast that wasn't covered by her mouth, drawing another long moan from Kirby. "God, you're unbelievable," Kirby said.

When Quinn looked up, Kirby pulled her to her feet again.

"Fuck." Kirby groaned and pushed them away from the door. "Bedroom."

Quinn nodded and started to walk backward, their mouths again fused together, but Kirby apparently thought she was moving too slowly and ran them into the back of the couch, tipping them over it.

They landed in a tangle of arms and legs, half-on and half-off the couch in the middle of the room. Quinn couldn't help but laugh as Kirby pressed down into her. "Are you okay?" she asked over their laughter.

"Yeah, sorry. I think I forgot to mention, I'm a bit clumsy."

"Probably good you waited until I was in deep. It might have been a deal breaker for me two hours ago." Quinn tried to deadpan but couldn't hold that tone for long and started laughing again. She awkwardly attempted to adjust into a more comfortable position, pulling her dangling legs over the back of the couch and bringing Kirby with her.

Kirby, laughing from deep in her belly, asked, "Now who's the clumsy one?"

"It may have been an inelegant maneuver, but it was effective. Now get back here." She pulled Kirby into her. In the shuffle, Kirby's thigh slipped between Quinn's again, and the friction had them both squirming.

Quinn reached behind Kirby and unfastened her bra, freeing her perfectly palm-sized breasts. Quinn cupped them and ran her thumbs over their nipples. Kirby said with a purr, "Please, Quinn."

Quinn was happy to oblige and rolled one nipple between her thumb and forefinger as she took the other into her mouth, alternating between delicately scraping with her teeth and soothing with her tongue. She wasn't sure if she had ever felt something more sensuous than Kirby sliding her hips back and forth along her thigh as Quinn ravished her breasts. Until Kirby unhooked Quinn's bra and wrapped her fingers around her breasts as well.

"Pants," Kirby mumbled. Quinn tried to shift her hips to allow Kirby to slide her hand into Quinn's pants and groaned in frustration when she still couldn't find the right angle.

"Bed. More room." Quinn released Kirby's nipple. They had both apparently lost the ability to speak like adults, but short fragments were getting the job done.

Kirby pushed up and reached to help Quinn stand. "Why don't you lead the way this time since you actually know where the bedroom is? And are unlikely to topple us over any other furniture." Kirby grinned when Quinn took her hand and led her to a door off the living room.

Quinn paused for a moment at the foot of her bed and took in the sight of Kirby, topless, in low-slung skinny jeans. She swallowed hard. Kirby had a trim waist and the perfect amount of definition in her shoulders. Her arms were sculpted like Michelle Obama's but sexier. Definitely sexier.

"You're overdressed," Kirby said.

"You too." Quinn pulled her closer and unbuttoned her pants, sliding them down her hips to expose black lace hipster panties that matched the bra that was somewhere out in the living room. Quinn felt a momentary pang of regret that she hadn't gotten to see Kirby in the full bra and panty combo but hoped she would have another chance later. She tried to drink in the view, but Kirby was already reaching for her pants.

Once she'd dispatched Quinn's remaining clothes and shoved her own panties down her legs, Kirby stood on her tiptoes and pulled their naked bodies together, starting with their breasts. At that light touch, Quinn's clit pulsed painfully, and she captured Kirby's lips again in a scorching kiss. The next thing Quinn knew, she was tumbling onto the bed with Kirby on top of her. If there was a heaven, Quinn was certain it would involve Kirby's body moving on top of hers, pushing all thoughts other than physical sensation from her mind.

Kirby's mouth began a trail similar to her earlier path, but rather than stopping at Quinn's ear, Kirby moved southward, pressing kisses and little love bites along her collarbone and chest. She paused at each nipple to smother it with attention before continuing farther.

Every place that Kirby kissed was set ablaze. Quinn threaded her fingers into Kirby's short hair, savoring the texture in the spaces between her fingers and loving the little purr Kirby emitted when she lightly massaged her scalp. When Kirby's slow journey reached the apex of Quinn's thighs, Quinn was certain she was going to combust and tried to press her hips into Kirby and bring her mouth where she most needed it.

But Kirby continued down the outside of Quinn's right leg and back up the inside. Quinn couldn't decide if she preferred the sharp bite or the soothing motion of Kirby's tongue, but she squirmed under her touch, silently begging for more. She prayed as Kirby reached the top of her inner thigh, but Kirby just exhaled a warm breath across her center as she moved to Quinn's other leg.

Quinn thought she might explode if Kirby didn't touch her soon. "Please touch me, Kirby. Don't make me beg."

"I *am* touching you. Can't you feel me?" she said and gently bit Quinn's sensitive inner thigh.

"That's not what I meant. Please, Kirby." Quinn groaned and arched her hips. Kirby finally took mercy on her and drew her into her mouth. Kirby's tongue on her clit was heavenly. Quinn didn't want to rush, but after all the teasing, she was so close. Kirby slid one finger into her, and she cried out with pleasure as Kirby found a steady rhythm.

Quinn began rocking her hips faster and faster. She desperately needed something to hold on to for leverage. She curled her fingers into the firm fabric of her mattress as her orgasm began to build. It started in her toes and then in her chest before, with one final thrust of Kirby's fingers, she shattered into a thousand pieces. She tried to halt Kirby's movements with her thighs and cried, "Oh God, please. Wait a sec. Wait. Stop. Please!"

Kirby pressed one final kiss to her outer lips before crawling upward, her finger still firmly inside Quinn. "Hi," she whispered.

Quinn tried to find some words—any words—but she was too tired. She rolled her head toward Kirby and smiled, despite how hard it was to keep her eyes open. Kirby softly brushed their lips together.

"Wow," Kirby whispered as she snuggled into Quinn's shoulder and draped her leg across Quinn's.

Quinn was finally starting to catch her breath and gasped when Kirby slowly slid her finger out. She felt the relief and loss simultaneously. "Wow doesn't begin to describe…" She sighed. "Just give me another minute and I'll be able to form an actual sentence. And be ready to go again."

"Take your time. I'm catching my breath too."

Kirby wound her fingers in Quinn's hair and rubbed her head in a soothing circular pattern. A wave of peacefulness washed over Quinn, and she wanted almost nothing more than to close her eyes and surrender to the post-orgasmic haze. But the one thing she wanted more was to bring at least a fraction of the same pleasure to Kirby. She shifted her hips to gain the leverage she needed, then flipped them over so Kirby was on her back.

Quinn loved the feel of their naked, sweaty skin sliding together. She ran one finger between Kirby's slick folds and groaned at how wet she was before rolling her hips between Kirby's thighs and pressing the lowest part of her belly into Kirby's very wet center. Quinn had never before realized that her abs were an erogenous zone, but the feel of Kirby's wetness pressing into her was so erotic, Quinn was pretty sure that any pressure, direct or indirect, on her clit might send her over the edge again.

Quinn started to rock her hips slowly as she brought her mouth to Kirby's in a long, slow kiss and interlaced their fingers above Kirby's head. Kirby's newly adjusted angle lifted her breasts up tantalizingly, and Quinn couldn't resist them. She broke off their kiss and moved her mouth back to smother Kirby's chest in light kisses.

Kirby began to push her hips harder into Quinn's stomach as if looking for more friction, and Quinn was happy to answer by sliding her hand between Kirby's legs and into her wet heat once again. Quinn still couldn't believe how wet she was and drove her hips into the mattress, looking for a little friction of her own.

Kirby freed one hand and gripped Quinn's back, her fingernails scraping lightly from the bottom of her ribs up along her spine, leaving fiery trails in their wake and driving Quinn a little wild. She slid two fingers into Kirby as Kirby moved her leg between Quinn's, allowing her to grind against it.

Quinn found a steady tempo, plunging her fingers into Kirby while riding her thigh. Looking at Kirby's face almost made her come again. She was flushed, and several rivulets of sweat ran down her forehead. Her hair was mussed, and she was biting the right side of her lip. Quinn lightly sucked on Kirby's neck as she pressed her thumb directly on Kirby's swollen clit. She didn't expect Kirby to rear up and sink her teeth into Quinn's shoulder as she came, but that sharp bite sent Quinn tumbling right after her. As her second orgasm ripped through her, Quinn collapsed half on top of Kirby.

"Holy Mother," was the last thing Quinn heard as she drifted to sleep, but she wasn't entirely certain if it had been uttered from her mouth or Kirby's.

CHAPTER FOUR

Quinn's hands shook in a private show of nerves as she buttoned the last button on the jacket of her pantsuit on Monday morning, the first day of her post-Navy professional career. It was the first time since she'd worked at Blockbuster in high school that she wasn't putting on a military uniform to start her workday, which seemed to be contributing to those pesky, first-day-of-school jitters. She wasn't as shy as she used to be, but she was still nervous about being the new kid on the block in a whole new industry. What if she wasn't good enough?

Stop. She reminded herself that she was ready for this. Her military experience and graduate degrees had prepared her, and she was ready to kick a little ass.

Quinn watched her chest rise and fall as she took a long calming breath and stared at herself in the mirror. She was grateful that she'd splurged for a few tailored suits. She was ready to start this next chapter, but knowing she looked good provided her with a modicum of additional confidence to face this first day. Until a few weeks ago, when she retired after putting in her twenty years, she had spent her entire adult life as a sailor, but at the tender age of thirty-seven, she was starting a new career while being lucky enough to draw a pension for the rest of her life.

She'd been living near Chicago for three years and was ecstatic to have been able to find a job so quickly in her adopted city. Especially one that allowed her to buy a condo within walking distance of her new office. It had never occurred to her as a child that she might someday find a home in the Midwest, but it had happened. There was simply something magical about this city.

Quinn loved its mix of big-city charm and culture with generally friendly people, not like the rude attitudes so common to people in the Northeast or the self-importance of so many folks on the West Coast. The food, the culture, the pizza, the people, the lake were a combination that had wormed its way into Quinn's heart, so while she'd always assumed that when she'd retired from the Navy, she would move back somewhere on the West Coast—though not her small, conservative hometown—she found that when the time came, she wanted to stay.

As Quinn turned her head from side to side, checking her reflection to make sure she was put together perfectly for her first day, her mind wandered back to Kirby, as it had been doing frequently the past few weeks since she'd run into her at Pride. Kirby had always loved it when Quinn dressed up. It didn't matter if she was in a suit, a dress, or her dress uniform, Kirby hadn't been able to keep her hands to herself when Quinn was in formal wear.

With her subtly pinstriped pantsuit tailored to her figure, her French twist, and her subdued jewelry, Quinn knew she looked good and was ready to impress at her new job. There was also a little piece of her that couldn't help but hope that today might be the day that she would run into Kirby on the street since they were almost neighbors, even though she didn't know exactly where Kirby lived.

With a frustrated huff, she pushed Kirby from her mind. She certainly didn't have the time for that distraction on her first day of work. She checked her hair one more time to be sure that no unintentional strands had slipped out of her updo, gave her rescue mutt, Fred, a kiss on the nose, grabbed her briefcase, and headed out the door. Since it was her first day, and it was already a sweltering July morning, Quinn decided to treat herself and take a taxi to work. She wouldn't do it every day, as she loved walking, and it was wasteful, but a sweaty mess was not the first impression she was looking to make.

The day was a blur between the HR meetings, benefits overview, getting an ID badge, lunch with her new team, and a whirlwind of paperwork, plus the added stress of meeting so many new people whose names she definitely wasn't going to remember, at least not without a reminder or two. With all of the bureaucracy of starting work at a Fortune 500 company, she felt like she was still in the Navy. As the day was winding to a close, one of her new coworkers, she thought her name was Nora, stopped by Quinn's office.

"Want to grab a glass of wine this evening once you wrap up that paperwork?" maybe-Nora asked. Her wide smile was warm and put

Quinn at ease. "There's a great place around the corner, Once Upon a Wine, that has the best selection in the city, and after all the drudgery of a first day, I figure you could use a glass. I definitely could."

"Sure," Quinn said. "Give me maybe fifteen more minutes here to wrap up?" It had been exhausting talking to so many new people all day, but the chance to connect with one person in a more relaxed setting, while still stressful, was much less scary. She also could use a glass of wine after being out of her comfort zone all day.

"Great." She smiled again. "Swing by my office when you're finished, and we can head down. I'm two offices down, in case you forgot." She pointed her chin to the left, and her voluminous mahogany curls swayed with the movement.

"Sounds good and thanks for the reminder. I suspect I'm going to be walking around a little lost for a few days. Probably normal in an office this size," Quinn said, feeling a little lift that she was already making a new friend on her first day. She was never the type who'd needed a ton of friends and tended to be a loner in general, but she still wanted to fit in. No one liked the awkward girl who didn't talk, Quinn reminded herself. She'd been reminding herself of that all day.

When Quinn walked down the hall, she noted a little nameplate on the door and took note. Thank goodness for the small favor of nameplates in corporate America, she thought. Although everyone walking around with their names plastered across their chests while in uniform certainly still made life easier, nameplates were something anyway. "Hi, Nylah. Ready for that glass of wine? I can hear it calling my name." Smile, Quinn, she reminded herself. Relax.

To Quinn's relief, she and Nylah fell into an easy conversation on their walk over to Once Upon a Wine. "Thanks for inviting me out this evening. The first day of a new job is like starting a new school in the middle of the year. Everyone is already in a clique, and I'm merely hoping to remember everyone's name. You would think with my military background, it would be easier, but it's a whole new world. All of that to say, I am definitely ready for a tall pour of wine."

Nylah let out a laugh. "Just wait until you're through all of the new hire stuff. Things are crazy right now with our expansion. They want everything yesterday. But I am absurdly happy that they hired another woman for the team. I've been working with these guys for more than five years, and I love them like brothers, but sometimes, the testosterone becomes exhausting. It's why I thought we could grab a drink together and get to know each other. As the only women on the team, we have to stick together."

"I feel you. I've been working in a male-dominated industry for twenty years, so I *am* at home but definitely value this." Quinn pointed her thumb back and forth between them, truly appreciating their developing sisterhood. In her over two decades as a working adult, Quinn always appreciated having a network of female friends and colleagues in an almost secret club amidst the never-ending sea of men.

"Definitely. Here we are." Nylah gestured to an unassuming storefront at the base of a high-rise with a cork on a corkscrew hovering over a wine bottle on the glass door.

Quinn was charmed by the little wine bar when she and Nylah walked in. It was relatively busy but not so busy that they couldn't get a table. The space had a classy, Napa Valley tasting room feel, with stone walls—faux, Quinn assumed—along the perimeter and mahogany racks of wine storage along the others. It also had an industrial chic feel to it that invited her to sit down and simply…savor. She couldn't help but think back to the amazing long weekend that she and Kirby had spent at a little bed and breakfast in Napa while they'd toured the countryside, visited too many tasting rooms, and worked in some hiking to burn off the extra wine calories. It was also the trip where they'd shared three simple words with one another that had changed everything and yet changed nothing at the same time.

"Hey, are you okay?" Nylah asked. "You look like you've gone somewhere else all of a sudden."

"Oh yes, sorry. I was thinking of how this place reminds me of a tasting room in Napa that I went to a lifetime ago. Didn't mean to zone out. I haven't looked at the wine list yet, but I am beyond thirsty. What would you recommend so we can order as soon as the server arrives? I'll peruse the list before our second glass."

"I like your style, my new friend. What's your poison generally? Red, white, rosé?"

"Definitely red. I know it's not the right weather for it, but I can't help it. I could drink red wine three hundred and sixty-five days a year. Plus, it's air-conditioned in here."

"No judgment from me. How about red blends? They have an amazing bourbon-barrel-aged red blend from Monterey County. To. Die. For."

Bourbon. Of course it had to be bourbon. Bourbon only brought one thing to mind. Or one person: Kirby and how bourbon tasted on her tongue, her skin. That sexy look Kirby got in her eyes after a sip of a particularly good old-fashioned. Shit. And Monterey County. Fuck. But she didn't want to explain why she didn't want to try it, so she plastered on a smile and said, "Sure, I've never had a bourbon-barrel-aged red, but it sounds intriguing. I'll give it a go."

"Adventurous. I knew we were going to be fast friends." Once Nylah had placed their order, she said, "I know you had a career in the Navy, and I've seen your resume, but I don't know much else. Who are your sports teams?"

Quinn chuckled at the abrupt change of subject. "That's not quite the question I thought you were going to ask."

"It's Chicago, it's the first question anyone asks when getting to know someone."

"True. I grew up in Oregon with few professional teams, so I don't have childhood allegiances." Quinn's family also didn't have patience for something as frivolous and immoral as sports and never allowed her or her siblings to watch any. Ever. Her dysfunctional family made her feel shame like nothing else and was *not* something she was planning to share with anyone, however. "Though I do like sports, all sorts. And in my adopted city, I've grown to love all of the Chicago teams. I'm a northsider, so definitely Cubs not Sox. I was here when they won their first World Series in a hundred years. How can that not win you over? How about you?"

"Ha. Ask a Sox fan. I think they'd disagree. I'm from St. Louis, so I'm a dreaded Cardinals fan…and a Blues fan. I was a Rams fan until they moved to Southern California, but I can't get past that betrayal, so now I cheer for my fantasy team."

"Ugh. I'm not sure if I can keep sharing wine with you after that. St. Louis *and* you have more loyalty to your fantasy team than an actual football team? This friendship might be over before it even begins," Quinn deadpanned.

Nylah laughed. "But then you wouldn't get my next wine recommendation."

"Fair point. And this one is delicious." Despite the baggage associated with it, the wine was spectacular, particularly for its price. "I suppose I can look past your poor taste in sports teams for wine recommendations. So what's up next?"

"One more, but then I have to get home, or my boyfriend Nate will get cranky since I didn't give him a heads-up that I was going to be late.

What are you in the mood for? Full-bodied like a cab? Or something a little lighter like a pinot?" Quinn felt a pang at not having anyone who cared when she got home. She'd thought that she'd been fine, but since running into Kirby a few weeks earlier, she'd been thinking a lot lately about what it would be like if she hadn't messed things up so long ago. Or if she had found some way to mend their relationship once she'd realized what an idiot she'd been.

"The cab and agreed on only one more. Tomorrow is only my second day. I need to be bright-eyed and bushy tailed. Though this is the most fun I've had in a while. We should absolutely do it again." Quinn was surprised that she meant that. She and Nylah had an easy camaraderie, and Quinn was able to simply relax and enjoy herself rather than stay on guard as she normally was in social interactions.

They laughed and talked through a second glass of wine, and Quinn was relieved at having established an ally at work and a new friend all on her first day. Also, a glass or two of wine always went a long way in settling her nerves when meeting new people. "Thank you for suggesting this. It feels so good to know that I have a friend amidst all of the newness, and the wine has definitely taken the edge off."

"Well, thank you too for coming. This has been fun, and I look forward to many more of these wine dates."

"Hope you don't get in too much trouble with your boyfriend."

"Eh, he'll be fine. Get home safe and see you in the morning. Do you have anyone waiting for you to come home?"

"Only a cranky dog named Fred. He's the canine equivalent of Fred Mertz from—"

"I love that you named your dog after *I Love Lucy*. Does he complain about his every ache and pain and try to prevent all fun?"

"Of course," Quinn said. "I met him at the shelter, and he just looked so grumpy I couldn't help but take him home. He isn't an old man, but he certainly acts like one. He loves love, though, and nothing makes him happier than snuggling all afternoon on a rainy Sunday." Fred didn't fill the hole she still had in her heart from breaking Kirby's, but he did help. He was a great snuggler and reminded her that someone thought she was worthy of love.

Nylah laughed out loud. "Well, don't keep him waiting too long."

Because it was about a fifteen-minute walk back to her condo, Quinn decided to use the restroom before she headed out. As she was pushing the door, she heard a familiar voice from behind her say, "You've got to be effing kidding me."

Quinn spun and felt that familiar pull in her low belly as she said, "Well, hello to you too, Kirby. Small world." Despite Kirby's open hostility, Quinn resolved to kill her with kindness, so she dialed the wattage up on her smile. It wasn't even hard because Quinn was practically giddy at seeing Kirby, despite the less than friendly greeting. And damn, was Kirby looking good in her light-charcoal-gray skirt suit and black silk camisole. She'd added a splash of color with an airy red scarf knotted around her neck that matched her anger and coordinated with her tall red pumps—not quite high enough to bring Kirby up to Quinn's eye level in her own heels, but close—and very sexy. She balled her right hand into a tight fist to keep from swiping an errant chunk of Kirby's bangs that was resting in the center of her forehead instead of being swept to the side with the rest.

"What are you doing here all dressed up?" Kirby asked through a tightly clenched jaw, as if Quinn were the root of her bad mood, which she probably was.

Quinn stumbled at the severity. She was excited to see Kirby, but it was hard to stay enthusiastic when Kirby was so blatantly irritated. "It's, uh, my first day at my new job. I work right around the corner, and one of my new colleagues invited me for a drink. It's a quaint little place."

"Eh. It's fine." Kirby shrugged as if feigning apathy.

"Doesn't it make you think of that little tasting room in Napa? The one that we bought all that wine from and joined their wine club? With the outdoor dining room?" As if it would actually take that many descriptors for Kirby to remember the place she was talking about. They had visited many vineyards on their Napa trip, but only one had become "their place." Quinn hoped that if she could appeal to Kirby's nostalgia, tap into all the happy memories they'd shared at the vineyard and over the bottles of wine they'd purchased, she might get Kirby to soften. Even a fraction.

Quinn saw a flash of something that might have been heat in Kirby's eyes and a slight flare of her nostrils before she said flatly, "That was so long ago, I can barely remember it." She looked around the room and shrugged again. "There might be some minor similarities."

Quinn was under no illusions that Kirby wanted to keep running into her or wanted to even be friendly, but she couldn't seem to help pushing. She didn't want to sound desperate. She wanted to give Kirby time to come around on her own, but being so close and not being able to touch her was physically painful. "I still belong to that wine club, you know. I've never been able to cancel it, and it's just as good as it ever was. I think of you every tim—"

"Well, that's great that you still enjoy it. I haven't actually had that label since 2010. Something about it just didn't taste the same after. Too bitter. Sorry, I have to get back." She abruptly stomped in the opposite direction to a table filled with other corporate-looking suits, and Quinn wondered if she had achieved her goal of becoming a high-powered financier. She certainly looked the part.

As Kirby stormed off, Quinn thought she heard something like, "In a city of almost three million people, why the hell do I keep running into her?" But she wasn't certain.

It wasn't exactly what she was hoping for, but Quinn felt a smile tug at the corner of her mouth from having run into Kirby again. Finding out that Kirby likely worked somewhere nearby, meaning they lived in the same neighborhood and worked near one another, was an unexpected bonus. Even if the interaction didn't give her a chance to actually do or say anything impactful, if she and Kirby kept running into each other, she might eventually be able to…she didn't know what, but she couldn't help but hope.

She had wanted to reach out to Kirby every day for the past nine years, but after behaving so poorly, so heartlessly, she hadn't been able to bring herself to do it. What could she possibly say or do to fix things? These chance meetings, however, gave Quinn a small spark of hope for…something. It was clear that Kirby still had a lot of anger, but it meant she felt something, and Quinn was reasonably certain something was better than nothing at all. It felt like for the first time in a decade, maybe the Fates were conspiring with them for a change rather than against them.

❖

Kirby stalked away from Quinn, pounding her feet so forcefully into the concrete that she could feel the vibrations in her teeth. Running into Quinn at Pride had been shocking but manageable. It was outside of her normal routine, and there had been nothing to indicate that there would be a repeat. But seeing her here, at her favorite after-work happy hour locale, simply was not acceptable.

At least she didn't lose her words this time. She was able to quip back and make it perfectly clear that she had no desire to chit-chat. Not that she'd had many witty comebacks, but at least she didn't stand there like a moron with her mouth hanging open or something equally embarrassing.

Even with her anger seething, Kirby was forced to admit that Quinn looked amazing in that pinstripe suit that appeared to be handmade for her, paired with those incredibly high heels that Kirby was never sure how she walked in. Shit, Kirby thought as she shook her head at herself. She had always been a sucker for a woman in a suit. Particularly that woman. She briefly wondered if banging her head into the wall would expel the image that she knew would stick with her for the rest of the night.

Kirby walked back over to the table and downed about three-quarters of her glass of wine. She tried to get back into the conversation with her colleagues to give Quinn enough time to clear out before she went back to the restroom, but it was difficult. Seeing Quinn threw her off her game, and Quinn had been right: this bar looked very much like that tasting room in Napa.

She was lying when she'd said she could barely remember it. In fact, almost everything she had said to Quinn in both of their recent meetings had been lies. She unfortunately could remember that tasting room in vivid detail, along with the rest of that weekend. It was one of the best long weekends she'd ever had.

CHAPTER FIVE

Napa Valley, California, February 2009

In the months since their first night together, Quinn and Kirby had spent nearly every waking moment together when not in uniform, so when Quinn asked if she wanted to go to Napa together for the upcoming Presidents' Day long weekend, Kirby had readily accepted. They were both eager to spend time together like a normal couple without worrying about who might see them, and after an afternoon spent hiking around the hills of Napa, alternated with a couple of tastings at vineyards around the valley, Kirby and Quinn headed to their B and B to get checked in and cleaned up for dinner. Kirby was eager to see what Quinn had planned for them; all Quinn said was to "dress up" and be prepared to be outside.

Because it was unseasonably warm, Kirby had chosen a simple but elegant one-shoulder black dress with a slim line through the hips and thighs and a slash of red across her chest. She knew Quinn would be wearing ridiculously high heels again, so Kirby went with a modest two-inch-heeled, strappy sandal that would be manageable to walk in but still keep her head in line with Quinn's shoulder. It was so frustrating how Quinn managed to walk with grace in absurdly high heels. Frustrating and yet hot, Kirby had to admit.

Kirby finished sliding the back onto her right earring and was checking that they looked good with her hair when she saw Quinn stepping out of the bathroom in the reflection, and Kirby lost her ability to breathe. It was the first time she'd seen Quinn dressed up in something more formal than her working blues, and Quinn had dressed to impress in a pair of slim-fitting dark pants, paired with a long-sleeved white dress shirt unbuttoned almost to indecency, and a vest that appeared to be tailored to emphasize her every perfect curve. With her blond hair flowing around her shoulders, she looked like something out of a sex dream. Kirby couldn't put into words exactly how stunning Quinn was and contemplated trying to convince her that they should stay in so she could unwrap this gift, but Quinn broke the heavy quiet first.

"You look exquisite. I cannot imagine how I'm going to take you to dinner tonight and keep my hands off you."

"You…we…uh…" Kirby struggled to find words, any words, a commonplace occurrence when Quinn was around. "Well, we could stay in, and I could take that sexy vest—and other things—right off you. With my teeth." Her clit twitched at that image.

"While that is an infinitely appealing idea," Quinn said with a heated gaze that made Kirby wonder if she might spontaneously ignite. "I want to take you out. Show you off. I am going to be the envy of every man and woman with you on my arm. Also, I wouldn't want my planning excellence to go to waste." She shot Kirby her patented cheeky grin.

"I think you have that backward. You are simply stunning this evening."

"We can agree to disagree." Quinn stepped behind Kirby and intertwined their fingers while holding eye contact in the mirror. "Have I ever told you what it does to me when you look at me with such desire? You look like you are in a desert, and I am the last canteen for miles. It's like a lightning bolt. And then you can't find your words, and it's the most adorable thing I've ever seen. I just…" Quinn looked like she was going to say something else, then stopped herself.

After a beat, Kirby laughed and broke Quinn's serious mood as she turned and said, "So I make you hot and bothered, but then I douse your flames when I bumble around like a teenager?"

"That's not it at all. I hope you can see that you've never doused my flames. Not once. Not ever." Quinn lowered her voice to a near whisper as she ran a finger from the edge of Kirby's jaw, down her neck, and finally to the top of her dress.

"I…uh…" Kirby sputtered.

"There you go again. I cannot get enough of you," Quinn said as she leaned in and swept her lips along Kirby's neck.

Kirby got her wits back by the time Quinn pulled away. "You know, I used to be suave. And have moves. And I meet you and there's something about you that makes me turn into a blundering middle-schooler going in for her first over-the-shirt boob grab."

Quinn let out a laugh. "You definitely have more skill both over and under the shirt than a blundering middle-schooler. Also, that body," she continued and gestured at Kirby's curves, "looks nothing like a middle-schooler."

"Charmer." Kirby grabbed the front of Quinn's shirt and pulled her down for a quick kiss. "If we *must* go to dinner, let's hurry. I *am* famished."

When they pulled into another winery, Quinn said, "We're having dinner here with a little more wine, of course. One of my classmates told me about it. She said it was 'divine.'"

"Who does your classmate think you're here with?" Kirby asked with mild discomfort.

"Eh, who knows. She made some assumptions about a stranger I met in a bar in early December, and I let her keep spinning the story as she would." Kirby knew they were all in a precarious position with having to be in the closet, but it seemed like Quinn was out to no one other than Kirby and *Kirby's* friends. She tried not to read anything into it, but it still seemed strange. She shrugged it off.

When they entered the tasting room, Kirby was taken in by the romantic ambiance in the space. The stone walls would have felt cold except for the soft light coming from rustic fixtures made of repurposed black pipes. The mahogany racks of wine along the walls lent a cellar feel to the room, yet the space had an industrial-chicness to it. A gentleman in a tuxedo greeted them. "Ms. Prescott and Ms. Davis?"

"Yes, thank you," Quinn answered.

"Right this way." He led them past several high-top tables repurposed from oak barrels and to the corner of a small tasting bar made of gorgeous, reclaimed wood finished with metal edging at the corners. "Enjoy your evening, ladies," he said with a small bow before walking away.

Kirby looked at Quinn and mouthed, "Ooh la la," when their sommelier walked up on the opposite side of the bar.

"Good evening, ladies. I'm Jesse, and I'll be taking you through your pairings this evening. I believe that you are having a full wine and cheese pairing, yes?" When Quinn smiled and nodded, he continued, "If you are agreeable, we will begin with a lovely sauvignon blanc and go from there." Quinn said yes, and Jesse walked off.

"I think you may have outdone yourself here with your 'planning excellence,' as you like to call it." Kirby ran her fingers along the grain of the highly polished counter. "This is gorgeous, and you are pairing my two favorite things in the world: cheese and wine. Make that my three favorite things: cheese, wine, and you."

Quinn laughed. "Glad to hear I rank up there with wine and cheese." She squeezed Kirby's leg to let her know she was joking. "Regardless, I have heard that the pairings are all to die for but have nothing on the full dinner, so we should be in for a treat. Hopefully, we worked up enough of an appetite on our hikes this afternoon."

Jesse returned with two glasses of the white wine and two small plates with what appeared to be soft white cheese. "First, we have a sauvignon blanc paired with a French goat cheese. The wine is light bodied and crisp, with notes of citrus and pear, and the cheese is an aged goat that has a hint of spice. I recommend trying them separately first and then together to fully unlock all of the flavors."

Kirby adjusted herself on the leather barstool, smooth and buttery against her fingertips as she anticipated the gastronomic delight to come.

"Shall we?" Quinn asked as she picked up her glass and arched one eyebrow.

Kirby lifted her glass in response. "Here's to you. Thank you for planning such a romantic little getaway. And here's to many more." Kirby brought her glass to Quinn's.

Kirby smiled and speared a bit of cheese on her small fork. "Oh my God, now that is perhaps the best goat cheese I have ever had." Quinn watched her, and after a long moment of eye contact that felt pregnant with significance, Quinn took a small bite as well. If Kirby had a bit too much appreciation watching Quinn's lips slide over the fork, she was quite certain no one would be able to fault her. Quinn's lips were perfection, and watching them move around the cheese and then slip along the tines of the fork, her tongue peeking out at the end to grab a bit of cheese stuck on her lip, had a blush working its way up Kirby's chest.

"The wine is okay, but that cheese I can definitely get behind," Quinn said with a sly smile that told Kirby she knew exactly what she was thinking. "I can think of something else—or should I say some*one* else—I hope to get behind later."

Kirby choked on a slightly too-large sip of wine and finally said with a headshake, "How is it that I can feel embarrassed and yet so turned on by you at the same time? Should we try them together then as Jesse recommended?" She pointed at the cheese.

They both tried the combination, and Kirby marveled at the way the two really did enhance each other's flavors.

They made their way through chardonnay, pinot noir, zinfandel, and finally, the crown jewel of the winery, the cabernet sauvignon.

"Each sampling has gotten better and better and better," Quinn said with a little giggle, making it clear that she was feeling a little buzz from the wine. She was not a giggler generally, though Kirby was feeling a little giggly herself, so she certainly couldn't judge. She also was having a hard time pinpointing whether her own giggles were from the wine or the company. Perhaps both.

"This cab is like heaven in my mouth. In fact, I can think of only one flavor that I enjoy more and am hoping to get to sample tonight. To confirm. For science of course," Kirby said, staring at Quinn's mouth.

"The zinfandel? I am certain we can arrange a sampling if you play your cards right." Quinn smirked.

Jesse walked up again as Kirby felt a rush of heat again at her throat. "Well, ladies, that concludes our little tasting this evening. I hope you enjoyed the sampling of our flavors." He looked puzzled at Quinn's laugh and paused for a beat. "It has been my pleasure, and when you have finished dinner, we will bring your cases of wine out to your car, but in the meantime, would you like to take a glass of something to either walk around the grounds with or take directly to dinner?"

"I would love to stretch my legs if you are up for a walk, Kirby. Fancy a glass of that cab?"

"Absolutely." Kirby was feeling the effects of the alcohol but knew that wasn't the only cause for her buzz. There was something magical about this winery, this tasting room, and this entire trip.

When their wine arrived, Quinn stood first and held out a hand. "Shall we?" she said.

Kirby placed her hand in Quinn's and allowed herself to be assisted to her feet. Rather than letting go once Kirby was standing, Quinn kept their warm fingers interlaced. It was amazing how the simple act of holding hands in public was so freeing. Fucking Don't Ask, Don't Tell. As if having a few gays in the unit would destroy morale. She wanted to scream at the Secretary of Defense that they were already there, and most were out to at least a few people. So far, the entire United States military hadn't imploded. Neither had half of Europe or Canada or even Colombia, for frick's sake.

Kirby apparently sighed too loudly because Quinn asked, "Hey, what's wrong?"

"Nothing at all. Just having a little internal dialogue with the Sec. Def. Nothing to be concerned about." High from the perfection surrounding them despite the stupidity of military policy makers, Kirby decided to be even bolder and leaned in for a quick kiss as they walked out of the tasting room and into the cool evening.

As they meandered down the crushed-gravel path lined overhead with filament string lights, Quinn asked, "Do I know you well enough yet to hear how you grifted your way through life for an undetermined period of time?"

"I thought you had forgotten about that." Kirby had wished she had, anyway.

"Absolutely not, and I was definitely more sober than you were at that point in the evening. I have been patiently biding my time for the right moment. Between the romantic evening, the ambiance of this vineyard, and a little wine to loosen your tongue, it seems like the perfect moment to find out all your darkest and deepest secrets."

As Kirby considered, the only sound was the crunch of gravel beneath their feet. "Well, I suppose you can be trusted to know the whole story," Kirby said while giving Quinn the side-eye. "But don't tell anyone any of this, or I might not be able to get my security clearance. To give you fair warning, you're going to get not only my dark and degenerate past, you're also going to get my 'why I joined the Army' story. Are you prepared for all that information? Also, what I say here can never, ever be shared with my parents."

With a laugh, Quinn said, "You make it sound so sordid. I cannot believe you have that dark a secret or that you held out on me for this long. Please, continue."

"Okay, well, keep in mind that you asked for it." Kirby stared, looking for some type of reassurance.

Quinn kissed her lightly. "I promise." Those two words settled the anxiety swirling in her stomach enough for Kirby to give her the whole tale.

"My story starts in the spring of 2006. I had recently graduated from college and had the bright idea to backpack across Europe for a month or two before I had to join the 'real world.' I had my newly minted finance degree and saw the whole boring world of corporate America, suits, and no fun beckoning, and I wasn't ready, so I decided to take a pause on life and bum around for a while. I had some savings and used it to get across the pond and live for a few months moving from hostel to hostel and taking the Eurail everywhere." Kirby remembered the feeling of first stepping out of the airport in Munich to start her adventure. She'd been young and inexperienced but ready to grab life by the horns. Now she still tried to be proactive and take control but understood that she couldn't control everything, and sometimes, the world wasn't cooperative to her grand schemes.

Kirby sighed softly. "My funds eventually ran low, but I didn't want to head home. Labor laws were so strict that I couldn't get a legal job, and honestly, I was no longer even there legally because I had stayed for so long. I got creative and thought maybe I could make a few dollars by hustling at billiards and darts. I was very careful not to get greedy, show my true skill, or hustle in the same bar more than once. It was a bizarre existence, but I did well enough that I was able to stay until the end of '07. I could have stayed longer, but after close to eighteen months sleeping in hostels every night with a bunch of strangers, I decided it was time to come home and start adulting. I missed my family, and the world was changing, so it seemed like the right time to buckle down and get a real job." She tried to read the look on Quinn's face, but she seemed to be staring with rapt attention. Kirby wasn't ashamed of any of it, but she was a little panicked wondering if Quinn's feelings toward her were going to change.

"Little did I realize that the economy was a complete and utter mess and was about to freefall. For someone a year and a half out of school with little work experience, finding a job was a near impossibility. It was a tough reality check and one hell of a blow to my ego to realize that I couldn't find a job in line with my dreams of becoming a high-powered financier when I got home, even though I'd done well in school. I moved back in with my parents and took stock. Part of me regretted wasting a year and a half when I could have secured a job and put in enough time to not have to worry about being on the chopping block. But three-quarters of my graduating class lost their jobs, so I tried not to wallow. Plus, I've always been the same glass-half-full girl I am now." She worked to hold on to this optimism as she bared her secrets to Quinn, but admitting she had failed at something was harder than she expected.

"I thought about going back to hustling, but if my parents found out, they would have been mortified. I thought about going to grad school, but with the economy in shambles, I didn't want to take on any more debt." She'd tried to stay positive during those weeks, but the bleakness of day after day not knowing what she was going to do had been the darkest period of her life up until that point and was likely the reason she was open to the radical move that came next.

"I happened to order a pizza one night, and it had a recruiting ad for the Army taped on top. I did a little research and realized I could get them to pay for my graduate degree, pay back my student loans, learn a language, and ride out this shitty economy, so I joined up within a week and shipped out in three.

"I hadn't fully thought through Don't Ask, Don't Tell." Kirby was embarrassed at her naivete and angry at the bullshit policy that had oppressed more than a generation. "I had no idea how hard it would actually be because I've never been in the closet. I came out to my parents at twelve, and they embraced me fully. I never had to hide, but I'm doing my best now. And I'm counting down the days until my discharge," Kirby finished with a nervous laugh. The wine in her glass sloshed with the unsteadiness in her hands, and she took a sip to try to hide it.

Quinn stared, her mouth slightly open as she fiddled with the charm on her necklace, and Kirby prayed she hadn't scared her. She wasn't ashamed of her past, but Quinn was quite the law-and-order type. After a long moment of silence, Kirby took another sip of wine to steady her nerves and relieve her parched throat. "Any reaction to dating an impulsive, former illegal immigrant who chronically leaps before she looks?"

That, thankfully, pushed a laugh out of Quinn. "Sweetheart." Quinn grabbed her hand and pulled her in. "I am so incredibly impressed with your resilience, and I am in awe of your free spirit and fearlessness." Her eyes were soft, and she ran her thumb across the back of Kirby's hand, soothing her fidgeting fingers. "I sometimes wish that I was a little—or a lot—freer and fearless. Your spirit is a big part of what drew me to you in the first place. I am so uncomfortable with myself most of the time."

So far, Quinn's response hadn't been bad, but Kirby's legs still felt a little unsteady, and she wished Quinn would tell her how she was really feeling about everything. "I joined the Navy when I was seventeen. I've never been formally 'out.' I always had a friend or two who knew, but I was too afraid to get involved with someone. I've lived in fear for the past decade, avoiding commitment like the plague for fear it would ruin my career. I thought, how could I possibly sustain a healthy relationship when I have to hide it from the world? I mean, I haven't even come out to my parents or my friends from school. They wouldn't take it well."

Ice flooded Kirby's gut. Were they getting too close now? She tried to interrupt, but Quinn continued, "But there is something in you that unlocks hidden pieces of me. You make me try to be freer, less uptight, and less fearful. You are my opposite in so many ways, but I feel like I've known you my whole life, and I just…I love you. You are perfect to me. Even if you are a criminal mastermind."

Kirby's heart fluttered as warmth spread throughout her chest. "You love me?" she said, feeling a little light-headed and worried she'd misheard.

Quinn nodded and looked luminescent in the moonlight with her eyes sparkling and her hair floating around her shoulders.

"I love you too," Kirby said quietly and leaned in for a kiss. She tasted the tang of red wine on Quinn's lips. As their tongues tangled, Kirby's heart inflated to near-bursting. She ran her fingers down Quinn's back and slid them under her vest, wishing Quinn wasn't wearing that crisp white shirt underneath, despite how delicious it looked.

Quinn groaned into Kirby's mouth before pulling back. "As much as I would love to continue this here and now, we should go have dinner." Her fingers continued to roam across Kirby's back, above the low cut of the dress, both soothing and stimulating Kirby's skin. She took a deep breath that sounded shaky. "Then back to the room for dessert. In the hot tub."

Kirby laughed. "Always the voice of reason. But are you sure I can't convince you to skip dinner and head back for dessert now?"

Quinn's hand slid down and squeezed Kirby's left butt cheek. "You are persuasive. However, we have nonrefundable reservations. Also, I'm starving, and we still have full wineglasses. Good things come to those who wait." Quinn arched her eyebrows as she stared.

Kirby yearned to go back to their room after the intimacy of the last few minutes, but she *was* a little hungry, and everything they'd had so far that evening had been divine. Reluctantly, she admitted Quinn was right. "This wine is heaven's nectar, and it would be a shame to waste it. I might also enjoy playing footsie under the table on this gorgeous night…but I promise to eat quickly if you do. Let's go." She interlaced their fingers and pulled Quinn back toward the tasting room. But one of her heels slipped on the gravel path, and she stumbled. Quinn somehow managed to steady her while not spilling a drop of wine.

"How the hell can you do that?" Kirby asked. "You toddle around on those skyscrapers like you were born in them and are still able to catch me without even spilling a drop. Where does that gracefulness come from?"

"Mad skills, darling. Simply mad skills."

"I hate you sometimes for those *mad skills*." Kirby huffed. "And yet, if I throw a ball, you're as likely to jam a finger as catch it."

"Fair point, but look at my calves. I'd rather have legs like these than be able to catch a silly ball." Her cockiness was surprising. And hot. Definitely hot.

Kirby laughed as she gazed longingly at Quinn's legs. "I can't disagree with that. I'd rather look at those legs than have you catch any balls."

"We're lesbians. We don't need balls." Quinn leaned in for another kiss. "Glad to hear you agree."

Dinner was as amazing as promised, but Kirby struggled to do anything other than stare at Quinn and count the moments until she could peel her out of her clothes. By the time they arrived back at their room, the sexual tension that had been building all evening was ready to bubble over.

"Do you still want to enjoy the tub for a bit before we go to bed?" Kirby asked.

"Sounds divine. Will you run the water while I slip out of these clothes?"

"Don't even think about it, Petty Officer. I have been dreaming of peeling you out of your clothes all night, and I don't want to be robbed of the opportunity."

Quinn laughed. "I thought you were kidding about unwrapping me."

"Absolutely not. Also, you might enjoy unwrapping me as well. I might be wearing a little present for you under this dress." Heat rushed through Kirby's body when thinking about the new lingerie she'd bought as a gift to them both.

"Well, I do *not* want to cheat either of us out of anything. I'll pour a little more wine, and then we can do all the unwrapping together." Quinn's eyes twinkled, and Kirby's heart soared.

She loves me. This goddess in heels loves me.

As the water began to run, Kirby walked over to Quinn, took her wineglass, and had a sip. She set the glass aside before laying her hands on the buttons of Quinn's vest. "I cannot believe how sexy you look this evening." She opened the first one. "Don't get me wrong." Then the second. "You are always sexy, but this..." Finally, the last button popped open, and Kirby moved to Quinn's white shirt. "This is a fantasy. Ribbon-tied and delivered to my doorstep." She trailed a finger along Quinn's sternum as she continued to slowly unbutton the shirt, exposing a cream colored, lacy bra. Quinn noticeably swallowed hard as Kirby ran her fingers over Quinn's hard nipples, visible though the nearly translucent material. She pushed the shirt and vest from Quinn's shoulders, then moved to her belt buckle. "Did you buy this outfit new for this trip?"

Quinn seemed to be struggling to get her words together as Kirby continued to slowly undo her clothing and casually brush all of Quinn's favorite spots. She nodded.

"Nice. Did you go shopping by yourself?" Kirby whispered as she slowly drew Quinn's belt out of the loops.

Quinn again nodded.

"Clearly, you know how I feel about it. I *am* hoping you'll wear it for me again soon." She reached for the clasp at the top of the pants and let them slide to the floor, so when Quinn stepped out, she was standing in her high heels, bra, and panties.

"You are so amazingly sexy, Quinn. Do you want to undress me, or do you want to sit and watch me undress myself?"

"I cannot imagine anything more erotic than watching you take that dress off."

Kirby barely whispered, "Okay," as she pulled the desk chair into the middle of the room and pushed Quinn into it. She turned off the water to the tub and turned on some slow R&B music on her phone.

Something about the way Quinn watched her made Kirby feel unbelievably sexy, so rather than slip out of her dress, she decided to do a little teasing. While holding eye contact, she began to sway her hips in time with the music. Quinn took another hard swallow, and Kirby knew she'd made the right choice.

She was wearing her sexiest red lace bra and panty set and wanted to make sure Quinn was able to fully appreciate it. She ran her hands up and down her body while still moving to the beat.

She turned her back to Quinn while she reached under her arm and partially unzipped the dress, still undulating her hips in a way that she hoped was sexy and not awkward; one glance back at Quinn's face, and she knew she was doing well. It was finally her turn to be the last canteen in the desert.

She turned around and let her dress slip to her waist and danced a few steps closer to Quinn before letting the dress fall to the floor. "Do you see something you like, sailor?"

"You're damn right I do. Come here." She softened the words with a delayed, "Please."

Seeing Quinn look at her that way gave Kirby crazy confidence as she sauntered over and straddled Quinn in the chair.

"Do you have any idea what you do to me?" Quinn asked.

"I might."

Quinn grabbed her right hand and slid it into her soaking underwear. "Can you feel what you do to me?"

Kirby wasn't sure what turned her on the most, but feeling Quinn's wet heat pooling in her panties sent her into the stratosphere. She crushed her mouth to Quinn's and began to touch her in earnest.

Quinn slid her underwear to the side and circled her clit at the same time. Kirby couldn't focus while sitting so openly on Quinn's lap and with those fingers caressing her. She rode Quinn's fingers as her own moved against Quinn's clit. They both picked up speed and, before Kirby was ready, tumbled over the edge together.

Kirby collapsed against Quinn's shoulder, both of them breathing heavy. "Do you think that is ever going to get old?" she breathed against Quinn's neck.

"If you continue wearing tantalizing lingerie like that, I cannot imagine it could. You are a feast for my eyes, Specialist Davis." There was something exciting about using each other's ranks in the bedroom when the UCMJ would consider their every expression of love illegal. A sexy defiance of a ridiculous law.

"You aren't half-bad either, Petty Officer, Prescott." Kirby leaned back to eye Quinn's matching underwear. "Should we make use of that hot tub now? The water should still be warm."

"You read my mind." Quinn stood, lifting Kirby with her. Kirby gasped and wrapped her legs around Quinn as she walked them to the tub. "I love you," Quinn said as she gently set Kirby on the floor.

"I love you too."

After removing their remaining garments, Quinn stepped lightly into the tub, holding a hand out for Kirby. She stepped in, positioned herself between Quinn's thighs, and leaned back into her chest, loving how perfectly they fit together. She had expected this weekend to be wonderful, but the day had blown her expectations away. Reclining in the hot tub with Quinn, knowing she loved her, made her feel complete in a way she'd never imagined possible. She didn't know that love could feel like this, had no idea what she'd been missing, but hoped to bask in this perfection every day.

CHAPTER SIX

Kirby's legs and glutes burned as she entered the homestretch of spin class. She was praying for relief as the sadistic instructor once again called, "Up," and the entire class groaned and stood. Well, Kirby groaned. The rest of the class seemed to be into it. It was sickening, really. "Ouch." Kirby yelped when her best friend, Emily, leaned over and punched her in the arm.

"Get your head in the game, bitch," Emily said only loud enough for Kirby to hear. "And stop whining. You're ruining my spinner's high."

"Ugh. Fuck you," Kirby mumbled. "Also," she said a little louder, "I don't think 'spinner's high' is an actual thing. I'm pretty sure your oxygen-deprived brain is making stuff up."

"Down," the artificially hyper degenerate yelled.

"As if. Pedal harder, girlie."

"Up, and give that dial a quarter turn to the right for a little more resistance."

Holy hell, Kirby's legs were about to give out. She tried to listen to Emily, found some inner strength, and stood. She closed her eyes and reminded herself that this class was taking her mind off how the Fates seemed to be conspiring to bring Quinn back into her life. The first two years after they'd split had been painful as hell, but she'd pulled on her big girl pants and had gotten through it. The last seven years, she'd barely thought about her.

Shit. Even Kirby couldn't believe the lie as she thought it. Double shit. She was supposed to be thinking about how her legs were burning or maybe even nothing at all as her she got into the zone and her body was flooded with endorphins. She was not supposed to be thinking about how hot Quinn had looked in that suit.

Great. Now the one and only thing she was trying to banish from her mind was the thing at the forefront. On the bright side, her legs weren't burning nearly as much since her brain kept wandering back to persona non grata. Kirby wanted to throw her head onto her handlebars in frustration, but she stood again as the damn hell beast in front yelled, "Up," once more.

After another ten minutes of torture, including pedaling a mountain the size of Everest, the devil finally said, "Okay, ladies and gentlemen, time to start cooling down. Turn your resistance dials to about forty percent. Take a deep inhale through your nose, and exhale through your mouth."

Kirby feared she might slide off her bike into a puddle on the floor, but she tried to do as requested. Breathed in through the nose. Breathed out through the mouth. *Don't think about Quinn.* Hell's bells, she was already failing. *Focus on the breath. Breathe in. Does it smell like sweet pea and lavender in here? Breathe out. Absolutely not. It smells like sweat. Dirty, nasty body odor. Not sweet pea. Sweat. Sweat. Sweat.*

"Okay, kids, let's move to our mats for a little yoga." What was with this girl? She couldn't be more than twenty-two and was calling them kids? "I know your legs are spent, but don't worry, we'll be in Savasana before you know it."

Hell. More time to fail at yoga. If she couldn't keep her mind clear while stressing her body on the spin bike, there was no way she was going to keep it quiet while focusing on her breath.

Thirty minutes later, Emily was poking Kirby's shoulder, pulling her out of a Savasana-inspired nap. "I guess I was a little too relaxed," she mumbled with a sleepy grin. "At least my mind quieted for a few moments."

"Maybe your mind but not your breathing. You were snoring like a drunken sailor."

"Whatever. And I was a soldier, not a sailor," Kirby said, not appreciating the reference to sailors, which brought one particular sailor in her working blues to mind. Great. "Want to grab a drink after this brutal workout? I want to do something to counteract all these calories I burned in that class."

"You're on. Let's clean up and hit the bar. Maybe have an app or two."

It was questionable whether Kirby's rubbery legs would stay under her on their walk to the bar around the corner, but she was hopeful she could fake it until she could sit. "Why did I let you convince me to take that damn class? I already ran seven miles this morning. I didn't need to burn another zillion calories."

"Your soul needed the burn, my dear, as you have been in a funk since Pride. Also, after seven miles this morning, your hamstrings will thank me tomorrow for those forward folds in the yoga class, so you're welcome."

Kirby stuck out her tongue with a sneer and flipped the middle finger, but Emily had a point. She had been stewing over the Quinn thing since she'd literally run into her a few weeks ago at Pride and then again last week at *her* wine bar.

She was constantly on edge, as if it was only a matter of time until she ran into Quinn again and needed something to break her out of it. She had been pushing herself in her morning runs to no effect, but maybe there was something to the half hour of yoga after exhausting herself spinning that had her feeling slightly more like herself. "You might be right. But regardless, let's go get a drink. It's already been a long week."

When Kirby got back to her condo that evening, she toed off her sneakers and walked to her small fish tank. She fed Frank the Tank and chatted with him for a moment. Typical Frank, he didn't talk much but seemed enthusiastic about his dinner, so Kirby counted it as a win.

She flipped through her mail as she walked into her kitchen and was unpleasantly surprised to find the notice of new condo assessments for the next fiscal year. Apparently, there were some structural issues with the pool that required significant capital, and the windows of the building needed to be resealed, which was going to require even more.

As a result, assessments were going up seventy-five percent. She needed to reassess her decision to not run for the board. It seemed like those yahoos didn't know what they were doing. If her department tried to increase expenses seventy-five percent year over year, she would get fired. These types of capital projects should have been budgeted for, and there should be some type of a capital reserve. Maybe they could take a loan rather than hitting owners with such a steep increase? Perhaps she would run for the board, although even as she thought it, Kirby dismissed it. Who had time for that?

❖

When Kirby's alarm went off the next morning at five a.m., she groaned and hit snooze. She hadn't been out late with Emily, and she'd only had one drink before heading home, but trying to banish all the inappropriate thoughts about Quinn via exercise was taking its toll on her body. She needed to listen and dial it back, but her morning runs were her source of Zen before the crazy day.

She decided to cut her mileage down, which meant she could sleep for another fifteen minutes, maybe even thirty. She rolled over, and the next time she opened her eyes, forty-five minutes had passed. Kirby's eyes popped wide open, and the adrenaline from realizing she'd overslept had her surging out of bed. She contemplated skipping her workout because it was so late, but the thought of facing all her clients without her morning run felt miserable, so she hurried to get ready and out the door.

As she headed east toward the lake and breathed in the cool, early morning air, she knew that lacing up her running shoes and getting out despite being late had been the right decision. It was so peaceful running at this early hour. She could feel herself loosening up with every step. As she crossed under Lake Shore Drive and turned south on the Lakefront Path, the sounds of the small waves lapping at the sidewalk along with her footfalls on the path lulled her into a trance.

She jumped about a foot into the air when someone said, "Good morning, Kirby."

Kirby stumbled as she turned and reached for her pepper spray but stopped at the sight of Quinn jogging next to her and looking unfortunately amazing in capri-length leggings and a racerback tank top. "Are you stalking me? I almost pepper sprayed you." Seriously. Three million people in this city and somehow, Quinn was everywhere. *Everywhere.* "Not that you wouldn't have deserved it if I had."

"That's a little harsh, don't you think? I saw you running as I was crossing Lake Shore Dive and thought it would be weird if I ran behind you at the same pace. Then it really would have seemed like I was stalking you, which I am not. For the record." Quinn sounded like she was a little out of breath, and Kirby wondered if she had it in her to pick up the pace a bit and leave Quinn behind.

"No, I mean, this is the third time we've run into each other in four weeks. You must be doing something to keep making this happen. I haven't been seeking *you* out." Kirby narrowed her eyes. There was no way they had run into each other so many times by chance.

"I'm not a stalker, I swear." Quinn lifted her hands in a show of innocence. "I think it's a weird series of coincidences that keep thrusting us together."

"Thrusting, huh?" Kirby laughed before she could censor herself. Why did she say that? Was she a teenage boy? She was clearly a glutton for punishment. Maybe she should jump in the lake and turn this workout into a swim before she did anything colossally stupid.

Quinn laughed in what should have been a gasp, given their present pace, but instead, sounded exactly like the laugh Kirby used to love inspiring. It was like a sucker punch. Kirby picked up her tempo, hoping that Quinn would get tired and fall back or would at least no longer be able to keep a conversation going.

"It is so gorgeous out here, isn't it? I thought I would hate being so far away from the ocean. But the sunrise and the lapping of the lake along the shoreline feels similar sometimes." Quinn paused for a few steps as she seemed to contemplate something, and Kirby was happy to leave her to it. "I always loved running along the bay in Monterey with you. First thing in the morning, before the rest of the world woke up, and as the sky was barely beginning to go pink behind the hills."

Kirby felt lost for words, which seemed the norm when she ran into Quinn now. The problem was that she didn't want to remember any of the good times that she and Quinn had shared. But Quinn kept evoking those emotional reminiscences that, despite Kirby's best efforts, continued to transport her back to the happiest period of her life. Wait. That couldn't have been the happiest period of her life. There was no way. Not with how it all ended. And yet, she could easily fall into those memories but couldn't quite remember how to tap into the sharp pain of the end the same way she used to.

"Monterey is one of those cities you can't help but love," Kirby found herself saying. "It's rather pretentious, but in those early morning hours, before all the people who can actually afford to live there wake up, there's something magical about it." The wave of nostalgia that rolled over her was poignant. She'd started to grow into an adult in Monterey, after her carefree youth, and it would always hold a place in her heart. Her mind also walked back to the innumerable mornings she had woken up entangled with Quinn, listening to the sea lions before they headed out for a run along the bay.

Panic struck Kirby as she realized she was thinking back fondly. Again.

Heart in her throat, she interrupted whatever Quinn was saying and nearly shouted, "Okay, well that's my turnaround point. I'm sure I'll see you again soon with the way things are going." She put some extra irritation in her voice as she about-faced, not giving Quinn a chance to say anything before she ran in the opposite direction, not caring about her mileage anymore. Now, the only distance she cared about was the growing distance between herself and Quinn. She couldn't afford any chinks in her armor. There was no way she could survive Quinn breaking her a second time.

She thought she heard Quinn yelling, "Bye," as she ran off, but she wasn't sure and told herself she didn't care. Just one of the many lies she was telling herself these days. She definitely wasn't going to look back. Absolutely not. One foot in front of the other to carry her away. Easy. *Watch the horizon. Do. Not. Look. Back.* She was almost chanting to herself. And yet, she glanced over her right shoulder. First at the lake, then all the way around and saw Quinn staring at her too.

Embarrassed, Kirby realized exactly how in trouble she was. She needed to stay the hell away from Quinn Prescott.

If it was only as easy to actually make that happen as it was to think it.

CHAPTER SEVEN

"Hey, Mom," Kirby said as she answered her phone Saturday morning.

"Good morning, sweetheart. How are you?"

"Good. Sitting on the balcony looking at the lake and having coffee. Reading a book off and on. What are you up to?" Kirby loved their weekend morning chat tradition.

"Usual Saturday stuff. Your dad and I closed the bar last night, and it was a little crazy. I got us to do a little yoga first thing to work out the kinks and sweat out the poison."

"Yoga sounds amazing. I've been pushing myself a little more than I should running in the mornings, so I am in need of a little stretching and Zen myself."

"Uh-oh. Want to talk about it?"

"It's nothing." The last thing Kirby wanted to think or talk about was Quinn. Though clearly, she was already losing that battle.

"Okay, I will respect it if you don't want to talk about it. I can tell you all about Brian Brady and the drama around his new twenty-two-year-old girlfriend. There's some good juice."

Kirby choked on her coffee and laughed at the unexpected subject change. She was interested in hearing her hometown's newest scandal, but her run-ins with Quinn were still weighing heavily on her mind, and talking it through with her mom might help. She was the only one who knew all the details about their past, and Kirby tended to share nearly everything with her. "I definitely want to hear about his newest scandal, but you're right. Something crazy did happen. Hell, it keeps happening."

"What's going on?"

"A few weeks ago at Pride, I was at a concert, and I ran into

Quinn. Quinn fucking Prescott." Kirby's heart started pounding as *that* name crossed her lips. She felt the equally strong rushes of distress and arousal that were becoming very familiar when it came to Quinn.

Her mom inhaled sharply. "That must have been a shock, sweetheart. I'm so sorry. But wasn't that two months ago or something? What's happened since then?"

"It feels like she's invading my life. Like that weird show on TLC where little parasites embed themselves into the worst places. I keep running into her. At my favorite wine bar right around the corner from my office. While I was on a run the other morning. I actually saw her at the grocery store the other day. I was so freaked out, I set down my basket and snuck out before she saw me. She's everywhere, and I don't understand why."

"Do you think she's doing it on purpose?" Concern laced her mom's tone.

"Not really, no. It's just...weird. She keeps turning up. And God, I've been unbelievably rude to her every time." She wasn't even intentionally being rude, but the part of her that was still aroused by Quinn scared her. Her body responded to Quinn's presence as though Quinn hadn't decimated her eons ago, and she immediately reacted, trying to get away from Quinn as quickly as possible. She said whatever she thought would push her away. Not that it had worked. It was infuriating. "I can't seem to help it. I thought I was over her, but every time I see her, it shakes me to my core, like my heart was broken last month, not nine years ago."

"It's not surprising. You had so many sparks, your dad and I felt like we were at a Fourth of July show. That first night after we met Quinn, your father said, 'She's going to marry that girl, isn't she?' and I thought for certain that he was right. And you've never had the closure you deserved."

"What is closure? I had my heart broken, but I moved on. You heal from cuts whether or not you get stitches." She started pacing on her balcony, needing some way to release the excess frustration.

"Yes, they will both heal, but if you get it tended, the scar is going to be much smaller."

"The scar is what it is. It feels like it doesn't matter where I go, I'm just waiting to run into her." She realized she was running her left hand over a scar from the surgery to repair her torn labrum after she'd landed wrong in softball. She could see it, feel it, but she didn't have any actual feeling in the scar itself. Why couldn't her heart behave the same way? "Everything is off tilt, so she's also on my mind. I just keep remembering, you know? I want to banish it all, but I can't, and I am so frustrated with myself."

"Go easy on yourself. You were blindsided, and she keeps popping up. Of course you're going to be out of sorts."

"I just want her to leave me alone." Kirby flopped back down into her chair.

"Maybe you should take this as an opportunity to get the closure you need. Talk to her a little. You don't need to be her best friend, but give it a little time. Say your piece. In addition to the sparks, you also were really good friends, so maybe start there. At least if you stop fighting it, you won't keep making your blood pressure spike."

"Mom..." Kirby huffed. "I'm thirty-six and fit, don't worry about my blood pressure." Kirby leaned forward and rested her elbows heavily on her knees. She squeezed the bridge of her nose to relieve the tension in her forehead. Her mom was a worrier, but she could have a point. She didn't think she needed any additional closure, but what she'd been doing so far wasn't working. "Regarding Quinn, maybe. I'll think about it later. Now tell me about Brian and his newest scandal."

Her mom giggled and gasped almost simultaneously, which would seem impossible coming from anyone other than her. She always was a bit theatrical and was exactly what Kirby needed that morning.

Chapter Eight

Quinn dreamed of the morning after she'd met Kirby and awoke aroused yet with the pressure of tears behind her eyes. She remembered how she had awakened a little sore and disoriented; she'd never spent the night with a near stranger, but as her awareness had returned, she'd realized Kirby had never felt like a stranger. They'd bantered and had a connection that belied the handful of hours that they'd known one another.

She had taken a moment to appreciate Kirby's warm breath on her neck, the comfort of Kirby's leg and arm coiled around her, and had felt an unfamiliar serenity. They'd shared several more orgasms before they'd talked about how they'd wanted to keep seeing each other in secret despite the risks to their respective careers. Even though simply being women was by far the riskiest factor, Quinn's rank would have also prohibited their relationship by military regulations, but there was no way she could have walked away then. She couldn't deny that there was something that defied logic between them. Something uncommon that they'd both acknowledged that first morning and from the first moment their eyes had connected across the bar.

Quinn could still taste Kirby on her lips and felt such a sense of longing that she didn't know what to do. She'd been too much of a coward to stand up for them at the time. The accompanying sense of loss, even nine years later, was almost too much to bear. A sob welled up in her chest that she didn't want to acknowledge but knew she needed to.

She'd never felt a connection like she'd felt with Kirby. There was something about Kirby that had always felt like they were being pulled together, almost like magnets. At the time, they'd both embraced the tug even though it was scary. They were young and in love and had never experienced betrayal.

Now, their continual meetings felt cruel, with all of the pain and hurt between them because of Quinn's callous actions nine years ago. And yet Quinn couldn't stop hoping that it meant that maybe there was still some spark, and the Fates were determined that they rekindle it.

She wanted to hope, and yet didn't think she deserved to believe, that she could repair the damage she had done. She could never win Kirby's love again—that would be gluttonous to entertain—but she hoped she could earn Kirby's forgiveness and maybe even the chance to be her friend again. Kirby still held her heart but was also the best friend she'd ever had.

On that melancholy note, Quinn rolled out of bed, placing her feet on the cold hardwood floor. It was 5 a.m. and time to hit the pavement. Having an alarm go off that early in the morning was brutal, but running along the lake this early in the morning could not be beaten. She also continued to hold out hope that today might be the day she ran into Kirby again.

She knew Kirby's habit of waking up before the masses and going for a run six days a week, and if she lived anywhere near water, that run would be along the shore. Here in Chicago, that would either be along Lake Michigan or the Chicago River. Or both, as the length of actual riverfront trails was relatively short in the city.

Quinn preferred the lake as it reminded her of the ocean—and it was along the lake that she'd run into Kirby before—so she headed east toward the lake rather than south toward the river. She couldn't believe her luck when she saw a familiar silhouette running at her as they both approached the Lake Shore Drive underpass to the lakefront path.

She watched Kirby's posture stiffen as they approached one another, but at least Kirby didn't turn and run in the other direction. Quinn cautiously raised a hand to wave as she said, "Good morning."

"It's a morning, and I'm running, so that's good."

Quinn awkwardly laughed at the pessimistic response but wanted to keep trying to engage. "What's your distance this morning?"

"Probably another mile and a half along the lake and then back. Give or take."

"About the same distance I was looking at. Any interest in jogging together?" Quinn tried not to hold her breath while she waited, but it was hard.

Kirby let out a huff and ran a few steps through the tunnel while she seemed to contemplate her response. Her voice echoed as she said, "Okay, something keeps pushing us together, and honestly, I'm too tired to keep being angry about it. We live in the same city and apparently, the same neighborhood. I don't want to be friends, but maybe all this happenstance will stop if I stop fighting it. So the long answer to your short question is, fine, let's run together. For a bit."

She was only agreeing out of frustration, but Quinn's heart still lifted. And maybe Kirby wouldn't try to shove her in the lake while they ran. A girl could hope.

The ease with which they fell into a rhythm was surprising, almost like the old days when they'd run together in the sleepy hours before dawn along Monterey Bay. Although this was a surprisingly comfortable silence, she didn't want to waste this time and felt compelled to talk.

"What have you been up to since you got out of the Army?"

"No small talk about the weather, huh?"

"You know me better than anyone else in the world. Was I ever into small talk?"

Kirby scoffed. "I don't think I know you at all anymore."

Ouch. Yet fair. "So?"

"So what?"

It felt like pulling teeth. "What have you been up to for the last few years?"

Kirby didn't answer right away, but Quinn decided to wait. Was Kirby trying to figure out another way to deflect? Ignore her? Quinn was contemplating prompting her again when Kirby finally said, "I used the Army's education benefits while I was still in to get my MBA in finance from Georgetown."

Vicarious pride flooded Quinn. She had always known Kirby was destined for great things. "That's impressive, Kirbs. You always said that was what you were going to do, but Georgetown. Wow."

"They're not a top ten school or anything but respectable. And it has served me well." Still not a chatterbox, but it was progress.

"How did you end up in Chicago? You finished out your years in Maryland, right?"

"It *is* a little creepy that you know that, but yes."

"Simple math with how much time you had left when we… ended." Quinn wanted to leave it at "ended," but the guilt she'd been living with for so long wouldn't let her. She genuinely wanted Kirby to know how sorry she was for everything. She cleared her throat and found her voice. "When I ended things. I cannot fully express how sorry I am for—"

"Stop," Kirby said. "I do not want to get into any of that. I don't want to talk about how you shattered my heart when you discarded me, as if the two years we spent together meant nothing. Since the Fates seem to be conspiring to bring us together, I am trying to be friendly, but I do not want to rehash anything we had or anything we lost. You lost that right about nine years ago."

Although disappointed Kirby wouldn't let her apologize, Quinn certainly wasn't going to push right now and ruin the tentative ceasefire Kirby was offering. She'd do almost anything to be able to spend more time with her. "Understood. I was feeling a little nostalgic because of a dream I had last night, and I'm probably about to start my period, but I will not talk about 2010."

"Or 2008 or 2009."

That was going to be more difficult as Quinn tried to bring down Kirby's walls, but she would try even though Quinn could think of little else aside from 2008 and 2009 these days. "Promise. Now, how about the story of how you ended up in Chicago?"

"Nothing fancy, and not a lot to it. I graduated with my MBA right before I separated from the Army. I scored an internship with a large bank in DC that spring and summer. When the internship ended, they wanted to keep me but didn't have anything in DC. I told them I wasn't tied down, and they offered me a job in Chicago on a new commercial lending team."

"Oh wow. Are you still with the same bank?"

Now that Quinn had gotten her started, Kirby seemed willing to share more than expected. "Yes. I'm now a Senior Vice President running several teams, though I still have several large clients of my own that I continue working with because of our long-standing relationships. I specialize in large commercial lending of one hundred million dollars or more. I work a lot. I network a lot. I drink a little too much, but I try to make up for it by working out, and that's pretty much me in a nutshell."

Quinn had always been stunned at how driven Kirby was, and clearly, nothing had changed. She was the high-powered financier that she'd aspired to, and Quinn was so happy for her. "That sounds very fancy, Ms. Vice President," Quinn said with a grin that she was pretty sure would milk a smile out of Kirby. She was right.

In her best royal accent, Kirby responded, "Well, yes, I am something of a big deal. But that *senior* was hard earned so don't forget it."

"My most sincere apologies, Ms. *Senior* Vice President."

"That's more like it."

Quinn risked a glance and found her staring back with a smile. Kirby had always been beautiful, but running while framed by the backdrop of the sun coming up over the lake, she had never looked more stunning. The years had been very kind.

Quinn drifted back to her dream and wondered what it would be like to wake up next to Kirby every morning again. A pipe dream—she had hurt Kirby too much to ever find their way back—but she couldn't extinguish that little ember of hope.

"What?" Kirby asked when Quinn apparently stared too intently.

"You've just never..." Quinn began but realized she'd promised not to go down that road. "Nothing."

"You had that contemplative, almost broody look on your face that I know means you were thinking something displeasing."

"I promised I wouldn't talk about it."

"Ah." After a few beats, with only the sounds of their footfalls on the pavement and the small waves lapping along the shore, Kirby said, "What have you been up to for the last few years?"

Quinn hadn't thought about having to answer a reciprocal question. Hell. She hadn't believed Kirby would care to ask about her situation. That had to be good though, right? She took a deep breath and steeled her nerves. "Well, after everything with us...the job, my career, everything lost some of its luster. I didn't feel like I could trust my team in Bahrain anymore after someone started the 'rumors' about me. I was lost and adrift, dealing with some self-loathing. At the same time, I was scared someone would find out that the rumors were true. I needed something different, so I applied to Officer Candidate School later that year. It seemed prudent to apply quickly before the rumors became widespread. I was accepted."

"No surprise there. You always were a great sailor and dedicated. To the Navy."

Quinn tried to shrug off the barb, but it still stung. "Probably, no, definitely too dedicated, but that's neither here nor there." She sighed. "I think we're at our turnaround point."

"Yeah, time went by quite quickly. Surprisingly."

Quinn missed the easiness of the time she'd spent with Kirby when they didn't have any hurt between them. Everything had always been so comfortable. "We always did lose time when we were alone together."

Kirby cleared her throat. "What happened after you were accepted?"

"My orders came through quickly, so I came back from Bahrain, reported to Naval Station Newport, and went through three months of hell. However, I graduated as an ensign with my little butter bar, did some more training, and then some more. I did some time in Maryland well after you were gone, some time in Hawaii, and I eventually ended up at Great Lakes. I retired as a lieutenant. I really wanted that lieutenant commander with the gold oak leaf, but truthfully, the money in the civilian world was too compelling, and I was tired of the military. Although I'd had some of the best experiences in my life, I'd also had some of the worst, and it was…time to be finished."

"Retiring at not-quite thirty-eight. Seems crazy."

"It's wild." Quinn knew how fortunate she'd been, but it was all at a huge cost. One that she wouldn't choose to pay again if she could go back and do it all over. "But I am excited for career version two-point-oh, you know?"

"How long were you at Great Lakes?"

"Eighteen months before I retired."

"Wow. To think, we've been living so close for two years, but now all of a sudden, we run into each other weekly."

"I was living in Evanston near Great Lakes, so it makes sense. It was only as I was starting terminal leave that I got a condo in the city, which was late May."

"Ah."

As they approached the underpass to get back off the Lakefront Path, Quinn chanced asking, "What direction do you head now?" Quinn didn't want Kirby thinking she *was* actually trying to stalk her, but if they were heading in the same direction, they might as well continue together.

"I live on Superior. I normally jog back that way, turning whichever way the lights guide me until I get to Michigan and then walk the last couple of blocks from there to cool down."

Quinn's mind began to race as she tried to figure out how to respond, given that she also lived on Superior and a few blocks west of Michigan.

"How about you?"

Quinn chuckled nervously. "Uh, despite how unhappy you are to run into me regularly, I don't think that's going to change. I also live on Superior. Superior and Dearborn."

Kirby stopped in the middle of the sidewalk and stared. Another jogger with a stroller almost bowled her over and glared as he detoured around them. "Are you kidding me?"

"I live on the thirtieth floor at Superior on Dearborn," Quinn said gingerly, hoping this new revelation didn't set their tentative truce backward.

"Fuckety fuck. Fuck. Fuck."

"Does that mean that you live there and not in one of the other condos on that block?"

Kirby finally started walking again. "Forty-seventh floor," she said through clenched teeth.

Quinn prayed this development wouldn't ruin everything, but her heart lodged in her throat. "Look, just because we live in the same building doesn't mean anything. We've never run into each other there. I promise not to stalk you if you promise me the same thing."

"I can absolutely promise that stalking you is the furthest thing from my mind." Kirby's tone was hurtful, but Quinn tried to shrug it off.

"We're both adults. We've proven this morning that we can talk without threatening to drown each other. If we see one another in passing, we can simply smile and wave and move on. No need for drama." Quinn ran her hand over her hair and tugged lightly on her ponytail, nervous.

"Fine, but I'm not happy about this."

"I'm not ecstatic either. Seeing you reminds me of the worst decision I ever made and what a coward I was." That wasn't entirely true. She'd been happy every time she saw Kirby, but that bliss was muted by the pain of regret. The longing for something she couldn't have. "But we can't pretend we're strangers. We have too much history."

"I beg to differ. We knew each other for two years almost a decade ago. I am definitely not the same person. I'm sure you aren't either. It's ancient history, and the only person I keep in touch with from then is Allie. I don't know you anymore, maybe I never did."

Quinn tripped over her own feet and took several steps to recover. Kirby denying she'd ever known Quinn nearly broke her. "I don't care what you think of me now, but please don't say you never knew me. In my entire life, you are the only person who has ever truly known me. I have friends, I've dated, but I've never opened up to anyone the way I did to you. Not before you and not since. I know I hurt you, but I have regretted that every day since then." Her heart was heavy with sorrow and remorse at the thought of Kirby trivializing their time together.

"You're breaking the rules, Quinn."

"You brought it up, Kirby." Quinn wanted to kick the newspaper box they were walking by. This wasn't fair. Their jog had been so peaceful, like they'd slipped back into their old rhythm, but now everything was quickly falling apart.

"Maybe it's too hard to see you and not have it come up. 2010 put a dark cloud over everything we shared. I don't want to talk about it, and I don't want to think about it, but seeing you brings all the pain back. I know you're sorry, but that doesn't help. It doesn't fix anything. Now I'm going to be on edge when I go to the mailroom, when I go to the pool. Hell, anytime I get in the elevator."

"I'm sorry, Kirby. I honestly am, but I don't know what to do." Quinn flung her hands up in frustration. "I only moved in a few months ago. I can't simply sell my condo and move because you don't want to see me. We don't have to be friends, but—"

"I told you. I don't want to be friends," Kirby snapped before continuing on a slightly softer note. "We can be acquaintances who occasionally exchange pleasantries but never ever talk about the past. Period. I know you can't easily pack up and move. I'm not keen to do that myself. But acquaintances only."

"Okay," Quinn said meekly. Acquaintances was better than nothing.

"In order to make this work, we're going to need to have some rules. Let's call them the 'Acquaintance Rules.'"

"Sounds official. I'm game." Quinn liked rules and defined parameters. Rules gave her a sense of control that had always been comforting, even when she disagreed with them.

"Of course you want something official." Kirby shook her head. "Okay, the 'Acquaintance Rules.'" God, she was sexy when she went into rule-maker mode. It elicited images of her teaching Catholic school and snapping a ruler.

Jesus, Quinn, focus here.

"Number one, no talking of the past, shared or otherwise." Kirby stared until Quinn nodded. "Okay, number two, no intentionally traveling to the other's floor unless there's an emergency. Number three, no lingering in the lobby, mailroom, or other common areas. If we see each other, we smile and nod and move on."

So far, that all seemed reasonable, but Quinn feared they might get more onerous as Kirby continued.

"Number four, we may occasionally run into each other on a jog. If we are both in the mood for company, we can jog together, but if either party isn't feeling it, we run in opposite directions with no hard feelings."

"Fair. What else?"

Kirby stared, lips pursed and eyes narrowed. "I reserve the right to add additional rules to this list whenever I deem necessary."

God, she was so adorable in take-charge mode. Quinn was captivated even with Kirby red-faced and sweaty. "I will accept, but I would like to add one more rule."

"What?"

"Number six, if we run into each other by happenstance, you can't assume I am stalking you and act as though you would like to wipe me off the face of the earth."

That drew an unexpected laugh. "Fine. I will try to tone down the hostility. Slightly. Maybe. If you're lucky."

"Deal." Quinn stuck out her hand. Kirby's hand, soft and warm, set off a faint but familiar buzz, and Quinn wondered if this tentative truce had any hope of lasting. She prayed it did. Regardless, she couldn't avoid feeling a little excited at the prospect of seeing Kirby more, even if Kirby wasn't. She hoped that maybe being "acquaintances" of sorts would help to fill the void in her life.

"You have changed in one way, Quinn."

"Oh yeah?"

"You're a lot better at running than you used to be." Kirby laughed as though she'd told the funniest joke ever. Granted, Quinn hadn't been the best runner when they'd met, and Kirby herself brought up 2009, which was pleasing to Quinn and gave her a free pass, right?

She didn't try to smother the laugh that bubbled out of her chest. "I got in the habit after someone who shall remain nameless used to insist on running together every morning. Now I have to go shower. Some of us actually have to work today."

Kirby's laugh stuck with her throughout all her meetings that day.

CHAPTER NINE

Quinn had just walked in from work as Jillian, the condo board president, was heading out to walk her dog. She smiled; she'd known Jillian for a long time and considered her something of a friend. Albeit a distant one, as they all were. "Do you have a second, Quinn?" Jillian called.

Quinn looked back at her, and although she yearned to get upstairs and take off her heels and suit, she nodded.

"Can we walk?"

Irritated, Quinn followed Jillian out of the building and suffered through her small talk as they walked down the street. She was only half-focused and hoped her occasional "Uh-huhs" didn't give away her attention level as she prayed for Jillian to get to the point. She was tired and wanted to change, kiss Fred, and have a stiff drink. It had been a long-ass day.

"I'm not sure if you heard or not, but we have an unexpected vacancy on the condo board. Marcus Jones passed away last week."

"Oh no, I hadn't heard." Quinn didn't know who that was and rubbed the back of her neck, trying to release the tension of the day.

"We're going to have to fill it as soon as possible."

"Okay," Quinn slowly said, still not understanding, but Jillian had been one of her sailors back in the Navy and was one of the reasons Quinn had looked at this particular building. She was willing to give her time to get to the point.

"The thing is…" Jillian paused, and Quinn was unsure if it was intentionally dramatic or if she was just trying to get her thoughts together. "I think you should run for the position. I know you just moved in about five months ago, so it is a little unorthodox, but if I throw my support behind you, unofficially, you should be a shoo-in."

Very puzzled, Quinn asked, "Why me? I don't even know the building that well or have a feel for what needs to be done."

"But you care how the community is run. And…" Again, another dramatic pause. *Please get to the point.* "Can you swear to keep what I'm about to tell you just between us? I know we weren't best friends in the Navy since you were my boss—or my boss's boss—but I still feel like I can trust you."

Quinn shrugged. "I'll keep whatever you say confidential."

"Okay." Jillian took a deep breath. "I think there's something afoot between the condo manager and a few of the board members. I'm not sure what it is, but our assessments went up an incredible amount this year, and despite all my pushing back, they held firm that such an increase was necessary. But something feels fishy about it. I'm not sure, and I don't want to say the word 'embezzlement,' but I want someone I can trust to take Marcus's place. Someone to look into this with me."

Quinn didn't feel equipped to handle something like this. She had no technical expertise, and she really didn't want to commit the time. But she did have a financial stake in anything going on in the condo. "That's heavy. Are you sure I'm the right person? It's not like I'm a detective or even a financial expert."

"You're smart, naturally curious, and I'd trust you with my life."

Quinn wished she'd just told Jillian she didn't have time that evening, but she also didn't want to get screwed on her assessments. And if she was Jillian's best choice, she didn't think she had a choice. "If you feel that strongly about it, sure. What's it entail?"

❖

Quinn was fifteen minutes into a phone call with their sales department about an upcoming presentation to a Qatar-based firm when her stomach started rumbling, and she began wondering what she could do to move this call along.

It was, of course, the chattiest salesperson at the company, William. He knew his stuff in a presentation room but had no idea how to read a room over the phone. Luckily, she didn't have to pay attention as her mind kept wandering to Kirby and their acquaintance rules, even though she hadn't seen her in a few weeks. Her heart stuttered at the thought of when she might run into her again and hoped it would be soon. She missed the lightness of their last run together. It had been starting to feel like they might be making progress to something mildly friendly, but Quinn had a niggling fear that if they didn't see each other occasionally, they might slip backward.

To keep from getting too nostalgic at the office, she thought about the first condo board meeting that she would attend the night after next. The speed of the election process had been surprising, as it had only been a couple of weeks since Jillian had approached her. She had no idea what to expect but definitely wasn't looking forward to it. She twirled her pen between her fingers as, despite her best efforts, her thoughts again drifted to Kirby and how amazing she looked in workout clothes.

After only ten more minutes, William's other line rang, and it was a call he needed to take. If she had known how easy it was, she might have called him from her cell phone to distract him from his monologue.

She put her suit jacket back on determined to head out for lunch before someone else waylaid her. She ducked into Nylah's office to see if she was interested in joining her, but Nylah was already on the phone and signaled that it was going to go on for a while.

Quinn tried to mime-ask if Nylah wanted her to bring anything back. She pointed at Nylah, pretended to eat with a spoon and bowl, and gestured two fingers pretending to walk.

Nylah cocked her head sideways and held up her index finger, asking Quinn to wait. Quinn had never been great at the games of charades they'd played with Kirby and her friends. Granted, there had been copious amounts of alcohol involved in those games, so she'd hoped she might be better now.

Nylah asked someone to give the group a rundown on demographics and hit the mute button. She whispered quietly, as if someone might still be able to hear. "Sorry, were you trying to say something about eating?"

"At least you got that part," Quinn whispered back, eliciting a smile. "I came to see if you wanted to join me for lunch. Or I can pick you up something?"

"That would be amazing. I am booked on nonstop calls. I'll be lucky if I can take a bathroom break before four o'clock. Where are you going?"

"I was thinking the food hall." It was only a few blocks away and had some of the best fast food in the city.

Nylah's face lit up, her dark eyes shimmering with excitement. "Tacos. Definitely tacos. If only you could also bring back a margarita." She laughed.

Quinn snickered. "I think I'd get fired. How about I buy you a glass of wine tonight after your marathon day of calls?"

"Divine."

❖

Kirby slipped off her aviator sunglasses and blinked several times, trying to get her eyes to adjust to the dim lighting of the food hall after the sunny September afternoon. The weather was about as perfect as it got in Chicago in September, sunny with a light breeze coming off the lake, temperature in the upper sixties. She'd always appreciated these last days of summer, before that warm smell in the air would turn crisp as the air cooled. She loved every season change, but for now, she would appreciate the warmth.

She'd almost ordered delivery because she had the underwriting on two three-hundred-million-dollar transactions to finalize for approval before her day could end, but as she'd looked out her office window and saw the sun reflecting off the lake, she needed to get out of the office for a few minutes.

On the walk over, she'd been torn between a grown-up grilled cheese from Qi-Zees, the bizarrely Zen-themed grilled cheese stall, or tacos from Te Quiero Tacos. Both were delicious and the comfort food she needed to get through the rest of the day, which she prayed would end by seven or eight at the latest. She ended up choosing tacos so she could buy an extra for dinner, and it would reheat better than the grilled cheese would.

After placing her order, Kirby stepped to the side to wait. She felt a slight buzz in the air but didn't have time to look around before she heard someone whisper in her ear, "Are you following me?"

Kirby jumped and whipped her head around to glare.

Quinn laughed and leapt back, hands in the air. She looked stunning in a charcoal gray skirt suit with a royal blue blouse. It was so unfair.

Before Kirby had the chance to say anything, Quinn stated, "Don't forget Acquaintance Rule Six. You can't look at me like you want to wipe me off the face of the earth." She shrugged with a cheeky smile that was as irritating as it was disarming.

"That's if we happen to see each other in passing. *You* snuck up behind me. And scared the shit out of me. I almost maced you. Again."

Her heart was still palpitating wildly with the adrenaline of the surprise and the excitement of seeing Quinn, though she hated to admit it.

"I didn't know you were so jumpy."

Kirby scoffed but knew it wasn't Quinn's fault that they'd both decided to grab tacos for lunch. Oh God, how close did they work to one another? Kirby was afraid to ask or even think about it. The wine bar, the food hall? The way her luck was running, they probably worked in the same building.

Kirby shook her head to shrug off her frustration. "Sorry, it's been a rough morning, and it's going to be an even worse afternoon, so I was in my own head a bit."

"I'm sorry. What's going on?"

"Just bad timing. Two of my largest clients are under contract to acquire office towers that are a few hundred million dollars, and I'm trying to get the lender commitments ready for final approval today."

"Sounds complicated."

Kirby ran her hand through her hair, tired just thinking about the hours of work still to come that night. "Yes and no. These are institutional investors, life insurance companies, who have conservative underwriting and very deep pockets. It's time consuming. And these are my clients, so the bottom-line responsibility falls to me."

Quinn laughed, provoking an irritating tingle in Kirby's stomach. She shook her head as Quinn said, "I'll say it again, sounds complicated."

"It means a late night for me, so I'm buying lunch and dinner right now. Tacos reheat well in the office toaster oven."

"Yuck."

"It's not every night, and it's worth it. I love my job, and this late night will be made up in a few weeks when I take a client to club seats at a Cubs game on a Thursday afternoon. It's a give and take." Kirby had never resented all of the hours that she put in before. It was just what it took to get ahead, but lately, she thought maybe there should be more to her life than her career.

"Still, that's rough. I'm going to Once Upon a Wine after work for a few drinks with a colleague. If you finish early enough, please feel free to stop by. I'm not sure how late we'll be there but probably seven or seven thirty. Maybe later. Do you want to text me if you can make it, and we'll wait?"

Kirby's heart and mind were racing with possibilities. Her turncoat heart was urging her to say yes while her brain was sounding the alarm. Her mouth felt dry, and it took a moment before she said, "I'm not sure if I'll be done early enough, but I might swing by." After hours of staring at numbers and reports, she knew her brain would be fried, but the thought of grabbing a casual glass of wine with Quinn in a setting that now was a reminder of their past seemed very scary.

"No big deal either way, but you are welcome." Quinn pulled her phone out. "What's your number?"

Kirby stumbled again. Why had she even given Quinn a maybe? The safe choice was to go directly home. "Uh, thank you. My cell hasn't changed."

Quinn looked ashamed as she said, "I lost my phone in a lake without a backup, and I lost all of my contacts, including yours."

Kirby blinked in surprise. Quinn never lost or misplaced an insignificant to-do list, no less something as critical as her phone. "Oh, sure. I'll put it in." She entered her number into a new text and sent a very quick "Hi" message to herself. "Done. You'll just need to save me."

The weight of exchanging numbers seemed much more significant, but she wasn't sure what else to say. She was also surprised that she'd given her number over so readily and without thought. Technically, Quinn should have already had it, so maybe that was why she didn't think twice about it?

Quinn's buzzer went off in her hand. "Saved by the bell." She laughed and stepped away to exchange the buzzer for her food. Then she seemed to hesitate before saying, "I should probably get back. I told a colleague I would bring her food, and I don't want it to get cold."

"Of course."

She stared at Kirby, again too long, before saying, "I did mean what I said. It'd be great if you wanted to join us this evening for a glass of wine. But no pressure."

"I'll think about it, okay?" She was certain she'd have a hard time *not* thinking about it.

"Okay. I hope to see you later. And if not, I'll see you soon."

"Yep." Kirby didn't mean to be so noncommunicative, but she was reeling. A part of her desperately wanted to spend more time with Quinn, and the rest of her wanted to run like Forrest Gump. Unfortunately, she wasn't sure which side of her was winning. She knew it was the run like hell half that should win, but she could feel herself softening.

Even as her internal deliberations prattled on, Kirby's eyes were drawn to Quinn's receding back as she headed to the exit. Although she couldn't hear the click of Quinn's stilettos above the ambient noise,

Kirby tracked from her perfect ankles up to her shapely calves that had even more definition than she remembered, the back of her knees, and the mere hint of the back of her thighs below the hem of her skirt. The pencil skirt emphasized her near-perfect ass, and her long hair swayed from side to side with every step she took, making Kirby's fingers itch to run through it. Quinn had always had perfect hair, and Kirby idly wondered if even the humidity would have the nerve to mess with it.

Right before Quinn reached the revolving door, she slowed and stepped to the side to prevent anyone who might be behind her from running into her while she took a quick look in her food bag. She glanced back with a half-smile, and Kirby was pretty sure she'd been caught. She could feel a blush blooming on her chest as she lifted a hand to wave. Quinn gave her a self-satisfied smile, as if to say she definitely had been caught, and waved back. Kirby hoped Quinn couldn't see the flush racing up her neck, but the way that interaction had gone, she was pretty sure she would have no such luck.

A buzz went off in her left hand, indicating her food was ready and drawing her gaze away from Quinn and the door. When she looked back up, Quinn was gone.

CHAPTER TEN

Kirby woke after nightmares of the terrible day Quinn got her orders to Bahrain, and the pain was particularly sharp. They'd been so certain that they'd both go to Maryland. Kirby had been devastated at the time, but she'd been so hopefully optimistic that they could make it, and Quinn had promised to never hurt her. They'd have Skype and thirty days of vacation every year. Technology wasn't quite like what *Back to the Future* had predicted, but they weren't living in the dark ages. It should have worked. *They* should have worked.

If they'd wanted it badly enough, they would have. Kirby would have done anything to save them, even "telling"—making a homosexual admission to get discharged—but Quinn had pushed her away in the end. She hadn't cared enough to try.

Kirby's chest burned at that memory now, and she struggled to draw a full breath. Why had she even considered meeting up with Quinn at the wine bar last night?

Since she began running into Quinn, she'd tried to relive the pain leading up to and following their breakup in an attempt to combat the powerful chemistry they still had. Until this morning, that pain had eluded her. She wasn't sure if the nightmares were because she was finally letting her guard down and almost enjoying their time together. Or maybe it was because a part of her—a larger part than she'd wanted to admit—*had* wanted to meet up with Quinn the night before.

She'd worked late enough that it didn't matter how the war between her heart and her head would have ended; she couldn't meet up because she hadn't left the office until after nine. But working that late into the evening hadn't been an actual necessity. She had wrapped up her "musts" list around seven, but rather than leaving, she'd gotten caught up on all the emails she'd missed during the day. Emails that could have waited. She hadn't wanted to make a decision and thus managed to find a thousand "productive" things to prevent her from having to make it. Classic procrastination. Clearly, her head had won the battle, even if it was a subconscious fight.

Unfortunately, her perfidious heart had still kept asking, "What if I'd gone last night? What if I'd gotten tipsy with Quinn and had seen where things went?" Her brain tried to remind her heart that Quinn had once lodged an ice pick in it, but her heart didn't seem to care. Or maybe it was only her libido.

Maybe she simply needed to get laid. Have an orgasm with another person to get this itch under her skin scratched. As she rolled out of bed, Kirby felt a new resolve to get a handle on her life, and she knew how she was going to do it. Before she laced up her running shoes, she shot a quick text to Marilyn.

Morning. Any interest in a drink and a nightcap tonight?

Straight to the point; that was how her situation-ship with Marilyn worked. They were friends who occasionally slept together. She was pretty sure Marilyn would be open to more, which made her feel slightly guilty, but she had never lied to Marilyn or misled her. She wasn't looking for anything more than someone she liked and respected to occasionally blow off steam with.

Kirby set her phone on the table by the door as she walked out for her run. No need to lug her bulky phone when she had a smart watch and wireless earbuds. As she got in the elevator, she was feeling optimistic for the first time in a while. She was taking control of her sex life again and wouldn't be a slave to awkward run-ins with Quinn anymore. She was in charge. She was a badass.

While mentally patting herself on the back and waiting for the elevator, "Girl on Fire" by Alicia Keys came on and put her into the zone. There was something about the beat and the empowering lyrics that always put a boost in her step. But she faltered in the lobby and lost some of that resolve when she saw Quinn stretching her hamstrings on one of the planters along the street.

"Fuck," she mumbled as she envisioned the needle being jerked off an imaginary record.

She reminded herself of her Acquaintance Rules promise to not be rude if they came across each other, so she plastered on the best face she could as she popped one of her earbuds out and said, "Good morning," as she exited the revolving door. "You shouldn't stretch cold muscles,

you know. You're going to tear something." Just because Kirby had to
be nice didn't mean she couldn't tease, did it? She also wouldn't be sad
if the teasing kept Quinn from lingering near the building before going
for a run in the future.

Quinn turned her head and smiled. "Morning. I warmed up in my
condo before I came down, but thank you for your concern about my
legs." She looked away and switched legs on the planter, pulling her
chest toward it.

The flex of her leg and glute muscles did unpleasant things to
Kirby's belly. Double damn. "My compassion knows no limits."

Quinn lifted her forehead away from her knee, smiling again. "We
missed you last night. How late did you end up being at the office?"

"I packed it in around nine thirty or so. Maybe a little later."

"Oof. Brutal."

"Not the latest I've ever worked but the latest in a long time."
She laughed as she thought back to how long it had been since she'd
actually worked that late. Probably before she added the Senior to her
job title.

"I'm surprised you're up and at 'em this early, given how late you
would have gotten home."

"Well, the plus is that, since it was so late, I didn't even have a
glass of wine when I got home. I'm in better shape than I would've
been if I had met up with you last night."

That drew a laugh out of Quinn, and Kirby joined in. It felt good
to chuckle after her crabby morning. Even if it was with Quinn. "I
wouldn't say that we tied one on last night. I think I left around eight,
but I did have two glasses. Luckily, I came home, drank some water,
and went right to bed. The secret to my success." She winked, and
Kirby was transported back to that first wink at the bar on the night
they'd met.

For frick's sake. Kirby pulled herself together enough to say, "We
can't all lead a life of retirement leisure, can we?"

"If this is retirement leisure, I'm definitely doing it wrong."
Quinn's laugh came from her belly that time.

Kirby had wanted to run alone, but now she…didn't. She wanted
to believe her change of heart was because sometimes it was nice to
run alongside someone. She wanted to believe it could be anyone. She
didn't actually believe that but, rather than heading off on her own,
found herself saying, "Do you want to run together or separately?
Either way. No hard feelings."

"Let's go together unless you would rather run alone?"

Kirby silently damned her spirits that were buoyed by Quinn's desire to run together. "Together works for me today." She could still feel the burn of Quinn's broken promise to never hurt her, but being around Quinn seemed to blunt the pain today. She was afraid to examine why too closely.

They ran in a companionable silence for four miles. Kirby felt uneasy at how comfortable that silence was. She didn't trust Quinn, nor did she trust herself around Quinn, but she convinced herself they were just acquaintances on a casual run. Rather than dwell on any of it, she focused on the sun coming up over the lake and whatever song happened to pop up next on her playlist. Unfortunately, as their run was coming to an end, "Pynk" by Janelle Monae came on. The song was an homage to the vagina, the last thing she wanted to think of when around Quinn.

Kirby hit the skip button on her watch. Then "Closer" by Nine Inch Nails came on. A throwback to her youth, but fucking like an animal was certainly not the sentiment that she needed to be channeling right now. Skip. Finally. "Independent Woman" came on and reminded her that she didn't need anyone. She made her own money, she had her condo with the amazing view of the lake, and *she* was in control.

And she probably had a date that night with Marilyn. Another independent woman who knew what she wanted. Marilyn rarely turned her down, so Kirby assumed they'd get together that night. She felt a twinge of guilt at how available Marilyn made herself for her. But Marilyn was an adult. She knew what she was doing. Kirby tried to ignore the sinking feeling in her gut and was happy they were almost home. As they approached the front of their condo building, Quinn said, "Well…"

"This was fun." Kirby was surprised at the truth of those words. They'd barely talked the entire run, but having the patter of someone's shoes along the pavement beside her had engendered esprit de corps and motivated her to run faster and farther.

"Really?" The look on Quinn's face was utter disbelief. "I mean, I had a good time, but I wasn't expecting you to agree."

"Don't overthink it, Quinn. That's my new life motto." If only embracing it was as easy as saying it. If only it wasn't terrifying.

"Fair enough. Want to share an elevator?" Quinn asked, as though they were sharing a cab across town. As if they actually had a choice unless one of them awkwardly waited in the lobby and called the next car.

"Why not?" she said. But more forced proximity to Quinn? Just what Kirby needed after a morning of too many confusing feelings to even begin to sort out. Thankfully, she was certain an orgasm or two with Marilyn would eliminate these lusty feelings. Her libido was just confused and needed some tending.

❖

Kirby was running a few minutes late, so she texted Marilyn to give her a heads-up while she briskly walked the last few blocks to her favorite neighborhood bar.

Np. You want me to get a drink started for you? Marilyn texted back. She was a mind reader. It had been an exceptionally long day.

That'd be amazing. Old-fashioned, Templeton rye, half-normal sweet.

It'll be here waiting for you. Like me. She added a winky face emoji.

You are a queen and my savior. So thirsty!

Why didn't she spend more time with Marilyn? She was a lot of fun and a good bar buddy. However, Kirby didn't want to give her the wrong impression. She never wanted to go through a heartbreak again and had resolved a decade ago to steer clear of anything resembling a relationship. Marilyn was an amazing woman, but Kirby wasn't willing to soften her stance, even for her. So she needed to keep her distance unless they were hanging out as a group, or she was looking for a little after-hours fun.

As she walked into the pub, she found Marilyn sitting at the bar chatting with the bartender. Kirby was pretty extroverted and made friends easily, but Marilyn had a way about her that put everyone at ease within minutes. It was probably why she did so well in her HVAC sales job.

She was also smart as a whip and could talk mechanics with the best of them, had a body to die for, and worked in a predominantly male industry. It was a deadly combination that she was able to exploit, and she did. She was routinely the top salesperson in her company. She wasn't in the closet, but she also didn't flaunt her sexuality, so all of the young building engineers tripped all over themselves to work with her in the hope that they had a chance. Kirby didn't condone anyone hiding their sexuality, but she begrudgingly respected Marilyn's ability to walk the very fine line of being out without fully dispelling all of the engineers' hopes.

Marilyn laughed at something the bartender said and tossed her chestnut hair back over her left shoulder. Kirby tried to will her stomach to clench with desire the way it did when Quinn did the same thing but was disappointed in her traitorous body. She was also frustrated with herself for thinking of Quinn when she should be thinking of Marilyn. She rolled her eyes and shook her head to clear her mind. She looked back as Marilyn caught sight of her and waved.

Marilyn's smile was infectious. "Hey, good lookin'," she said as Kirby slid onto the stool next to her and hung her briefcase on the hook under the bar.

"Hey, Marilyn." Kirby leaned in for a hug, and Marilyn brought her in for a light kiss.

Kirby's stomach finally clenched at the kiss but not with desire. She instead felt a pang of guilt that she was using Marilyn, one of the kindest and most unassuming friends she had, to try to take her mind off Quinn. Kirby reassured herself that Marilyn knew what she was getting. She was pretty sure she could push the guilt away. Definitely. She tried to ignore the way the lies to herself were piling up now that Quinn had been foisted into her life.

She plastered a grin on her face and took a large gulp of the old-fashioned Marilyn had kindly ordered for her. "Sorry to keep you waiting, but thank you for this," Kirby said as she gestured to her glass. "It's been a week."

"That's what friends are for. Here's to a long overdue catch-up," Marilyn said as she lifted her glass in a toast.

Kirby brought her glass up, enjoying the little clink as their glasses touched.

"Also, I know you've had a week, but I closed a sale today after four months of work and negotiations on a huge automation project for one of the largest buildings downtown. That is going to earn me the best commission check I've ever gotten, so I am ready to celebrate." Marilyn danced in her seat and grinned from ear to ear.

"Congrats. That's awesome." She was an impressive business-woman, and Kirby knew she'd continue to be successful when she inherited the company from her father in a few years.

"I've been working on this one since before Pride. It's been a long road, but this is going to be an amazing project. Hanging out with you seems like a perfect way to celebrate."

Another clench of discomfort. "I'm happy I'm here to celebrate with you," Kirby said, which produced another huge smile from Marilyn. Shit.

The bartender placed a plate of cheesy tater tots in between them. "Here you are, ladies. Enjoy. Are you ready for another round?"

Kirby looked at her glass and was surprised to see only about a quarter left. "Sure."

"Thirsty tonight, huh? Guess I'll have to catch up. I'll take another one too, Jimmy."

When Jimmy walked away, Kirby laughed. "Tater tots?"

Marilyn gave her a sheepish grin. "I'm hungry. We've gotta keep our strength up for later." She bounced her eyebrows twice and looked at Kirby lasciviously. "Also, what better way to celebrate my big win today than with cheesy tater tots and a cocktail?"

"Good point." Kirby grabbed a tot that was dripping with cheese and placed it in her mouth. "Oh my God, these are so good." The tot was perfectly crunchy around the edges even though it was covered in cheesy goodness.

"I know, right?"

Two drinks and a lot of laughs later, they left the bar reasonably buzzed. Marilyn had her arm around Kirby's waist and was pulling her down the street. "Your place or mine, babe?" she said as she leaned in and kissed the side of Kirby's neck.

Three old-fashioneds in, and Kirby was finally starting to get into it. She had a faint flutter in her belly as Marilyn took a little nip along her neck. "Mmm. My place. I'm only two blocks from here." Selfishly too, she would appreciate the extra fifteen minutes she wouldn't have to spend before falling asleep to take a taxi home.

While they were waiting for the elevator, Marilyn kissed her with enthusiasm. She felt a little uncomfortable with that level of PDA in the lobby, but no one was around, so she tried to enjoy it and not worry about someone coming along. While Marilyn wasn't grinding against her, they were pressed tightly together, not exactly fit for polite company.

The elevator dinged, and Kirby delicately pulled back as the ugliest dog she'd ever seen came running out of the elevator and put his front paws on her leg. She bent to pet his homely little face. "Hey there, little guy."

The dog was tiny and had to be a crazy mix of chihuahua, terrier, and who knew what else, but he had an absolutely adorable underbite a little reminiscent of Gomer Pyle. Little Gomer was apparently an attention hog as he spun in a circle and gave Kirby's hand and wrist a good bathing. "Have a good night, Gomer," she said as she stood and finally took notice of the person whose wrist Gomer was attached to.

"Hi, Quinn," Kirby said, trying to be nonchalant but knowing that she was failing. How could she expect to be casual while standing between her first love and her present-day fuck buddy? The stricken look on Quinn's face, almost certainly the product of seeing the tail end of her and Marilyn's make-out session, made Kirby feel nauseous. She didn't want to care what Quinn thought, but, in that moment, she couldn't deny that she did.

Quinn stared for another beat, and the elevator doors started to slide closed with her still inside but her dog standing in the lobby. She put out her hand to catch the doors, and that seemed to snap her out of her paralysis. "Uh, sorry about Fred. He's a little exuberant at times."

"No problem. He's a sweetheart. I didn't know you had a dog."

"He's a rescue. Three years now."

They both stared for another awkward moment. The elevator doors started to close again, but this time, when Quinn pushed them back open, a buzzer sounded. Yet Quinn stayed in the elevator, staring at Kirby while Fred pulled on the leash, his short, stubby legs sliding on the terrazzo floor as they looked for purchase. Kirby squelched the urge to comfort Quinn. That wasn't something acquaintances did.

Marilyn cleared her throat. Shit. Kirby had completely forgotten she was standing there.

"Sorry, where are my manners? Marilyn, this is Quinn. We knew each other in the military eons ago. Quinn, this is my...uh, friend, Marilyn." Could she make this any worse? She didn't think so.

Quinn was silent for another awkward pause but finally said, "Sorry, nice to meet you, Marilyn. Let me get out of your way." She paused again as she walked past them, seemingly conflicted about what to say. "Have a nice night." And then she was gone.

"Shall we?" Marilyn asked with less enthusiasm than before.

Thick guilt coated Kirby's throat. She tried to smile and grabbed Marilyn's hand as she pressed the call button for the elevator. Quinn's had departed as soon as she'd finally stepped out. "Yes."

The elevator ride upstairs was terrible and lasted for an eternity. Kirby had nervous sweat pooling under her arms and dripping down her back. She continued to hold Marilyn's hand, but there was nothing comfortable about the silence. As they approached the amenity floor, Kirby prayed that another person would get on the elevator and break the tension. No such luck.

Kirby's bourbon buzz had evaporated at the look of pain on Quinn's face. So had her desire for Marilyn, and she felt…empty. She couldn't decide how to handle this when they got to her condo. Should she try to get back in the mood?

She was disgusted with herself at the thought. After seeing Quinn, she couldn't fool herself. She didn't actually want to sleep with Marilyn tonight. Or any night, for that matter. She enjoyed spending time with her and had enjoyed the physical aspect of their relationship in the past, but it was now painfully clear that she was trying to run from her problems and hide in Marilyn's arms. She wasn't so much of a cad that she could sleep with Marilyn while pretending Marilyn was someone else. Kirby was sad at needing to end their situation-ship, but it came with a little relief too. But that also meant she had to admit she still wanted Quinn rather than a quick lay, and that was a lot harder to accept.

Kirby sighed when they finally arrived at her door. Her fingers were still intertwined with Marilyn's, so she released her hand to pull out her keys. Not that she was surprised, but the uneasiness between them did not evaporate when they went inside.

"So," Kirby began, though she had no idea where to start. Deciding to buy herself some time, she asked, "Do you want something to drink?"

"Sure, that would be nice." Marilyn looked uncertain in a way that pulled at Kirby's heartstrings. She hated the self-doubt in Marilyn's eyes, and it was undoubtedly going to get worse before it got better.

Kirby walked to the kitchen and pulled out wineglasses. From the other room she heard, "So you and that woman from the elevator. Quinn, right? You knew each other years ago?"

"Yeah. A different life."

"I don't know how to ask this, but—" She paused as if carefully selecting her words. "Is there…something going on with you two now?"

"Definitely not." Kirby walked back into the room and handed her a glass of the cab.

"But you want there to be."

"No," Kirby said. Probably too quickly, but she didn't want there to be anything, did she? The chemistry was clearly as strong as ever, and she was enjoying the casual time they'd spent together, but she did not want to rekindle anything. It had been too painful the first time around. She couldn't risk her heart the same way again. Maybe she was still attracted to her, but she didn't *want* anything with her. "No," she said again softly.

"But she wants there to be?" It was a question this time.

"No." But she didn't actually think that was true. "I don't know." She sighed.

"She looked gutted when she saw us together, and you looked…I don't know, guilty? Like you were doing something wrong. Which as far as I know, we aren't."

"We weren't. We aren't. It's…complicated. Quinn and I have a bit of history."

Marilyn grabbed her hand. Not in a romantic way, rather as a supportive friend. "Anyone with eyes can see and feel that there's something between you," she said gently. "Do you want to talk about it? I know you said you don't want to be with her, but maybe you're conflicted."

"I…" Kirby trailed off and looked into her glass of red wine. The color depth should have been gorgeous but looked like blood in the current light. Or perhaps it was her current mood. Did she want to talk about it? She'd spent so much time repressing everything with Quinn, but that clearly wasn't helping her move past anything.

When Kirby looked back up, Marilyn was watching with kindness and compassion, and before Kirby even knew what she was doing, she started to talk about the past. "We met shortly after I joined the Army in 2008. It was crazy intense between us from the moment we met. We had this powerful chemistry that I'd never felt before and haven't felt since, but it was a complicated time. Don't Ask, Don't Tell was still in force, so we had to hide everything from the outside world, except for a few select people."

"I cannot begin to imagine. I am so sorry, Kirby."

"The funny thing is, we had a perfect first year and a half, even in hiding. We traveled together on long weekends, I basically moved into her house off base, she even met my family. My parents loved her. When we weren't on duty, we were inseparable. I never believed in true love, but I knew she was the one almost from the moment we met. But she showed me what *shit* true love actually is a few months later." The bitter taste in the back of Kirby's mouth made it difficult to talk. She took a gulp of wine trying to cover it. Despite that lingering bitter taste, she felt a...longing for the days when life and love had been less complicated. She did not appreciate that subconscious longing. Not one bit.

"What happened?"

"A year and a half after we got together, I got stationed in Maryland, and she was sent to Bahrain."

"As in, the Middle East?"

"That's the one."

Marilyn winced. "Oh wow, that must have put a strain on your relationship."

Kirby laughed scornfully. "It was hard, but we were doing okay until someone overheard one of our Skype conversations. They started some rumors about Quinn being a lesbian, which was still illegal under military law."

Marilyn scowled and asked, "What did she do?"

"Broke things off. Over the phone. Painfully. And I never saw her again. That is until Pride, when I literally fell into her arms."

"When you were coming back with beers for all of us," Marilyn said, realization dawning on her face. "I knew you looked like you'd just seen a ghost. Why didn't you tell me what happened? Why the complete blackout?"

Sheepish at being called out, Kirby said, "Yeah, it's been a weird couple of months. I *am* very sorry for going radio silent. Quinn's rather infiltrated my life since in a random sequence of the Fates hating me. I ran into her at my wine bar, at the grocery store, my lunchtime food hall, on my runs, and a few weeks ago, I found out she lives in this building."

"That's almost unbelievable."

"You're telling me. I've been off-kilter for weeks." The number of random run-ins they'd had seemed implausible, and yet they kept happening. Kirby shook her head in disbelief and frustration.

"Do you think she researched you and was stalking you?"

"At first, I did, but I don't anymore. She acted as horrified to find out we live in the same building as I felt. She seems to have a lot of guilt over everything. Kind of the way I have a lot of anger. I think she said something along the lines of 'seeing you everywhere reminds me of the worst mistake I ever made, how callous and cruel I could be, and I don't want to be faced with that every day.' I think she was telling the truth." As irritating as seeing Quinn regularly was, she understood her.

"Wow."

"Yeah, and in her defense, she and I were in very different places as far as what the military meant to us. For me, it was a short detour to ride out the economic crisis and get my MBA on Uncle Sam. For Quinn, it was her career, her life. And it was more important to her than we were."

"Do you really believe that?" Marilyn asked lips pursed and brow furrowed.

"I didn't always. But after the way she broke things off, the military clearly was more important."

"At least on that day. That moment in time."

"What?" Kirby had never framed their breakup as a singular point in time. That decision had been made in one moment, but the impact continued for the last nine years. Every day in between that Quinn hadn't reached out had affirmed that she'd chosen the Navy over Kirby, whose life's course had been completely altered that day. It couldn't just be one moment on one day.

But was that entirely true? Quinn had looked so earnest when she'd said that breaking up with Kirby was the biggest mistake she'd ever made. Did she really mean that? Then, with a rare hint of tears in her eyes, she'd said Kirby was the only person who'd ever known her. How could Quinn say something like that, feel that way, and have also chosen the Navy over her every day for nearly a decade? It didn't quite add up, and it terrified her. "Maybe the military was more important to her that day, but it doesn't mean you *never* were more important."

Kirby's head was spinning like an out of control merry-go-round that she couldn't hop off of. Marilyn had a point. After Don't Ask, Don't Tell had been repealed, it was no longer Quinn choosing the Navy over her, but she still hadn't chosen Kirby either. "But why didn't she ever reach out after Don't Ask, Don't Tell was repealed? Could she be as remorseful as she seems? Could I have been as important to her as I used to believe?" Kirby knew the answer to the last question even as she asked it. She had no doubt Quinn had loved her, but still, even after all of these years, she hadn't come to terms with how Quinn could have loved her and torn her apart at the same time.

Marilyn smiled softly. "Maybe you should be asking Quinn these questions."

Kirby knew Marilyn didn't have the answer to any of these questions but hadn't fully realized she was vocalizing them until Marilyn had spoken. Marilyn, who was a better friend than she probably deserved. "I *am* sorry, you know. I'm sorry for dumping on you tonight.

I'm sorry for bait and switching you. I'm sorry for not being available for anything more than fun. Clearly, I still carry around more baggage than could fit in a C-17 cargo plane from my two years with Quinn, but I didn't realize until now how unfair I've been, Marilyn. You are an incredible woman and human." Kirby hoped that, even though she'd tried to ruin their friendship, they'd be able to find a way back to it.

"Kirby, you know I would have been open to more if you had wanted, and a little piece of me always hoped you would come around, but I've been fine with our relationship as it is, our situation-ship, as you like to call it. I knew what I was getting when we started fooling around. You have nothing to be sorry for." Kirby could feel Marilyn's eyes on her until she looked up. "I truly mean that."

"Thank you." Kirby squeezed her hand.

"Well, that might not be completely true." She looked at Kirby as if she was staring into her soul until she squirmed. "What you should be sorry for is that we actually used to be friends. Pretty good friends, I thought, but when we started sleeping together, you pulled way back, so we only hung out as a group or if we were going to hook up. That wasn't cool. We went from friends to friends with benefits to me being a booty call, sans the friends piece. I suspect that this is the end of our situation-ship period, but I truly hope we can go back to being actual friends again."

"You're right. I'm an idiot, and I've spent a lot of years running away from any type of 'romance' because I don't believe in love anymore. I *am* sorry, and I promise to try to be a better friend to you." Regret lay heavily across Kirby, pressing her into the couch. As if she sensed it, Marilyn pulled her into a hug, and Kirby relaxed into the embrace, feeling some of the pressure release. "You are one of the kindest, sexiest, most amazing women I know. I wish we were meant to be, but there is someone out there who is way more emotionally available for you. She is probably sexier and less of a workaholic than I am too."

Marilyn tossed her head back and laughed. "I know, darling. Doubtful on the sexier, but I agree with the emotionally available portion. The real question is what are you going to do about your sexy downstairs neighbor?"

"I have no clue." Kirby gnawed on the inside of her cheek as she considered. "My mom told me to embrace that she has been forcefully rammed back into my life so I can get closure. We've taken a couple of not-altogether-unpleasant runs in the morning. We came up with some

Acquaintance Rules where we promise to be civil to one another, not loiter in the lobby or the mailroom."

"You came up with actual rules? Did you sign them in blood?"

Kirby chuckled. "No signatures in blood, but rules help me feel like I'm in control. I know this about myself. I embrace it."

"Self-awareness is crucial."

Kirby pressed her lips together tightly and bit down until she felt a twinge of pain. "So what am I going to do with her? We still have this chemistry. I had hoped it would fade with time, but it hasn't. It's like my body hums when she's around." She trailed off as she thought about how drawn she was to Quinn despite the pain they shared. Then it occurred to her that, although Marilyn was being amazing, maybe she was not the person to talk to. "Sorry, is it too soon for us to talk about this?"

"Kirby, seriously, it's fine. Do you really think you're the only person I have this arrangement with?"

"Wait, what? You have other situation-ships?" Kirby was embarrassed by the prickle of jealousy that flared in her and suppressed it. She certainly had no right to feel jealous.

"Um…yes." Marilyn dipped her chin. "I've always known we weren't serious."

"Wow."

"I'm sorry. Does that offend you? I didn't think it was a big deal. You were always very clear that we weren't and never would be a 'thing.'" She made air quotes.

Kirby was reeling with this new information. She'd always thought, at least a little bit, that Marilyn was pining away over her. "I'm being stupid. I've been fighting my guilty conscience over our situation-ship because I thought you wanted more. I can't tell you what a relief it is to hear that is not the case." Near-hysterical laughter bubbled up within her at that, and before she knew it, she had tears rolling down her cheeks. But they were not of the fun variety. She wasn't entirely sure if she was crying over the mess of things she'd made with Marilyn, over the loss from nine years ago, or over not knowing what to do now, but they just kept coming.

Marilyn pulled Kirby into her arms again. "Just let it out." Kirby had no idea how long she cried for, but Marilyn's arms were solid, and the hand on her back was soothing. For the first time in a long time, Kirby felt safe just letting go.

When she finally got herself under control, she pulled back and looked at Marilyn through teary eyes. "I'm a fucking mess." She grabbed a tissue from her side table to wipe her nose and hoped she hadn't snotted on Marilyn. Because wouldn't that be a great nightcap?

"You're not. You're just trying to get past a decade-old broken heart. A heart that you told yourself was healed, but you're now figuring out isn't. And to make matters worse, the subject of your pain has popped back into your life. You need to cut yourself a little slack."

Kirby hiccupped and lay her head on Marilyn's shoulder. "What *am* I going to do?"

"I don't know. I'm your friend, and I can be here for you, but at the end of the day, you have to decide what to do in your heart and your head. Decide what you can live with."

"Right now, I think the only thing I can do is play it by ear. I don't know if I can ever trust her. What if she breaks my heart again? I don't think I could come back from it." Kirby closed her eyes and took a long inhale. When they had broken up the first time, she had been shattered. She went through the work, eat, sleep, and repeat motions of life, but it was years before she had her head on straight again. Years before she could actually envision a future for herself. She was too old and didn't have years to waste on that level of pain, which could so easily be avoided this time around.

Marilyn leaned in until they made eye contact. "Yes, but what if she doesn't? Would it be worth the risk to find that happiness again?"

Kirby shrugged, not ready to think about that yet. If ever.

"I know you feel like you're in an impossible position, but I think that's what you need to figure out, and you're the only one who can decide."

They finished their wine and chatted about inane things that Kirby couldn't remember later. During that time, Kirby's mind was on Marilyn's words, playing over and over in her head. *But what if she doesn't?*

After Marilyn left, Kirby stared into her empty glass and was transported to the wonderful days that she'd spent with Quinn: the long weekend at the winery, all of the perfect Sundays under the covers, the early morning runs before the rest of the world woke up. They'd clicked in a way that she'd never dreamed possible, and she felt the ache of the loss deep in her soul. And yet, she'd also never been hurt the way Quinn had hurt her. How could she possibly open herself up to the misery, even if it meant that she could find that happiness again?

Kirby stood and placed their glasses in the sink, too exhausted to wash them. On autopilot, she trudged through brushing her teeth and putting on her pajamas. When she lay down that night, she'd hoped for sleep to swiftly take her out of her own cyclical thoughts. But Quinn still plagued her dreams. She was haunted by both the devastation on Quinn's face in the lobby and glimpses of what the future could look like if only she could find it within herself to forgive Quinn and try again.

CHAPTER ELEVEN

When Quinn opened her eyes, Fred was standing over her licking her face. It was a rather rude way to wake up, not to mention a bit gross, but her alarm was going to go off in ten minutes anyway. Which made it four fifty in the morning.

"Geez, buddy. You're kind of a dick this morning, aren't you? As if yesterday wasn't bad enough, you have to wake me before the damn alarm even goes off?"

Fred cocked his homely but adorable little head and licked her from her chin to her right eye. She contemplated bopping him with the pillow and rolling over for some pity sleep but instead said, "Okay, okay. I'm getting up."

She rolled out of bed, and Fred did his little happy dance in a couple circles before lying back down on her pillow and taking a nap while he waited for her to get ready.

"I wish my life was as easy as yours, my friend."

As she put clothes on, she thought back to the previous evening when she'd seen Kirby making out with that very hot brunette. Kirby had mentioned a girlfriend when they'd first met, but Quinn had forgotten because she'd never seen her with anyone. It had always seemed that wishing they could put the past behind them was a childish dream, but seeing the proof in black and white had been almost more than she could bear.

She understood that she didn't deserve Kirby. She'd ruined that chance when she'd chosen to be pessimistic about life, her career, and the end of Don't Ask, Don't Tell and had thrown away the most important person she'd ever had in her life. Because she had been stupidly afraid. And just plain stupid. And entirely cowardly. She was like the lion in the *Wizard of Oz*, but unfortunately, she hadn't realized she had courage until it was too late. A few short months after they'd broken up, the winds of change had begun to blow in earnest, and less than a year after that, Don't Ask, Don't Tell had formally ended.

But by then, it was too late.

If only she had actually listened to Kirby, who'd tried to tell her that Obama was close to making it happen, but it had already been two years at that point, and no serious progress had been made. She could see the debate going on for another nine years, by which time she would be retiring. Or not, if she'd already been dishonorably discharged due to homosexual conduct.

Her cowardice had led to another very successful nine years in the Navy. Years in which she hoped she'd been a positive influence on her colleagues in general about how "the gays" were normal people, no different from anyone else. Years in which she hoped she'd helped some young sailors struggling with their sexuality to come to terms with it and realize that the military of this decade was not the military of the past. She hoped, despite making the biggest mistake of her life, that she'd done some good.

But that didn't mean she wouldn't go back and change it all.

For the nine years that she hadn't seen Kirby, she'd tried not to think about her, sometimes more successfully than others. She'd never dated anyone other than that disgusting attempt right after they'd broken up to give herself cover. When Kirby had popped into her mind and her old friend guilt had reared its ugly head, she couldn't help but hope that somehow, some way, maybe she'd done enough good to make atonement to the universe for breaking Kirby's heart.

She couldn't squelch that little seed in the back of her mind that she and Kirby were still meant to be, and the universe would bring them back together. And until then, she would continue to volunteer at gay outreach centers and animal shelters.

After Pride, a piece of her had prayed they would have a second chance, even though she didn't deserve it. Her head told her there was no way Kirby would ever forgive her, but her heart…it insisted that this had to be fate. They lived in the same city. In the same neighborhood. In the same building, for fuck's sake.

But Kirby was so angry. The weird Fates who kept pushing them together and lifting Quinn's heart seemed to make Kirby furious. Their chemistry was still off the charts, and there was no way Kirby didn't feel it too, but it seemed to fuel her anger.

As they'd almost gotten to a tentative understanding, Quinn had been forcefully reminded that Kirby had a girlfriend. An exceptionally hot girlfriend at that.

When she'd brought Fred back the night before, she'd poured herself an embarrassingly tall glass of rye and had tried not to cry. She'd failed miserably and finished the glass, which meant she was not only heartsick this morning but also plagued by a headache.

So of course, this was the one morning that Fred, the laziest dog to ever live, who was never even awake before she got back from her morning run, was ready to relieve himself before her alarm went off.

"Okay, Fred. Let's go downstairs to the pet relief area."

He unhurriedly stood and walked across the bed to her.

"You don't realize how good you've got it." She carried him over to the front door where his harness and leash hung on a hook. "You don't have balls or sex hormones. You're in love with me, and I love you back, and all we have to do for you to have a perfect life is eat, take walks, and snuggle on the couch while we watch movies. No unrequited love for you. No watching your true love with her new love."

He sniffed at her shoe as she pressed the elevator button and then lay down again while he waited for it to come. He had a hard life.

"You've never broken the heart of the only woman you've ever loved. Well, maybe you did before we met, but even if you did break some poor girl's heart, you seem to have gotten past the guilt to give me your whole heart. What can I even do, Freddie boy?"

He stared at her as they rode down to the building's amenity floor and blinked adorably with his little under-bitten chin sticking out.

"I like you more than ninety-nine percent of all humans, buddy, but I'm guessing you aren't going to have any sage wisdom for me."

He continued to stare. At least he was a good listener. Thankfully, the elevator doors opened, and they walked out to the dog run. Since the clock had not yet turned to five a.m., they had the place to themselves, and she unhooked him from his leash to let him roam.

He ran to a fake fire hydrant—as close to running as he ever got, anyway—sniffed at it on all sides for approximately twenty-five seconds and then proceeded to lift his leg and pee for an inordinate amount of time. Quinn wasn't sure how he could possibly balance on three legs for so long. When he dropped his leg and meandered back to her, she clipped the leash back on him, and they headed upstairs together.

"Anyway," she said as they hopped back on the elevator, "what am I supposed to do? I can't get her out of my head. Or my heart. Or my life, as I run into her everywhere I go, and she happens to live in the same building."

Fred, ever helpful, continued to blink at her, though this time, his tongue was hanging out, and he had as close to a smile as he seemed capable of giving.

"Is that the answer? Staring and giving unconditional love?" She laughed at how absurd it seemed, but as they walked back into her condo, she ruminated on that. Fred, clearly oblivious to the emotional turmoil his mother was in the midst of, trotted across the room, jumped onto the couch and snuggled into his favorite blanket once she took his harness off. Typical Fred.

But maybe she was actually doing the right thing. Just existing in the same space as Kirby. Not being pushy but giving friendship like Fred would. Loyalty.

Who knew what the future held? Maybe Kirby would marry the hot brunette, and they would move out. If they didn't, Quinn would definitely have to because there was no way she could handle seeing them making out all the time in the lobby. Maybe she'd end up heartbroken and alone…which she already was.

Or maybe Kirby wouldn't fall in love with the hot brunette. Maybe they would break up. Maybe she and Kirby would forge something of a friendship that would help her get past this unrequited love and lust.

Well, the lust wasn't unrequited. She could still read *that* in Kirby's eyes. Or maybe it was something else altogether, maybe something that Quinn shouldn't dare hope for but had been hoping for since she'd run into Kirby at Pride, regardless of how futile it all was.

"Shit, Fred. You might be on to something here." He didn't even lift his head despite Quinn's agreement with his advice. "Accept things the way they are. Don't push and see where it goes. Solid. However, I will not stare at her like a creeper like you are inclined to do. I will also not lick her hand or her face the next time I see her."

He let out a loud snore, and she was certain that meant he was in agreement with this new plan.

Although she still didn't feel good about the situation, she felt more at peace with it than she had since running into Kirby months ago. Hell, perhaps ever. She'd never been an optimistic sunshine and rainbows person—she'd always considered herself a realist—but embracing the fact that she didn't have control over the situation, that all she could do was try to be a good friend and a good person, lifted a burden that she hadn't realized she'd been carrying.

Despite the newfound peace, she still snuck out the service entrance into the alley rather than out the front door and then ran in the opposite direction to avoid running into Kirby. She wasn't ready to face her after seeing her so obviously enjoying herself with another woman.

❖

Quinn hung up her office phone and let out a sigh of relief. It had been a long day, and she just wanted to get home and snuggle up with Fred. She felt guilty for not spending as much time as she would like with him, so she promised herself she would get him a special treat on her way home to apologize.

She scrolled down a little further in her Outlook calendar and remembered she had her first condo board meeting that night, which would significantly shorten her snuggle time. Ugh. She still wasn't sure why Jillian had wanted *her* to join the board, but Jillian had been right. She'd handily "won" the recently vacated seat. Perhaps because no one else in the building decided to run, she thought as she chuckled to herself. Having no one run against her didn't really say much about how much anyone actually wanted to be on the board, though, so hopefully, it wasn't too tedious or time-consuming of a job.

Later that evening as the board meeting wrapped up and everyone was moving the furniture in the lounge back to its normal configuration, Quinn whispered to Jillian, "Are board meetings always that long and dull?"

"Yes," Jillian said flatly, dragging out the short word to three syllables. "But it's good having some control over what's going on in the building. I feel like it's my responsibility as an owner to keep these louts from doing who knows what. I'm glad you joined us. Another voice of reason."

"I can't believe someone is trying to establish a dog breed ban. How ridiculous," Quinn said. She seethed thinking of people who tried to blame a dog's breed rather than the owner's training.

"I know. This isn't the first time, but with no incidents from any dogs in the building regardless of breed, there are no grounds." She rolled her eyes. "Thank you for being normal. That vote was closer than it should have been."

"I know, right?"

"Hey, do you have time to chat for a few minutes?"

"Sure, I need to get Fred, but want to go grab a tea at the café around the corner? I could go for a slice of pie too, and they have a great patio so Fred can sit with us."

"Sounds good."

"Meet you in the lobby in ten?"

"Actually, let's meet over there? We don't need to hide, but I'd rather none of the board members see us walking together after the meeting, you know?"

"Cloak and dagger," Quinn stage-whispered as she raised her eyebrows twice. "Sounds fun." She thought Jillian was exaggerating the "danger" of it all, but it was a little exhilarating to be wrapped up in intrigue. And at a minimum, it gave her something to think of other than Kirby.

Quinn quickly ran up to her apartment to use the bathroom and grab Fred before meeting Jillian. When the elevator doors slid open to whisk her and Fred downstairs, Kirby was standing on the other side. Of course. Quinn froze, not quite ready for this interaction.

As the doors started to close, Kirby pressed the open button and asked, "Were you planning to ride the elevator, or did you decide to take the stairs?" She smiled. God, Quinn loved that smile. It was entirely unfair how it made Kirby's entire face shine.

"Oh yes, sorry. My knees definitely wouldn't enjoy thirty flights of stairs. Especially carrying this lug." Quinn forced herself forward one step at a time into the elevator as she indicated Fred.

"Is he injured or something?"

"No, he just sometimes doesn't feel like going for a walk. But he needs to get outside so he can pee, so we play this game. I carry him, and then occasionally, he walks so he can do his business."

"Is he actually even a dog?" Her laugh reverberated low in Quinn's belly.

"A very lazy dog. He knows what he deserves, and it's anything and everything he could possibly want. And he's right." She had never seen herself as a dog person before Fred, but now, she couldn't imagine life without the little guy.

Kirby leaned toward Fred, who perked up as she scratched him behind the ear. "You have such a sexy ugly face, Fred." Quinn felt Kirby's breath on her arm that came out in a poof of surprise when Fred licked her chin. "Such a friendly boy. Though I would have named you Gomer with that adorable underbite. How old are you?"

Even with Kirby speaking in baby talk to her dog, Quinn felt liquid heat pool between her legs at Kirby's nearness. Her mouth was dry as she racked her brain for the answer. "He's, ah, five."

"Only five and you're too lazy to even walk outside? Poor baby. Is there something wrong with him? Like medically?" She finally looked up and made eye contact. Her eyes went from innocent puppy love to something weightier. She also seemed to realize how close they were standing, their arms touching right above where they were both touching Fred.

Kirby took a small step back and visibly swallowed, dropping the hand that had been petting Fred. "I…" she began but didn't continue, staring at Quinn's mouth. Quinn glanced at Kirby's mouth as well, and vividly remembered what those lips felt like against hers, even though it had been a decade since last she'd felt them. She gently bit the corner of her lip and wondered what Kirby would do if she moved closer and brought their mouths together.

The elevator made a banging sound, lurched to a halt, moved a few more inches, and stopped again. Heart in her throat, Quinn asked, "What the hell was that?" She pressed into the corner as if she would be safer if squeezed herself between two walls, the rail pressing into her hips. She also found herself squeezing Fred a little too hard and tried to relax at his grunt. "Shit."

"Feels like the elevator stopped. Probably a minor mechanical issue. No big deal."

"What?" Quinn felt lightheaded and swiped her hand across her forehead to remove the beads of sweat. "Are we going to plunge to our deaths?" There was something terrifying about being trapped, suspended however many hundreds or even thousands of feet above the ground with no control. She fanned her face trying in vain to alleviate the heat.

"Relax, Quinn. It's going to be fine. We aren't going to plunge to our deaths, I promise." Kirby looked at her again, but rather than being heated and heavy, her eyes made Quinn feel warm all over. "This happens more often than you think. An elevator is like a car. Even with regular maintenance, every once in a while, it's going to break down. But elevator safety standards have come a long way, and there are about ten fail-safes in place to keep us safe." She pressed the button with the little firefighter's hat on it, but nothing happened. "Now that's weird."

"What?" Quinn had been feeling slightly less panicked, but her anxiety began to rise again.

"Probably not a big deal, but the security line seems to be dead." She pressed that same button three or four more times. "Shit. Do you have your phone? I think I forgot mine upstairs." She ran her hands around her hips and pockets.

"Oh God, we're going to die. They're never going to know that we're trapped, and we're going to run out of oxygen."

Kirby laughed. She laughed! What the hell response was that? "You know the last time passengers died in a standard passenger elevator in the US due to a mechanical issue?"

"No."

"Well, I don't either, but I've never heard of it, and I bet it was at least one hundred years ago. My career is in lending money for companies to buy buildings. Elevators are a risky part, but we have very rigid safety guidelines, and before we lend money on a building, we thoroughly review all inspections and safety records. I have never had a building not be compliant on elevators."

Quinn didn't even realize she was breathing rapidly until Kirby placed a hand on her arm, and she felt her breath begin to slow.

Kirby looked her in the eyes, "I don't remember you being afraid of elevators before. Did you develop claustrophobia over the past few years or something?"

"It's not the small metal box itself, so it's not claustrophobia. It's the small metal box suspended hundreds of feet in the air seconds away from plunging to a terrifying and excruciating death."

Kirby let out a breath that sounded strikingly like a muffled laugh, but she wasn't laughing when she looked at Quinn again. "I promise you, we are perfectly safe. We are not seconds away from plunging. This elevator has brakes upon brakes upon brakes. Even if the cable broke, which it didn't because that sound wasn't nearly loud enough, and the first set of brakes failed, there are other backups. We're just stuck in place until either the fire department or the elevator company shows up and gets us out. You could be terrified of my company for the next who-knows-how-long, but that's the only thing you have to fear right now."

Kirby's smile was catching, and Quinn found herself feeling better as she smiled back. "At least you're no longer flat-out rude to me. This would be much more unpleasant if we couldn't have a conversation." She winked to take any bite out of her words, even though she wasn't sure if Kirby would have felt the bite anyway.

"Thank God for the genius Acquaintance Rules allowing us to be civil, huh?"

Quinn scoffed. "*I* was always civil to you."

"Whatever. Now, do you have your phone? It would be good to call the security desk and verify they are aware that we're stuck."

Quinn nodded as she placed Fred on the floor while still keeping pressed into the corner. Fred gave a little dissatisfied grunt, and inexplicably, Quinn found that comforting as well. Clearly, Fred wasn't worried about being trapped in an elevator. She unlocked and then handed her phone to Kirby.

"I love this picture on your home screen. Was this at the lake?"

"Yes." A selfie she'd taken of her and Fred lying in the sand, eyes closed and heads touching, was her wallpaper. It was one of her favorite pictures of them together. She'd taken it a few months after she'd adopted him.

"Fred is such a handsome devil."

"No need to lie. He knows he's no Julie Andrews or anything, but he also knows he makes up for it with charm."

Fred chose that moment to roll onto his side and made a sound that was suspiciously like passing gas. Quinn wanted to crawl into a hole and hide. Fred had no sense of decorum. He was going to ruin Quinn's chance to have a few civil moments with Kirby with his smell of death.

"Did he just do what I think he did?" Kirby giggled.

"Yep, we'll probably smell it in less than five seconds. So much for class, Fred-O."

Kirby broke out into a laugh. "We really do need to get out of here. It smells like he ate a rotting skunk and then shit it out right here in the elevator." Kirby was laughing so hard, tears were beginning to leak out of the corners of her eyes, and her hysterics were contagious despite the skanky smell permeating the air.

Quinn was laughing so hard that she had a hard time speaking. "That is a big sign that he needs to go number two, so we need to get out before he passes another one. Or decides he can't hold it and poops in here. Trust me, it won't smell any better."

Kirby looked at the phone and then back up at Quinn. "Uh-oh, do you have security's number in here?"

"It never occurred to me." Quinn gasped. She felt the beginning of panic creeping in again.

"Well, hell. You only have one bar of reception, and it seems to come and go, so the page for the condo won't load. Do you know anyone else who lives here? And have their number saved?"

"Oh! I was heading to meet with Jillian, the condo board president, for tea. I have her number." Quinn took her phone back and tried to dial. The phone indicated that it was calling but never started ringing before saying Call Failed. "Fuck, we're never getting out of here. How else can we send out an SOS?"

"What if you text her? Sometimes texts will go through with less of a signal than a call needs."

"Okay." She typed a quick text and sent a little prayer up to the heavens that it would go through. *Stuck in elevator at building. Emergency phone dead. Can u call security?* "I don't know if it went through," Quinn stated, sucking on her bottom lip.

Kirby laughed quietly. "Give it a minute. Why don't we sit? You're going to wear a hole in the carpet pacing like an animal at the zoo, and given the increase in our assessments this year, I don't want to have to add anything new like replacing the carpet in this elevator."

Quinn didn't realize she'd been pacing until Kirby grabbed her hand and guided her to the floor next to Fred. As they both slid down, Kirby continued to hold her hand, then seemed to realize what she was doing, gave Quinn's hand a squeeze, and let go.

A ding from Quinn's hand drew both of their eyes down. "Oh, thank God," Quinn whispered. "Jillian is calling security now."

"See, help is already on the way." Kirby kindly smiled. "Now, back to my question before all of this. Does Fred have some medical issue? Thyroid? Metabolic problem?"

At the sound of his name, Fred stood from where he had been sleeping next to Quinn's leg and climbed into Kirby's lap.

"Traitor. She thinks there's something wrong with you, Fred, and yet you desert me, your mother, who rescued you from the pound? So much for loyalty." Not that Quinn could stay mad at him, or hell, even begrudge him. Given the option, she would crawl into Kirby's lap for comfort as well.

Kirby lightly grabbed Fred's face. "Don't you believe your mean mommy. I think you're perfect exactly the way you are."

Quinn again thought she should be put off by Kirby's baby talk, but curiously, the expression on Kirby's face as she talked to Fred was endearing.

Kirby looked back at her before continuing in normal adult speak.

"I was wondering because it seems odd for a young dog like this to be so lazy."

"No." Quinn laughed. "No medical condition. He had a rough life before he was picked up as a stray. If you look, he's got a piece missing on the back of his left ear. He's also missing three teeth, and he has some scarring around his head and shoulders that you can see when he's shaved, which he was when I adopted him. He was so skinny when he was brought into the Chicago shelter too. About half his current weight."

Kirby felt around Fred's left ear. "Oh my gosh, you poor little guy. How did you survive? You're so tiny." Quinn melted when Kirby pressed her face to Fred's head and gave him a kiss.

"I think he realizes he's got a good life now and embraces it. Why go for a walk when he can lie on the couch? Why run around when, with one look, his mom will pick him up and carry him wherever he needs to go? He had a lifetime of exertion in his first couple years."

Kirby cuddled him closer. "Don't you worry, Fred. If your mom is ever mean to you, you just run away to my floor, and I'll take you in. I will give you all the cuddles. All. The. Cuddles. Do you hear me?" He licked her chin and then nuzzled between her elbow and hip as though he was trying to block out the light. Which he probably was. It was close to his bedtime.

"Traitor," Quinn said again but couldn't fault him. She'd love to cuddle into Kirby too. She'd always loved Kirby's hips.

"So…" Kirby began but didn't seem to know where to go next.

"So…" Quinn mimicked, also not sure what to talk about.

"I didn't realize you and Jillian were…friends?" Kirby asked with a noticeable pause.

Quinn wasn't sure if that was a slight tinge of jealousy in her voice, but a girl could hope. "Yes, she was one of my sailors when I was at Great Lakes. She's actually the reason I looked at this building."

"I don't know her well, but she always seemed like a bit of a… well, a bit of a bitch, to put it indelicately."

Quinn chuckled at the very apt description. "Oh, she absolutely was as an NCO. It's what made her great. She didn't put up with any bullshit. But if you did your job, there was nothing to fear from her. It's probably also what makes her a great condo board president."

"It's why I vote for her." Kirby laughed and ran her hand through her short hair, which fluttered around but fell exactly back into place.

Quinn's fingers ached as she wished she could run them through Kirby's hair again. "Speaking of, I saw you ran for the board. I voted for you, by the way, so you're welcome."

"I ran unopposed, but I still appreciate the vote."

"You still have to get a quorum for the election to count. I helped make that happen."

"If you want to be technical about it, yes, thank you for helping to meet the quorum. I promise to take my responsibilities as board member seriously and will do my very best to represent the best interests of my constituents," she deadpanned, drawing a laugh out of Kirby.

"I…" Quinn paused, second-guessing whether she could be open. Kirby cocked her head but didn't say anything. Deciding she could always blame what she wanted to say on the stress of their situation, she continued, "I've never had such easy conversation with anyone other than you. I don't know what it is about us, but even when you're angry, something about you makes me feel comfortable, like I can talk and not sound like an idiot." She had been staring at her hands, afraid to make eye contact but found the courage to look up when she finished. She couldn't read Kirby's expression, but it wasn't anger, so that was a start.

"I'm sorry about last night, Quinn. I never meant for you to see that." Kirby bit her lip.

"You have nothing to be sorry for. You told me at Pride that you had a girlfriend. I apparently chose to forget it."

Kirby chucked sardonically. "It's not like that. We…"

As Kirby trailed off, Quinn said, "Look, you don't have to explain anything. It's not my business."

"I know, but I want you to understand. The look on your face last night, I—" She looked at Fred. "I hated it. Marilyn isn't my girlfriend. We're friends who run in the same circle and who occasionally enjoy each other's company a little more intimately. Nothing serious or formal."

Quinn's heart fluttered to life. She didn't know what to say, but the fact that Kirby cared enough to make sure she understood that what she'd witnessed wasn't serious had to be a good sign. Right? She was saved from coming up with a response by another ding in her hand.

"Jillian says the elevator company is on the way and should be here within thirty minutes."

"Whew." Kirby sighed, and Quinn shared in her apparent relief. "Speaking of Jillian and the board, why did you decide to run? I must admit, I was surprised when I got the special election ballot with your name on it."

"A bit of a bizarre story. I had no interest in it, but Jillian asked me to."

"Weird. Why?"

"I probably shouldn't tell you this, but I'm emotionally fraught at the thought of swinging hundreds of feet in the air. Can you please keep it between us?"

"Of course."

"Jillian thinks there might be something weird going on with a couple of board members and the condo manager. Weird stuff with the books and she asked me to join because she knows she can trust me. Though since I'm sitting here spilling my guts to you, she probably can't actually trust me as much as she thinks."

"Those motherfuckers. When I got my new assessment notice, I thought it seemed crazy and briefly thought about running for the board myself, but I didn't want to commit that much time. Shit. Have you found anything so far?"

"No, but that's why Jillian and I were going to meet this evening, so we could talk about her suspicions. I think she wants me to dig into the financials to see if I can figure out what's going on. It isn't an area of strength for me, but I told her I'd try."

"Wow. Well, if you need some help, I spend a lot of the day looking at financials for towers similar in size to this. Apartments and office buildings mostly, but I'm sure there are a lot of similarities."

"Really? You would do that for me?"

"Yes, and not just for you. If something is going on, we're all getting screwed."

"You're a savior. I'll talk to Jillian but will likely leave out the part where I already told you all this."

Quinn looked at Fred to make sure he was still doing okay but instead found herself watching Kirby's very long fingers as they delicately played with the hair on his head and around his ear, scraggly as it was. She remembered those fingers wrapped around a dart in the sexiest way possible. She remembered those fingers tracing lazy patterns along her back after they were both spent. She remembered the feel of those fingers tangled in her hair while her face was buried in Kirby's pussy.

In an effort to bring her dirty thoughts back to the present moment and change the subject, Quinn blurted, "Do you still play darts?"

"That was an abrupt change of subject." Kirby chortled. "Yes, I do. Does that surprise you?"

"Of course not." Quinn had always pictured Kirby continuing to hustle unsuspecting dart players. "I always thought you could have gone on the pro circuit."

"You're too kind. I've never been *that* good. But I do still play. Not for money any longer, normally, but sometimes, some fragile male ego needs to put up money in front of his friends to try to prove that he can beat *the girl*. I have a hard time saying no to those douchebags. There are a group of people who meet at a bar nearby a few nights a week, and I join them when I can."

"You are something else, Kirby Dav—"

The elevator lurched downward, and the lights blinked out. Quinn screamed as she used her feet to press farther back into the corner and braced for impact, certain that they only had another breath or two before they were splatters in the basement.

A warm body pressed against her side, and an arm slid around her shoulders. "Hey, we're going to be okay."

Quinn inhaled sharply at the unexpected contact but quickly settled into Kirby's embrace.

"This probably means the elevator company is here and is resetting the system or something. Nothing to worry about," Kirby said softly.

Quinn's breaths were choppy, and she had a hard time getting them back under control, but Kirby sat there holding her, rubbing her back. Fred even seemed to understand that Quinn needed some comfort and stretched across both of their laps. "I thought for sure that was it. But I'm not ready to die. Holy shit."

"It's okay. I'm not either." Kirby reached around with her outside arm and pulled Quinn into a tighter embrace. "I'm not either," she whispered again.

Quinn wasn't sure if they stayed like that for minutes or hours, but she lost herself in Kirby's embrace, in her scent, despite sitting in a dark elevator that she still didn't feel confident about.

"Thank you," Quinn said, breaking the silence that had grown heavy.

"You're welcome." Kirby released her outside arm but left her other arm around Quinn's shoulders. Quinn didn't mind; she still had her head resting on Kirby's shoulder.

"How are your parents?" Quinn had felt the loss of Kirby's family almost as much as losing Kirby herself. They had been more like parents to her in two years than her own had ever been.

"They're good. Great, actually. They still have the bar but have finally agreed to bring in some additional staff so they don't have to work quite so many hours. I think my sister is looking to buy them out so they can do a little traveling, but Mom and Dad haven't agreed yet."

"That's so great to hear. I always wished your parents could be my parents. They were so amazing." Quinn reached to pet Fred, and as she was running her fingers along his back, her fingers brushed Kirby's. "Sorry," she muttered and pulled her hand back up to Fred's head.

"Dad is still creating new cocktails. It's hilarious. And awesome. Still talk to Mom almost every weekend."

"You are so lucky with them." Quinn thought she was imagining it when she felt a warm finger graze hers on Fred's head the first time, but then she felt another warm brush and another. Until a finger linked with hers on the top of his head and stayed there.

"I know."

They slipped into a remarkably comfortable silence, their fingers connected in Fred's wiry fur, Quinn's head still on Kirby's shoulder. She'd always loved the way Kirby smelled and turned her head into her neck, taking in a deep breath. She felt Kirby shift slightly, giving her a little more access. She was pretty sure that was why Kirby shifted anyway.

Quinn couldn't see, but she could feel Kirby's breathing. The rise and fall of her chest, the occasional hitch that said Quinn wasn't the only one feeling something. Perhaps it was the complete and total darkness that made her feel bold as she turned her head a little farther and brought her lips softly to Kirby's neck.

Her senses were overwhelmed. The softness of Kirby's skin under her lips, the scent of her hair filling Quinn's nose. She heard Kirby sigh and followed suit. She began to shift to get the leverage to find Kirby's lips when the lights abruptly came back on, and the elevator began a controlled descent.

Quinn pulled away and blinked as her eyes tried to adjust to the bright light flooding the cabin. She saw Kirby's chest heaving in time with her own. Quinn wanted to say something but had no idea what the right thing was. She watched as Kirby's eyes shifted from being overwhelmed by the light to panic and didn't know what to do to stop it.

She started to open her mouth, even before she knew what she was going to say, but before she had a chance to speak, Kirby slid out from under Fred and jumped across the car. "Well."

"Well," Quinn parroted. "I think we are going to survive this elevator debacle."

Kirby cleared her throat. "I think you're right."

"Yep," Quinn said as she felt the elevator decelerating as they approached the ground floor.

"Yep," Kirby echoed.

"So."

"So. Ah, I meant what I said earlier about helping on the financial deep dive stuff. Just let me know."

"I will. I'll text you."

"Okay, good."

"Good." The tension in that elevator was thicker than the afternoon fog in Monterey Bay. Quinn wanted to do or say something—anything—to reestablish the casual banter that they'd had while the lights were off, but she didn't know what that might be.

"Good."

"Do you think one of us could say 'good' one more time?"

"Good," Kirby replied, but at least she also laughed.

"Think you're going to go for a run tomorrow?"

Kirby continued laughing. "After the stress of this evening? I can pretty much guarantee it."

"Great. Maybe I'll see you?" Quinn hoped that the desperate longing in her voice didn't ring through.

As the doors to the elevator slid open, Kirby said, "I…I think I might like that. Five thirty?"

"It's a date. Shit, I mean, not a date. I just meant, I'll be here."

"I'll see you then."

Jillian came running around the corner saying, "Oh my God, ladies, I am *so* sorry!"

"No worries, Jillian. These things happen." Kirby was surprisingly calm, though she had been the calming presence in the elevator, so maybe it wasn't that surprising. She'd never truly seemed worried at all, while Quinn fought off a panic attack. "As a heads-up, you might want to push the condo manager on why the emergency phone didn't work in the elevator. I thought they checked those daily or something for safety reasons."

"I was wondering why you had to reach out to me. I'll definitely address it with the manager. Ugh. If it's not one thing it's another. Thanks for the heads-up."

"Of course." Kirby shifted her attention back to Quinn and sighed. "See you tomorrow, Quinn. I've got to go get my can of black beans from the convenience store that I am now too tired to cook. Jillian, great seeing you. Thanks for the help. As an aside, Quinn don't forget to save security's phone number in your phone."

"I will, but maybe you shouldn't forget your phone when you leave the house. Just an idea." Quinn shrugged.

"Ha, funny girl. Okay, g'night."

Quinn thought that Kirby *might* be running away, but they had a running almost-date in the morning, and she'd kissed Kirby's neck under the cover of darkness, so despite the near-death experience, Quinn was pretty sure she was winning.

"Holy shit, this dog is getting heavy. Want to walk outside with me for a few minutes while I let poor Fred stretch his legs and relieve himself?"

"Sure. I can't believe you were stuck in that elevator for more than two hours!"

"Holy hell. That was two hours?" Quinn brought her tone down to a more normal level as they went through the revolving front door.

"From when you texted me, it was two hours and twelve minutes, but I don't know how long you were in there before you texted. It felt shorter than that, huh?" Jillian smirked.

Quinn gritted her teeth, not sure exactly where this was going but suspecting it was going to be meddlesome and counterproductive. "I would have never guessed two plus hours, though it was emotional and traumatic. I'm afraid of heights and kept envisioning plummeting to my death, squashed like a sardine in a little tin can."

"Are you sure it wasn't the company?" Jillian bumped her shoulder. "I know for a fact that Kirby is gay or is at least into women anyway. And, damn, is she good looking. If I weren't already off the market, I might let *her* turn me gay. And I'm pretty sure you're still single. Perpetually single, unless something has changed." Jillian laughed so loudly, it almost sounded like a bark.

"I can confirm that Kirby is gay. I know from personal experience, but we have a history that is way too complicated to get into tonight. So, changing the subject, since my little lazy Fred doesn't have much stamina and we can only really go around the block while he tries to find a grassy patch to poop on, let's talk condo business."

"Got it, no Kirby talk, and keep it quick for poor little Fred. To summarize, basically, the same guys who voted for the breed ban this evening are on the capital expenditure committee. This committee oversaw the pool and window capital expense bids, but in years past, they have also overseen the bidding of all major capex work in the building. But something is up. I've got all the bid documentation, the close-out packages on recent work, the general ledger, and more. I want you to take a look and see if anything looks fishy to you. I smell a rat, but I can't fricking find it."

"When do you want me to pick everything up? Do you have the files in your condo?"

"Whenever and yes."

"This is probably a little unorthodox, but what would you think if I had Kirby help in the financials review? She works in lending, and I think she looks at financials regularly. This isn't in my wheelhouse, and while I'm happy to help, I'd feel better if we had an expert's opinion as well."

"Do you know you can trust her?"

"Absolutely."

"Okay, but please make sure she knows she has to keep her mouth shut on this. We can't risk word getting out to the other board members and the damn management staff on our suspicions."

"Promise. I'll come by tomorrow evening and pick up the files."

By the time Quinn got back to her condo, she was so far past exhausted from the emotional roller coaster of the day that it took all of her energy just to take her makeup off. Despite the fatigue, the tiny seed of hope that had been in her chest since Pride was blooming into a sunflower of possibility. She knew the chance at a real relationship was still unlikely, that in the light of day, Kirby wouldn't have linked their fingers together or allowed Quinn to kiss her neck. But she couldn't help the optimism she was feeling for the first time in nearly a decade. For the first time, she thought maybe there was a chance after all.

Chapter Twelve

Quinn kicked the door to her apartment closed behind her as she struggled with the hand trolly holding four banker's boxes containing the files she'd picked up from Jillian. What an odd day it had been. Kirby had met her in the lobby as promised at five thirty, and they'd had a pleasant run. Surprisingly pleasant.

They'd talked about the weather and how they were looking forward to fall, how the Cubs were having a decent year. They agreed this probably wasn't a repeat of 2016 but were still hoping to see a good showing. They talked about men's basketball, women's basketball, more about Kirby's family. Quinn wasn't sure how they'd run so far at such a quick pace, given the amount of talking that they were doing.

She was afraid that after the previous evening and Kirby's "deer in the headlights" expression that Kirby wouldn't even show. And if she did, Quinn assumed it would be another "cold" morning in the game that they were playing. But Kirby had shown, and she hadn't brought the cold. Hot and cold didn't even aptly describe their interactions. Prior to last night, their interactions had been frigid with occasional moments of cool. Last night, however, was definitely running hot, and this morning's run was still very warm. The optimism that started after the elevator was still running rampant, and she longed for more time together. She ached to feel even a slight connection again.

Now Quinn was sitting in her living room with four boxes of 2017, 2018, and 2019 condo files and had no clue where to start. It was Friday night, the best night of the week, and here she was with boxes full of non-work-related papers that needed to be scrubbed. She was, perhaps, the most exciting woman in Chicago. Maybe the world.

She dropped her head onto her kitchen table and groaned at how pathetic she felt. It had been a long week, and what she wanted was to have a glass of wine and go the hell to sleep.

However, a bigger part of her wanted to reach out to Kirby. For any reason, but she could use the files in her living room as an excuse. Ugh. She felt disgusted with herself, but at the same time flashed back to the night before, when she'd found the courage to kiss Kirby's neck. If the elevator had stayed stuck for another breath, she would have been kissing Kirby's mouth. She was confident Kirby would have kissed her back. How far might they have gone if they'd had more time? Fuck. Quinn groaned and tried to shake off that train of thought.

Quinn felt so tightly strung that she might break at any moment. She picked up her phone, looked at it, then set it down, feeling like a creeper. Yet she couldn't get Kirby out of her mind. Would it be so wrong if she reached out to say hi or happy Friday or something about this morning's run?

She took a sip of wine and picked up her phone again. What was the harm in a quick text? If Kirby was out, she might think Quinn pathetic, but she could choose to respond or not. And if she asked about the files on her own with no false pretenses, Quinn could tell her she had them. Yes, that seemed good.

She typed *hey you*, then deleted it. Nope.

She tried again, *Happy Friday*, and quickly backspaced again. Nope.

Third time's a charm perhaps. *What are you up to?* Immediate backspacing again. Absolutely not. This was not a booty call.

She chastised herself for her foolishness and started typing again. *Checked my fitness tracker watch this evening, and that was the fastest 4 miles I've run in months.* Maybe, but she still deleted it.

Ugh.

She finally settled on *Happy Friday. I am a little sore after our run this morning, but that was the fastest 4 miles I've run in months. How are you feeling?*

She hit send before she could overthink it, but even though it was too late, she still obsessed over whether she'd said too much. Or not enough. Why was this so flipping hard?

Within seconds, however, the little dots appeared, indicating that Kirby was texting back. She felt a tingling in her chest that she was afraid might explode, excited and yet afraid of what Kirby might text back.

She took another long sip of a wine that was delightful on the palate. Unsurprising, as it was from her favorite Napa vineyard, Baglioni. A bold 2016 cab that was smooth and delicious.

Sorry if I made you sore this morning...

Heat blazed through her abdomen. "What the literal fuck, Fred? Why would she say that?" Before he could answer, Kirby texted again.

Sorry, it's been a long day. I'm only walking home from work now. Almost brain-dead. Desperately in search of a drink.

Quinn's first thought was, "Well, at least she won't think I'm a loser for being home on a Friday night." She only waited another beat before she replied: *I happen to know a place on your way home. With an open 2016 Baglioni cab that is breathing, and I can attest to its tastiness. If you have some interest.* She again hit send before she could obsess.

Against her better judgment and despite her best efforts to not be a creepy asshole, she added, *I also have the financials from the condo. We don't have to review tonight, but I could give you a sneak peek.* Send.

Shit. Why did she say that? A sneak peek? Really? She was a mess. A hot mess. She dropped her head to the table again and let out a frustrated sigh.

But again, those three little dots popped up and gave her hope.

Interesting.

Shit. How was she supposed to respond to that? Okay, maybe she needed to go out on a limb: *It was a* very *good year. If you're interested and don't just find it interesting, on your way home, stop off at the 30th floor. Turn right. 3005.*

She hit send and waited. And waited. No little dots appeared. No indication that she'd even read the text. Damn. Maybe she'd gone too far? She'd invited Kirby to break the Acquaintance Rules. Kirby had never been a stickler for rules but seemed to be these days. Shit.

❖

Kirby stopped in the middle of the sidewalk and stared at her phone. Quinn had invited her over. With an apparently delicious bottle of wine that was going to be a throwback to their past.

She had no fucking clue what to do.

Marilyn's words—but what if she doesn't break your heart this time—had been reverberating through her head for the last forty-eight hours. The thought of opening back up to Quinn was terrifying, but how was denying what she felt any less painful? It was emotionally exhilarating and yet physically painful to see Quinn and not touch her. To keep running into her. And in the elevator last night…her skin sizzled at the thought. She'd adjusted to give Quinn better access to her neck. They'd been about to kiss.

She'd lost her mind for a moment. And yet, what if she took a chance to see where it led? Could it hurt more than it already had?

She was only about a half-block from home and started walking again, still undecided. She still hadn't responded and was sure Quinn was freaking out, but how could she respond when the inner civil war between her head and her heart was still raging?

When she stepped into the elevator, she still hadn't decided if she would go straight home or make a detour. Her heart desperately wanted the detour, but her head was sounding the alarm and telling her to go directly home, so she pushed the buttons for both the thirtieth and forty-seventh floors. When the doors slid open on the thirtieth, Kirby found herself compelled out of the elevator, but she told herself that she could still come back and call another car without anyone knowing.

She turned right and quickly came upon 3005.

But what if she doesn't break your heart this time?

Kirby couldn't answer that question. She stared at Quinn's door for what felt like an eternity, trying to push past her indecision.

But what if she doesn't break your heart this time?

"Yeah, but what if she does?" Kirby whispered to herself. But if she did, would it be worse than the way she was currently feeling?

Before she could hesitate any longer, Kirby lifted her hand and knocked.

Quinn opened the door so fast, Kirby wondered if she'd been standing next to it, but she looked fantastic in a simple, soft V-neck T-shirt, jeans, and bare yet perfectly manicured feet. On her face was a look of shock, yet Kirby was sure she also saw excitement mixed in.

Quinn wasn't making any motions to invite her in, so she went with a very safe and generic, "Hi, there. Hope it's not too late for that drink?" She tried to plaster on her best, most charming smile.

"No. No. Where are my manners? Sorry, please come in. My mother would be mortified if she knew how I was just standing here. Well, if she knew you were a lesbian, she would block you herself, but otherwise, she'd be mortified. Sorry, I digress. There are still three full pours left in that bottle, and I am willing to share one and a half of those with you." Quinn's rambling hinted that she was just as flustered as Kirby was, though why Quinn would be flustered made no sense. Quinn was the one who'd invited her over.

Kirby couldn't decide if she wanted to follow Quinn in or turn and run. She'd come this far, though, so she decided to step in. She looked around, curious as to the tastes of present-day Quinn. The kitchen and living area were similar to Kirby's, with an open floor plan and a wall of windows along the far side of the living room, though Quinn's flooring was stone gray hardwood with deep blue cabinets and a light marble countertop, almost the opposite of Kirby's. She normally associated the color of this flooring with commercial spaces, but Quinn made it work. The living area was a little smaller than hers and lacked a balcony, but she'd filled it with warm furniture that looked more comfortable than Kirby's own.

"I was surprised to see you at my door." Quinn handed her a generous pour in a bulbous wineglass with tasteful red lines swirling up the sides.

Kirby ran her index finger along the swirling line. "Honestly? So was I. I didn't fully commit until I lifted my hand and knocked on your door." Afraid of what Quinn might see on her face, she turned, unbuttoning the two buttons on her suit jacket and slipping it from her shoulders. She draped it across the back of the barstool at the kitchen peninsula before she slid onto a seat. She was wearing a short-sleeved blouse, and the cool air on her newly freed arms felt amazing, letting them breathe for the first time that day.

"I'm glad you did. I'm happy to see you." Quinn did look happy, with that shy smile that always undid Kirby. Her head and heart continued their struggle, and Kirby tried not to stare at the bottom of the V in Quinn's shirt.

She shook her head at herself and looked at her glass, tilted the contents to the side, and watched the legs of the wine. It appeared to have a fairly high alcohol content, given the number and length of the legs. Focusing on tasting was much easier than trying to figure out what to say to Quinn now that she was in her kitchen.

Kirby swirled the wine and watched its beautiful deep ruby color. "I love the complexity of this color," she said quietly, almost to herself. "It actually is very close to the accent wall in my kitchen."

That extricated a laugh from Quinn. "Why am I not surprised that you have a wine-colored kitchen?"

Kirby made eye contact that felt too significant and smiled anyway. "It's a beautiful color, wine or no, don't you think?"

Quinn continued to look at her with new heat and shrugged. "I don't know how you can draw the anticipation of tasting out this long." "Sometimes, the anticipation makes it even better. Especially when you know how good it's going to be." The subject of wine no longer felt so safe, but Kirby wasn't sure if there was a safe subject where Quinn was concerned. Hell, she wasn't sure she was even still talking about the wine. Her heart and libido seemed to be uniting against her brain.

Kirby managed to break eye contact, slightly altering the tension. She swirled her wine again, closed her eyes, and brought her nose to the rim of the glass, breathing deeply to get the full aroma. "Mmm. Black cherry, vanilla." Keeping her eyes closed despite feeling the intensity of Quinn's gaze, she repeated the process. "Maybe a hint of tea? This smells amazing."

"Wait until you taste it." Quinn's voice cracked.

Kirby's mouth began to water at the thought, but she wasn't certain if it was the thought of tasting the wine or Quinn. "This can't be a cheap bottle. It's, like, special occasion quality, and you're drinking it on a random Friday night? Alone?"

"I'm not alone now, am I?"

"You didn't know I was coming by when you opened it."

"No. But I already felt like it was a bit of a special occasion."

Kirby wasn't sure what that occasion could be, but despite the tension in the room, she wanted to appreciate the wine before changing the dynamics of the moment further. "Interesting. Let me taste this beauty, and then I want to understand why it was already a special occasion."

"I don't think I can tell you due to the Acquaintance Rules, but please, go ahead. We can talk once you've had a taste."

Kirby was afraid to look. Afraid of what she might see on Quinn's face. And afraid of what she might do, so instead, she continued to focus on the wine. It still seemed to be the safest topic in the room. Barely. She swirled it one last time before guiding the glass to her lips and taking a sip. She held it on her tongue for only a moment, but her palate exploded with sensation, cherry, but also berries, vanilla, and a subtle hint of leather. She left her eyes closed and took another small sip, in awe of how tasty it was. "This is beyond delectable. I think it's just as good as the wine we had at the vineyard all those years ago."

"I think it's better."

Unable to ignore the feel of Quinn's continued gaze, Kirby found herself looking up, drawn almost hypnotically. Her throat dried up under the passion in Quinn's eyes, and she took a gulp, not even noticing the delight that it was. Then another. Was it getting warmer? She reached to unbutton her suit jacket before she realized she had already taken it off. She might be losing her mind.

"Which Acquaintance Rule are you trying to break?" she squeaked out.

Quinn appeared to be concentrating for a moment. "Technically none, but I feel like it would be breaking the spirit."

"I'm not sure you noticed, but I willingly broke rule number two this evening by being here."

Quinn giggled. "Good point. Though I probably also broke the rules by encouraging you. It wasn't a rule, but again, in the spirit..."

"You do seem to be quite the rule breaker these days. Look at last night." Kirby's brain continued to sound the alarm, but she couldn't stop. "And since you're the unexpected rebel here..." She cocked an eyebrow and made a continue gesture. She also couldn't resist another sip of the cab.

"Since I am the rebel, what?"

"Why were you already celebrating?"

"Maybe the end of a long week?" She was cute when she tried so unsuccessfully to deflect.

"Nice try, but that wouldn't come close to violating even the spirit of the Acquaintance Rules." Kirby wasn't sure why she was pushing. She still felt nervous at having come over. Nervous at sharing a bottle of wine, particularly a wine that provoked a lot of memories. And perhaps most of all, nervous about what might happen if she set her wine down and walked over to Quinn. Her heart couldn't be trusted. But the squeeze in her chest, the pull of her heart, the unanswered question of "what if she doesn't" kept her pushing.

Quinn turned a faint shade of red. "I shouldn't have said anything."

"But you did, and you can't take it back." Why wasn't she heeding the alarms? Kirby should excuse herself and go home before things got even more out of hand, but she wanted to know. Needed to know.

"Fine. I was celebrating because we have spent three hours together out of the last twenty-four, and they were all pleasant. Friendly, even, despite the threat of possible death. Maybe a little more than friendly. Because we didn't die last night...and maybe, maybe a little because I almost kissed you. And you almost let me. I was pretty sure you were going to let me." She looked into her glass as the red in her cheeks became more pronounced, and Kirby felt that pressure in her chest grow. She couldn't decide if it was telling her to go to Quinn or run. Run far and fast and anywhere but there. So instead, she stayed rooted in place, watching Quinn stare into her glass. Could two people in the same room spend any more time not looking at each other?

Kirby had made the decision to go home when Quinn looked up with hooded eyes, and Kirby was a goner. She'd known this was where the evening would go the moment she'd hit the button engraved with "thirty" in the elevator. With more calmness than she felt, she took one last sip, walked over, and took Quinn's face, tilting her head down.

They stayed like that for a moment before they lunged for each other.

The kiss wasn't soft or sweet. It was rough and passionate and messy. It seemed to embody Kirby's feelings about what was still between them. She didn't know what it meant, but she did know it felt amazing.

No kiss in the last ten years came close to how Quinn was making her feel in that moment. It was almost as though the last decade hadn't happened, and they were still standing in Quinn's living room at her house in Monterey, feasting on one another. The feeling of Quinn's lips pressing against hers, the feeling of Quinn nibbling her jaw felt exciting, but it also felt like coming home.

That feeling of home jarred Kirby back into consciousness. It wedged just enough room into her brain to allow the panic to set in and expand. This was all too much, too fast. Too much period. The pain of Quinn calling her to break up. The pain of being cast aside, of not being enough. It was too real, and this was too much. She couldn't do it.

She pushed away, only now realizing they were both topless in Quinn's kitchen. Kirby's eyes were pulled to Quinn's breasts moving ever so slightly against her silver bra as her chest heaved.

Quinn stared at her with a heart-wrenching expression.

Kirby tried to speak but couldn't quite get the words right. She was more out of breath than at the end of her last half marathon. "I can't...we can't...I thought I could do this, but I...this is a—"

"Please don't say this was a mistake. I'm so sorry that I pushed us too fast, but please don't call this a mistake." Quinn's pleading tone was heartrending, but Kirby stayed strong. "Please, can we maybe take a little break and try to talk in a day or two? Maybe on Sunday. Once we've had a chance to think?"

"I don't know. I just, I just don't know." Her chest was split open again, and all the pain from a decade ago crashed back into her at once.

She needed to get out of there. She swept her top off the floor, frantically trying to flip it so she could pull it back on.

"I know you don't want to, but I really think we need to talk. About how stupid I was. About how I would trade anything to go back. About how I was afraid but I'm not anymore. But I don't think tonight is the right time. Please, can we talk Sunday? Or tomorrow? Or Monday? Any day."

Kirby couldn't breathe and needed to get out of there if she had any hope of thinking clearly again.

"If we talk and you still want me to leave you alone, I will put my condo on the market and look for someplace new. Please, I just want the chance to try to explain and apologize. I know I can't make up for what I did, but I…I don't know. Please, please, don't shut me out. I can't take it."

The tears that had been filling Quinn's eyes began to spill over. Kirby's hands froze as she drew her blouse over her torso. She wanted to run, but seeing Quinn so vulnerable, so exposed, held her in place. "I'll text you, maybe. I won't promise anything, but I'll think about it. I'll try." She grabbed her jacked off the stool and walked backward until she hit the door and fumbled with the doorknob behind her. "Good night," she whispered as she opened the door and backed out.

As she walked to the elevator, she heard a gut-wrenching sob. She tried to convince herself it was coming from somewhere else, some stranger was having a bad end to a bad week, but she knew exactly where that sob had come from, exactly *who* that sob had come from.

She somehow made it into the elevator before her own sob echoed back.

CHAPTER THIRTEEN

Maryland, 2010

Kirby grinned when she looked at her ringing phone and saw Quinn's face smiling back at her. It had been a long few months, but Quinn was finally coming to visit, and she couldn't wait.

She wished Quinn had been stationed in Maryland with her, or in her absence, any of their old crew, but they had been spread all over the world, and no one else had landed in Maryland. It felt weird being alone, but she was excited about her little one-bedroom apartment fifteen minutes from base, and she was excited for Quinn to see it in person, to be in it with her.

In a little less than forty-eight hours, she would have Quinn in her arms again for the first time in months. They Skyped at least once every day for a few minutes, longer if they could, but nothing compared to holding Quinn in the flesh. The feel of their bodies together. The scent of her hair in Kirby's nose. The taste of her skin on Kirby's tongue. In a moment of ridiculous lovesickness, Kirby had bought Quinn's shampoo and began using it herself to be surrounded by Quinn's scent, but it hadn't worked as well as she'd hoped, and she felt more forlorn after every shower.

Kirby didn't understand why, but she could feel them growing apart as the weeks went on, and they didn't see each other. She was confident, however, that a week together would be exactly what they needed to get back on track.

She slid her finger across the bottom of the screen to answer. "Hey, sailor. Lookin' for a good time?"

"Hey. Kirby."

Odd response. Normally, Quinn said something along the lines of, "You know it, but don't tell my girlfriend. She's got a jealous streak a mile wide." Or more simply and to the point, "Mm-hmm. What are you wearing?" To which Kirby always responded, "Nothing," whether it was true or not.

No reason to panic, though. Maybe someone was around, and Quinn couldn't talk candidly.

"I'm excited to see you."

"About that…"

"Uh-oh, that doesn't sound good." Kirby spoke over the small lump forming in her throat.

"I don't think it's a good idea for me to come out this week."

"What? Why? I've been looking forward to this and planning for it for weeks." She heard the whiny tinge in her voice but ignored it. This visit had been getting Kirby through all the lonely months. Quinn had to come. She needed to see her. "I miss you. I miss your face. I miss your arms. I want to see you. I have so many plans for us together in DC. Please."

"I miss you too, but someone started rumors about me. Bad ones that are gaining traction. They aren't one hundred percent true, but true enough that if someone started an investigation, I'd be completely fucked."

"What kind of rumors?"

"Rumors that I'm a big dyke and have a girlfriend in the Air Force in Maryland."

Kirby scoffed. "Really, the Air Force? I am *much* tougher than that. Clearly, they don't have good intel." She was not feeling as worried as Quinn sounded. "Sounds like someone making up shit because you won't go out with them." Rumors had a way of petering out as long as there was no fuel thrown on them. Especially for someone like Quinn, who easily passed for straight with her long hair and propensity to wear high heels all the time.

"Unfortunately, it's more than that. This command. They're so homophobic. It's supposed to be Don't Ask, Don't Tell, but it feels more like deny, deny, deny, hide, or you're going to get crucified."

"But that's not legal. They can't start a witch hunt. And Don't Ask, Don't Tell is going to be a memory in less than a year." Full of indignation, she began pacing around her living room. This was such bullshit. There was no way something as trivial as rumors could keep them apart.

"I don't think I have that long. My fucking roommate apparently overheard us a few weeks ago on Skype, and now the entire fucking division is talking about how surprising it is that I'm a dyke because I look so femme."

"If that's it, then just lay low for a bit. I'm sure it'll blow over. Make up a lie about going to visit your family in Oregon or something this next week."

"That bitch saw my tickets and already knows I'm going to Maryland. She has apparently told the entire division that as well. There's no way I can come." She sounded defeated. Kirby knew she'd been struggling with mild depression since getting to Bahrain, but she'd never sounded so hopeless.

"I know it seems bleak, but we can get through this." Kirby couldn't believe that the situation actually was hopeless, despite Quinn's tone. Her stomach was churning, but she was certain they could figure something out, even if it meant they couldn't see each other that week. "I don't want you to skip this trip. I *hate* the thought of it, but look, I love you, and we can reschedule. We can meet somewhere else in a few weeks. We could do London or Paris or Barcelona. Somewhere that wouldn't be connected to either of us. You can tell them you're meeting your brother or parents or even having a holiday alone."

"I can't." Quinn sighed heavily.

Kirby's hand shook, and she almost dropped the phone. "You can't what? Meet me for a holiday?" That didn't make any sense. A holiday with no one who knew them would be perfect. Like Napa had been. There was no way Quinn could be talking about something else. About them. About their love.

"I can't do this anymore, Kirby."

"What?" Kirby's stomach fell to the floor as she could no longer deny what Quinn was doing. She leaned against the wall before her legs gave out.

"I can't do *us* anymore. Before you, I never got attached to anyone. Who I am in my chosen profession is a crime. I can't do a relationship right now." Her voice was devoid of emotion. How could she sound so cold?

Kirby pleaded. "It's not going to be a crime for much longer. Things are going to change so soon. *Please* don't do this." She had to see reason. "Listen, Obama promised that he was going to end this shit."

"It's not going to be in time, Kirby." Quinn's voice hitched, and

Kirby began to cry in earnest. "There's no way. You don't understand what it's like here."

Kirby refused to accept that this could be it. That the love of her life was going to walk away without a second thought. Their love could conquer this. She knew that it could. "I might not understand what it's like there, but I know us. I know our love. We can get through this. I'll do whatever you need. Whatever you want. Please, just give us a chance. Do you need us to talk a little less often? Maybe only write letters and use code names, no Skyping?"

"It's too late. The rumors here are spreading like crazy. I have to toe the line. I can't. I just can't be who I need to be to survive this with my career intact and be with you. This is my livelihood, Kirby. My life."

"*You* are my life, Quinn. *We* are my life. Please don't do this. I'll wait for you. I've only got two years left here. You've got two years at most in Bahrain. We can hit pause. Once this is over, I'll come to you. I'll move wherever you are. I don't care about the military. I care about *you*." Kirby's heartbeat was roaring in her ears, threatening to drown everything else out. She fought to keep her thoughts together. Quinn had to see. Kirby would give anything, everything up without hesitation to make things work with her. She slid to the floor, her legs no longer able to hold her up.

"I don't have that luxury. The military *is* me. You may see these four years as a blip in your life, but it's been my life for the last eleven. It's my career. It's my future. It's my retirement. I can't throw it away like it hasn't been my life for my *entire* adulthood."

"I'm not asking you to. Work with me to find a way. I know you love the Navy. I know you've committed yourself. But for fuck's sake! You love me too. And I love you. I will do anything to make this work. If you need me to disappear for a year, I will. If you need me to not talk to you until Don't Ask, Don't Tell is repealed, I will. Please. People search their whole lives for what we have. You know it's true. You don't have to pick between me and the Navy, Quinn."

Kirby knew she sounded desperate as she begged Quinn to love her, to not cast her aside. She felt a stab of embarrassment at herself, at how pathetic she must sound, but couldn't find it in in herself to care or stop. Her skin felt too small for her body and was compressing her limbs, her torso. She had to make Quinn see that she didn't have to do this. Her entire future as she'd planned it was vanishing, and she had no idea how to stop it. If only Quinn was standing there in front of her so she could touch her, or even on the computer screen so Quinn could see the sincerity in her eyes. But Quinn was so closed off. Her mind was apparently made up.

"I can't be who I need to be in order to fight this if I'm with you. If I'm thinking about you, wishing I was with you, I can't do it. I have to make everyone think I *am* the perfect, straight sailor, which means I have to *be* the perfect, straight sailor. I don't have a future without the Navy."

The final shreds of Kirby's disbelief vanished, and she dropped her head onto her knees, resigned. She could barely find her voice. "I thought *I* was your future. I thought we together were the future. I guess there's nothing I can do to compete with the fucking Navy. *Your* life. *Your* future."

"I'm sorry, Kirby, but I just…I just can't."

"Fuck you and fuck the Navy. I would have done anything for you. In six or twelve months, when Don't Ask, Don't Tell is repealed, you're going to regret this. We should have been together forever."

"I'm sorr—"

"Fuck you!" Kirby yelled and slammed down the phone before slumping over until she was lying on the floor. It had to be a terrible nightmare. She tried pinching herself, but nothing happened. How could Quinn know what they had and walk away? They'd made plans. Their love was forever, like what all the romance novels talked about. Like what her parents had, and Quinn had just thrown it away like it was nothing. Maybe it had never been anything after all.

CHAPTER FOURTEEN

When Quinn awoke the next morning, all of her optimism from the previous day had evaporated. It was Saturday, but it felt more dismal than any day in recent memory. She should have known better than to try to push things with Kirby. But Kirby herself had been so pushy regarding why Quinn was breaking the Acquaintance Rules. She had to know where pushing down that road would eventually lead.

Quinn had been so nervous and yet so hopeful when Kirby had kept asking what she was celebrating. By the time they got there, she had been sure Kirby knew what she was going to hear.

And that kiss? My God, that kiss. It was everything Quinn remembered between them. The spark, the heat, the intensity. When Kirby had pressed her against the countertop, kissing her like it was their last day on Earth, Quinn had thought she might die. For a moment, it had felt like no time had passed since their days in California, but as quickly as it had started, Kirby was pushing her away again.

Quinn desperately wished there was someone she could call to talk this through with, but there wasn't. She sure as hell couldn't call her family. She saw them once a year at most, in a bad year, but they had never been supportive of anything she'd done. They hated that she'd joined the Navy; they pretended they didn't know she was gay.

She had no confidants. She genuinely liked Nylah but wasn't comfortable getting that personal with a new colleague. She had acquaintances like the ones she went to Pride with but no close friends from the Navy. She didn't want to think about the last close friend that she actually had. Kirby had made it clear last night that they were not friends again and didn't have much hope of becoming anything other than acquaintances.

Regardless, there wasn't much anyone could tell her. She'd fucked everything up all those years ago, and until Kirby was willing to talk to her, there wasn't anything she could do. So rather than get herself together and go for a run, she pulled on sweats and gathered Fred to take him downstairs. As soon as he was done, she curled up on the couch under a blanket with a pint of mint chocolate chip ice cream to eat her way through her feelings despite it barely being nine a.m. She put on a movie that matched her mood, the one about a dog that keeps dying and getting reincarnated. That tear-fest allowed her to cry her feelings out without acknowledging what she was actually doing. She wasn't a big crier, but sometimes, even she needed to let her emotions out.

❖

Kirby picked up her phone, looked at the screen, and set it back down. She repeated the motion again. And again. She walked away and made herself a cup of coffee but was drawn back to that damn phone like a moth to a flame.

She unlocked the screen, scrolled to her contacts, pulled up Quinn's name, and slammed the phone back down on the coffee table. What was there to say?

Why couldn't she walk away? What was wrong with her? Last night, she had allowed her hormones to get the best of her. There was still an attraction between her and Quinn, but everything else was long since past. No lingering feelings. None whatsoever.

Quinn had asked for help, and she should have known better than to go over after dark. Nothing good happened after dark. That was the saying, wasn't it? Or was that after two a.m.? Either way, no good decisions were made. Especially when wine was involved. Especially when they had a history with that wine. That wine had been a key player in the most romantic weekend of Kirby's life, so it was no wonder she had been emotionally whisked back in time. It certainly didn't mean she still had feelings for Quinn. Why would she?

For a while after they had broken up, Kirby wasn't sure if she even had feelings anymore, and in the decade since, she'd never had any real romantic feelings for anyone. She surely hadn't been celibate, but she'd also never seriously dated or gotten attached to anyone either. She had barely survived their breakup, and that was all she could think of when she'd pushed Quinn away.

Yet thinking back at the look on Quinn's face as she walked away, at the sob that she'd heard from the hall, pulled at her heart more strongly than she would have imagined.

As Kirby reached for her phone one more time, it began to vibrate. She pulled her hand away as though she had been burned, thinking it was Quinn, but she realized how foolish that was. It was Saturday morning, so it was probably her mother.

She flipped the phone over, but it was only a text from Emily. *Hey.* Kirby rolled her eyes. Emily likely wanted to give her a hard time about not going out with the group last night, and Kirby definitely wasn't in the mood for that. She also wasn't in the mood to talk about what she'd actually been up to the night before. She didn't want to think about it herself, much less talk to anyone about it.

She flipped her phone facedown once again and went into the kitchen to make herself another cup of coffee. She tried to put Emily out of her mind, but when she did, her thoughts were engulfed by images of Quinn, and she just kept replaying that kiss over and over in her head.

The softness of Quinn's lips. The scent of her hair, exactly same as she remembered. It was like a scratched record that just kept playing the same track over and over again. She wished it would stop entirely, and short of that, she wished the offending track would start over the moment before she'd pushed Quinn away. Instead, it played all the way through Quinn's stricken face as Kirby had run and Quinn had sobbed. The sick feeling of guilt churned in her stomach along with the low hum of arousal she'd had since walking into Quinn's place.

She grabbed her vanilla coffee creamer out of the refrigerator and added a splash to her cup. She stirred the coffee with more force than necessary, stopping only when some of it sloshed over the edge of the mug. "Shit." She grabbed the sponge from the sink and wiped up her spill, scrubbing with more force than was necessary until she hit her mug and spilled more. "Hell." She was apparently now taking her frustration out on her coffee. And her counter. She didn't know how to get Quinn out of her head so she could get some peace, but she needed to figure something out before she wore a hole in the granite.

She threw the sponge back into the sink and took her coffee to the living room while trying to think about anything other than Quinn. Completely unsuccessfully. When her phone buzzed again, Kirby snatched it off the table for something to distract herself and prayed it wasn't Quinn.

Another text from Emily. *Hello? I know you're awake. You're always up this early.*

That was true. Kirby was an early riser. And she always did better sorting her feelings out when she could talk them through with someone. Even if she didn't want to. Before she could change her mind, Kirby dialed Emily. Perhaps Emily wanted to talk about something that would take her mind off Quinn for a bit too.

"Morning, sunshine," Emily said after only half a ring.

"You're very chipper after having been out last night." Kirby was occasionally jealous of how easily Emily could rebound after a night out. She'd been able to do the same thing when she was twenty-three. but now that she was pushing forty, it was a lot harder.

"Nah, it wasn't a late night. What about you?"

Kirby sighed as she decided where to begin. "A little crazier than I expected. Why'd you text so early?"

Emily laughed. "What are you trying to say? That I'm lazy and don't get up on Saturdays? Can't a girl text her best friend because she misses her without an ulterior motive?"

The sincerity in Emily's voice made Kirby smile even as she knew that there was, undoubtedly, an ulterior motive. "I'm not sure how to answer that and am instead going to plead the Fifth."

"Maybe instead start by telling me why you had a crazy night?"

Kirby sighed. "I…well…I had an encounter. With my ex. With Quinn. You rem—"

"Of course I remember. I'm coming over."

"No, please don't. I'm not really in the mood for company. I just wanted to maybe talk this through with someone. With you." Kirby feared Emily's intensity would be unbearable in her current condition.

"Nonsense. This needs to be handled in person. I'll grab brunch and be there in thirty minutes."

Kirby could hear Emily start to shuffle around. and Kirby envisioned she was throwing on her shoes to come right over. She was still reluctant to have Emily over, but the thought of brunch was enticing. "Brunch from where?"

"Your favorite place with the fried green tomatoes. You know you can't resist."

It was true. She couldn't. Softening, Kirby said, "Fine. I'll be here and let security know to let you up."

Forty-five minutes later, Emily arrived at her door in gray sweats and with her hair in a messy bun with the promised brunch as well as a surprise minibar in tow. The food smelled heavenly, and Kirby's stomach responded with a growl.

"Hungry much?" Emily laughed and pushed her way past Kirby. She set her bags down on the counter and began to unpack.

"Hungrier than I thought." Kirby grabbed plates and glasses. She made their drinks, complete with cheese cubes and celery, while Emily doled out breakfast skillets, fancy pancakes, and fried green tomatoes.

Once they settled at the table, Emily spoke first. "It's not why I texted you, but I had a little inkling that something was going on with you and your ex. Marilyn said something to me last night, and I thought, 'There's no way that's true because my best friend would have called me if she was living in the same building as her ex. Especially if she might be entertaining something a little more. Doubly so with the woman who broke her heart ages ago.' And yet, the more I thought about it, the more your behavior of late made sense. You've been ignoring my calls half the time, which you never do. You haven't gone out with us at all. You seem…different. I wanted to find out the truth."

"I am *not* different." Kirby speared a little cheddar-jack cheese cube with more force than necessary.

"That's what you deny out of all of that? Not that you didn't call me to tell me anything about what was going on with you two? Or that you have been avoiding me?"

Chagrined, Kirby ducked her head. "I unfortunately cannot deny the rest. I've been stewing with it for a while. But I can't believe that Marilyn told you all that."

"She was slightly inebriated at the time and made a comment in passing about your old flame coming back into your life. I wouldn't leave her alone about it until she told me more, and you know how annoying I can be when motivated, but that's all I got out of her. So you better start talking because I cannot live knowing that Marilyn knows more about your past and present love life than I do. And I think you need to talk. Actually, I know you need to talk. It's why you called me this morning."

Kirby was rarely one to share her feelings—that had ended with Quinn—but Emily was sentimental and not emotionally stunted like she was. She knew shutting Emily out was torture for her and that she needed to make it up to her. And talking it through was why she'd called her this morning. Getting it off her chest and bouncing her thoughts off someone would have to help.

"You are a good best friend. A better friend than I am to you." They gave each other a hard time constantly, but Emily was the best.

"I do try," Emily said as she preened and patted her hair as though it was perfectly coiffed rather than in a messy bun. Kirby laughed at her silliness.

She took a bite of a melt-in-your-mouth fried green tomato and sighed in pleasure. "Your gifts are softening me up. So, my exciting night. I'm not sure if exciting is really the right word for it, but something did happen. I've been trying to process this shit, unsuccessfully, I might add, on my own for weeks, so thank you for coming over to let me blabber on about it."

Kirby took a sip of Bloody Mary to steel herself and tried to decide how much to share, but once she got going, she talked for longer than she would have believed possible. She told Emily everything, from her and Quinn's first meeting to the intense relationship they had for almost two years, to the breakup and everything that had happened since seeing her again at Pride, including their fast and furious make-out session the night before where both of their shirts ended up on the floor. And how Kirby freaked out and pushed Quinn away and the devastated look on Quinn's face.

When Kirby finished, she still had no idea what to do, but a weight did feel like it had been lifted from her.

"Holy. Shit." Emily stared. "So that dog you mentioned, he's scruffy, pretty small with a crazy underbite?"

"I spill my heart out, and you zero in on her dog?" Kirby looked quizzically at her, not sure why that was the detail she was asking about.

"Trust me. That's him, right?"

"Sounds right."

"And Quinn, is she about five-seven, blond, pretty, yet kind of eerie, amber eyes, absolutely gorgeous face?"

"How did you know any of that? Though I wouldn't describe her eyes as eerie."

"I saw her in the elevator carrying that ugly-ass dog when I was coming up here."

"You what?"

"And her eyes might not have looked so eerie if they hadn't been puffy and red-rimmed."

"I've only actually seen her cry once before last night. The night she got her orders to Bahrain."

"You guys were together for almost two years, and you only saw her cry once?"

"Yeah. I saw tears of laughter a bunch. I think she cried a couple of times over the phone but never when we were Skyping."

"Not even when you broke up?"

"She called me, not Skyped, and I'm not sure if she cried or not. She sounded cold and detached."

"Well, judging from this morning, I'd say she's been crying pretty much nonstop since last night. And after seeing her, I can understand why she'd try not to cry in front of anyone. She isn't an attractive crier."

"Judgmental much? Who *is* an attractive crier?"

Emily snickered. "Jumping to her defense. Interesting." She stared with pursed lips, and Kirby threw an empty container at her.

"Ugh. Whatever." Quinn *was* objectively beautiful, and no one was attractive when they cried. Emily was being judgmental, and Kirby was certain her comment didn't have some hidden message for Emily to decode.

When Emily just laughed at her, Kirby groaned and dropped her head onto the table. "But what am I going to do?"

"First, let me apologize for giving you such a hard time about not being open to love. You clearly had love PTSD. Hell, still have."

"I do not!" Love PTSD. What bullshit.

"Then why did you push her away when you started to feel something other than lust?"

"I—"

"Why haven't you dated anyone seriously at all in almost a decade?"

"I—"

"Why do you jump to her defense when I make fun of her?"

"I—"

"Why have you been circling around her for the past few months? You intentionally try to spend time with her, but whenever she gets too close, you panic and pull back. Face it. You are still drawn to her like crazy, but you're so afraid of getting hurt again that you refuse to let her get close, even though every fiber of your being—not to mention the universe—is pulling you to her."

"Bullshit."

"You've spent the last decade running away from something that you seem unable to avoid."

"You don't understand how much she hurt me. I'm not sure if she ever loved me the way I loved her."

"Do you truly believe that in your heart?" Emily clinked her ice cubes before reaching for the pitcher and splitting the remaining dregs between their glasses.

"Yes," Kirby said as she thought of how cold Quinn was when she'd broken up with her. But as she thought back to what they'd shared all those years ago before the heartbreak and how Quinn had been over the past few weeks, she was no longer as certain that was true. "Maybe not?" she whispered. "But then how could she have thrown everything away like she did?"

Emily grabbed Kirby's hand around the empty containers from their demolished brunch. "I can't answer that question, but Quinn can. But if I were going to guess? She felt like she was in an unwinnable situation and made the wrong decision. A decision that I would bet my life she regrets more than anything."

Could that be right? She looked at their joined hands and confessed something she refused to admit, even to herself most of the time. "I'm afraid."

"I know. And understandably so. But if you keep running away from your past, you're never going to be able to move forward."

"My mom said something similar. It's when I started being more friendly with Quinn actually."

"Your mom is a wise woman. So is Marilyn. So am I. What's the worst that could happen if you get your shit together and talk to her?" Emily stood and started clearing their carryout containers from the table.

"She breaks my heart again, and I never recover?" Kirby stared into her empty glass and took a bite of celery. The rhythmic crunch between her teeth lulled her into a near trance.

As she continued to clear off the counter, Emily looked over her shoulder, and Kirby felt her intense stare. "It's been ten years, and you still haven't recovered. Don't you already worry about never recovering? If you don't do something, I think never recovering is a greater risk than if you try a different approach."

"Fuck." Kirby flattened the side of her face on her table, the press of wood cool against her vodka-heated cheek.

"I'd love to stay and keep agonizing with you, but I think my work here is done. I've got a date in a few hours, and I definitely need to shower first. Try to make myself presentable, you know? The messy bun and sloppy clothes are good for brunch in your dining room but not so good for public consumption."

"So you come in here, pull off all the bandages from my battered heart, pour lemon juice over the raw wounds, and then run off for your little romance? Cruel, Emily. Very cruel." She smiled so Emily would know she was kidding. Mostly.

Emily shrugged. "It's my gift."

"So who are you going out on a date with? Did you meet someone new last night?"

"No, but sort of. She's actually the reason I texted this morning."

"What does that mean?"

"That hot bartender at the wine bar—"

"Oh, the one you've been pining away for?" Kirby was excited for her. Emily had been obsessed with her for months.

"Yes. She was at the club last night, and we started talking. Actually talking, you know? Not just about what types of wine I like. She's apparently as smart as she is attractive."

Kirby squeezed her shoulder. "That's great."

"I figured if you, Ms. Perpetually Single, were going to take a shot at love, I should pluck up my courage too. So I did and asked her out." Her self-satisfied grin was adorable.

"Good for you, but I'm not—"

"Hush. And don't say something you don't mean. Stop letting the luggage that the airlines should have lost years ago drag you down."

Kirby laughed. "That is a ridiculous metaphor."

"Ridiculous or genius. I'm going with genius." She kissed Kirby on the cheek, stuck out her tongue, and was gone.

"Well, that was a whirlwind," Kirby said to no one. She slipped out onto her balcony and buried herself on her lounger, snuggling into her favorite throw blankets to ward off the chill. She gazed at the lake, enjoying the crispness that only October could bring, and tried to clear her mind, but Marilyn's words continued to infiltrate her thoughts. *But what if she doesn't break your heart this time?* Her years with Quinn were the happiest of her life, but the pain of their ending could still bring Kirby to her knees if she let it.

Looking back through clear eyes, Kirby couldn't deny that Quinn had loved her. She knew Quinn had been in a terrible position, but how could she have chosen the Navy over Kirby? Over them? It didn't make sense.

Before she knew it, Kirby had slipped off to sleep, a memory of Quinn's smile on her mind.

Chapter Fifteen

By Sunday afternoon, Quinn hadn't showered in two days but didn't much care. She hadn't heard from Kirby since Friday night and was beginning to lose hope that she would. That afternoon, she was still curled up on the couch with Fred nestled on her chest, exactly where she'd been for the last forty-two hours or so, and was about ten minutes into streaming another movie she'd likely sleep through. She was starting to doze off again when a pounding on her door startled her back to reality.

Quinn's heart thundered so loudly, she suspected the neighbors could hear it as the adrenaline from being startled awake coursed through her body, and she limped to the door, trying to work the kinks out of her back from lying on the couch for two days. It was probably Jillian trying to see if she was through with the condo files yet. The answer to that was unequivocally no since complete inertia had set in on Friday.

She was so certain that as she pulled it open, she started to say, "I haven't reviewed anything yet, Jilli—" She didn't get it all out, however, as an angry Kirby standing on her threshold brought her up short. Quinn cleared her throat. Seeing Kirby had her heart start it's pounding again, and sweat coated her palms. "Hey, sorry, I thought you were Jillian."

A small smile flitted at the corners of Kirby's mouth before her scowl set back in. "Clearly."

"Clearly," Quinn echoed. "Do…you want to come inside? Fred and I were watching a movie." As she stepped back, she realized with horror that she was in ancient Navy sweatpants that barely had any stretch left in the waistband and a holey T-shirt, and she wasn't certain that she had even brushed her teeth that day. Maybe not even yesterday. "Would you excuse me for a minute? I was heading to the bathroom when you knocked. I'll only be a moment."

"Oh, uh, sure."

Quinn wondered why it looked like she'd taken the wind out of Kirby's sails, but she desperately needed to freshen up. "I'll be back in a sec. Please feel free to make yourself comfortable." She threw the blanket she'd been using over the back of the couch and tried to surreptitiously grab the take-out containers spread on her coffee table but suspected Kirby saw. Because she had eyes and Quinn didn't have an invisibility cloak.

She nearly ran into the bathroom, splashed some water on her face, and brushed her teeth. She left her sweatpants on but exchanged her shirt for one that didn't look like a mouse had chewed its way through multiple times. She looked at her puffy eyes, but there wasn't much she could do there. She wished that she had time to shower but was afraid that if she took more than a couple of minutes, Kirby might flee again. With a final swipe of deodorant and a tousle of her hair, she walked back into the living room. "I wasn't expecting to hear from you today. Don't get me wrong. I'm happy to see you, just surprised."

Kirby turned from her seat on the couch and raised her eyebrows, no doubt at the wardrobe change. "I'm a little surprised by it myself, but here I am." She ran her fingers through her short hair as she often did when anxious. Knowing she was nervous too made Quinn feel a little more settled as she sat on the couch.

"So," Quinn began, "what—"

"How could you do it, Quinn? Did you ever even love me?" Kirby's eyes flashed with anger as she turned sharply. She had seemingly rediscovered the emotion she'd shown up with.

Quinn marshalled her emotions as she prepared to fight for the only woman she'd ever loved, knowing she was going to have to lay herself bare to give Kirby everything she had in her, every emotion in her, in order to stand a chance at winning. "I loved you with my entire being. My entire soul." Quinn slid closer to her and reached for her hand, but she slid it out of reach. That hurt, but Quinn couldn't blame her.

"Then how could you? How could you call me so cruelly and dump me without even a backward glance? And then never try to reach out again? Even after Don't Ask, Don't Tell was repealed. It was barely a few months later that the law changed, and nothing. Not one peep."

"Oh, Kirby. I wish I could go back and handle things differently. I was so afraid of everything at the time. I was a coward. I hate myself for the way I treated you. How could I call you after I had been so terrible? And with what I did after I broke up with you."

"What do you mean?" Kirby furrowed her eyebrows.

Quinn squeezed her eyes closed as the torrent of bad memories washed over her. She didn't want to talk about it, but Kirby deserved the truth. The full truth. And after that, she could only hope. "My command in Bahrain was unbelievably homophobic. Shortly after I arrived there, a young male sailor was sexually assaulted on base by another man. He didn't know who did it, but he was roughed up pretty bad and had to go to the hospital. He reported the assault, and the command chose to start a witch hunt. They investigated him even though he was the victim. Typical victim blaming, and they found out that he was gay, assumed it must be his fault, and began dishonorable discharge proceedings."

"Oh my God, Quinn, how did you not tell me that?"

"I didn't want you to worry about me being safe, and I didn't want you to worry about us getting caught. We were so careful."

"I know, but still. Was he a friend of yours?"

"I wouldn't say friend, but he was a nice guy. I met him at a party, and we were friendly before the incident. After the incident, and I hate myself for this, but I distanced myself from him because I was afraid of guilt by association. It wasn't like we were best friends, but given the climate of the command, I was too afraid to even talk to him. In the time when he probably most needed a friend, I was such a coward."

"Oh, Quinn."

She wondered if Kirby was either judging her or trying to absolve her of her sins, but she'd come this far and needed to get everything out. "Shortly after, that bitch eavesdropped on one of our Skype conversations and started spreading rumors about me being in a relationship with you. Well, not specifically you, but the idea of you. The rumors began to spread like wildfire." She stood and began to pace. "I had no idea who I could trust, but my chief sat me down one day and didn't 'ask' per se but told me what a mistake it would be if the rumors came out as true. He told me he knew I'd make Chief soon, then he proceeded to remind me my future as a sailor was at risk and what would happen if the rumors found their way up the chain."

Quinn relaxed her tightly balled fists and rubbed at the half-crescent indentations in her palms from her nails. That command was the worst she'd ever served under, and she still had hatred for most of the sailors there. "I am still not sure to this day if that chat was a threat or a reminder, but from that moment, I couldn't think of anything other than the witch hunt that poor sailor had to endure. The brutal questions about his past. The interviews of his friends in the command, previous duty stations, and in his hometown. Somehow, the command didn't recognize the second half of the Don't Ask, Don't Tell edict. You know, Don't Pursue, Don't Harass. Fuckers."

Her voice broke as she felt awash in the hopelessness from all of those years ago. "I'm sorry. I need a glass of water. Do you want anything? Water? Wine? Bourbon?" She cleared her throat. When she finally looked at Kirby, she saw compassion. Kirby's eyes were a small spark of hope trying to see her through her own self-loathing that was so hard to fight.

"Sure, water would be nice."

She brought back a glass of water for each of them and handed one to Kirby.

"Thank you." Kirby smiled, and Quinn took that as a prompt to continue.

"I denied the rumors at first, but it seemed to have no effect. My roommate kept telling people how many hours I spent on the phone with my lesbian lover back in the States, and it kept going around and around."

"That's when you started to pull back, isn't it? You put a distance between us that even the miles couldn't."

"Yeah." Quinn watched a drip of condensation slide down the side of her glass and onto her thumb. "I didn't feel like I could talk on the phone to anyone without it fanning the flames. I didn't know what to do or how to make it stop, but I was so afraid."

Looking back, she felt so stupid. "I was afraid of losing my career, my pension, and you were so far away. I felt like we were growing apart, and I no longer felt so confident that we could make it through anything. It wasn't until later that I realized we were growing apart because I was pulling away. It wasn't the distance. It was me."

She felt tears pricking her eyes and tried to force them back in as she continued to stare into her glass. "I thought I needed to do something drastic in order to kill the rumors."

The hardest part of the story was coming, so Quinn took a sip, wishing it was something stronger, a little burn down the back of her throat to settle her nerves. "There was this guy, Dave. He'd been asking me out periodically since I arrived. I had kindly but firmly turned him down every time, but then I thought if I went out on a few dates with him, it would stop the rumors. I would never—could never—do that if we were still together. I could never do that to you. But then came the drama of my plane tickets and my roommate telling everyone that I was going to see my lover in Maryland. I have no idea what set her off, but she was on a mission to smear my reputation. I didn't see any way out other than Dave."

"So to squelch the rumors, you decided to date a guy?"

Flooded with shame, Quinn said, "Looking back, I know I could have done a million things differently, but at the time, I saw no way out. All I could see was you breaking my heart anyway and me getting a dishonorable discharge. I didn't have a backup plan. So I broke up with you. And then I said yes to Dave."

Kirby grimaced. "Dating a guy would be fine if you were into guys too, but you aren't. We talked about it."

"I know. Not my proudest moment. In fact, I was disgusted with myself the entire time. Every time I went out with him and he'd grab my hand or lean in to kiss me, I had to force down my gag reflex. And the worst part is, he was a really good guy. Like, the guy you want your little sister to marry."

"I don't have a little sister," Kirby said with a little chuckle. "Neither do you."

Quinn smiled slightly. "No, but you know what I mean. The type of person you would want for her if you did. He had no idea that I was using him as my beard. Honestly, if I had told him the truth, he probably would have agreed to pretend date me rather than actually date me. My absolute lowest point was when I tried to sleep with him. He was so sweet and never pushed me, but the dating was only helping the rumors a little bit, and I thought if I slept with him, he would tell his buddies, and they would talk, and then the rumors would go away."

"Oh God. I'm guessing that didn't go well for you, then?" Kirby winced before she placed a hand on Quinn's leg and lightly squeezed.

"God, no. When he slid his hand down my pants, I burst into tears." Quinn did laugh scornfully at that repulsive memory. "Poor guy had no idea what he did wrong that would cause me to go to pieces. That was pretty much the end of that farce, though to his credit, Dave apparently never told anyone about the crying, as the rumors didn't get worse. It is, however, when I realized I needed a change and ended up choosing OCS. The officers in my unit were happy to recommend me, as they hadn't yet heard the rumors. Such bullshit." She ran her thumb along the outside of her sweating glass, trying to force herself to continue. The worst was out, but her stomach was still roiling.

"I was so disgusted with myself—at how I treated you, at what a coward I had been, at how I had taken advantage of Dave and his kindness—I just couldn't find the courage to call you even after Don't Ask, Don't Tell was lifted. You were right when you hung up on me. Every single day of my life since I made that horrible phone call to you, I have regretted it. And then you suddenly walked back into my life. Or should I say, fell back into my life when you fell on me at Pride. And I have been hoping against hope that you could find a way to forgive me. That we could find a way to be friends. A secret piece of me was praying we could find a way to be more, but I tried not to let her be the voice in my head often."

Kirby's look was hard to read with tears leaving tracks down her face, and Quinn couldn't decide if she should continue or not. "I don't think there are words to fully communicate how sorry I am. I'm sorry I broke your heart. I'm sorry I broke my own too but not nearly as sorry as I am that I broke yours. I've tried to karmically make up for the damage I did. I volunteer at gay outreach centers, I chaired the LGBTQ+ club in the Navy, once having those wasn't illegal, I volunteer at animal shelters…I wish there was some way I could regain your trust. Even if just to be your friend." She swallowed the lump in her throat as she watched Kirby, still waiting for her reaction.

"You really hurt me. My best friend came over yesterday and told me I have love PTSD. I want to deny it, but I think she's right. I haven't dated anyone seriously since we broke up. I didn't fully realize it, but you really messed me up."

"I know. I am so, so sorry."

Kirby laughed. "Please stop apologizing. At this point, if I didn't know you were sorry, I haven't been paying attention."

"I just—"

Kirby didn't pause. "What I've been struggling with is, how can I trust you again? How can I trust you to not run again if we encounter an obstacle? How can I open myself up and risk that kind of pain again?"

"I—"

"Please let me finish, okay?" When Quinn nodded, Kirby continued, "The thing is, I'm already in pain. I have been miserable since I started running in to you again."

Quinn's heart dropped, but she managed to not interrupt.

"It seems like no matter where I go, there you are. You have invaded my condo building, my favorite wine bar, my running route, my grocery store...the list goes on and on. And yet, I keep finding myself drawn to you even as I fight it. So, yes, I am unhappy, but it has turned from being unhappy because I'm seeing you to being unhappy because I'm not *seeing* you seeing you, you know?"

"You're unhappy because you're not seeing me? Like, as much?" Quinn understood every word individually but couldn't make sense of them together.

"No, I'm unhappy because when we're together, it feels like it used to. I want to take your hand and hold it. I want to hold you. I want to kiss you. And it hurts my heart because I keep denying myself. When I kissed you Friday night, it felt right. It felt like home, and it scared the shit out of me, so I ran. But that didn't make me feel any better. My heart and my head were warring because my heart wanted to run to you and hated how I hurt you on Friday, but my head was so afraid of getting hurt. But the more I thought about it, with a little help from my best friend, I have to acknowledge that I'm already hurting and have never actually gotten over you. We clearly still have something between us, but I needed to understand why you chose the Navy over me and decide if I could get past it or not."

Quinn slid her hand a little closer, sliding their fingers together. "So now what? How do you feel now that you know the whole truth?"

"Honestly? I don't know, but I do understand a little more." She squeezed Quinn's fingers and flipped her hand over and slid it under Quinn's, palm to palm, with her fingers grazing the back of Quinn's wrist. "When you broke up with me, I couldn't understand how you could just let us go. With the end of Don't Ask, Don't Tell on the horizon that everyone could see coming, I didn't get it. But I didn't realize how homophobic the command there was. I didn't realize that even with the end being near that you could be dishonorably discharged before that happened. And although it still hurts to know you picked the Navy over me, I understand that it was a moment in time." Her fingers were beginning to make Quinn feel lightheaded.

"The worst moment of my life. The worst decision I have ever made."

"I know. I don't think I can—nor do I think I want to—keep fighting this, but I'm not sure what happens next. Do we go out on a date? Would you want to go on a date with me?"

"There is nothing in the world that I want more than to go on a date with you." She stared at her hand on top of Kirby's and tightened her fingers. When she looked up, she saw Kirby staring at her mouth. She didn't want to move too quickly, but the pull was too strong to resist. Millimeters before their lips touched, Quinn paused and looked into Kirby's eyes. All she saw staring back at her was anticipation and desire, and before she had a moment to breathe, Kirby closed the gap.

Unlike the previous night, this kiss was gentle and sweet. She could smell Kirby's lip balm and mousse. She reached into her hair, feeling its silky softness and sank more into the kiss. She had fireworks going off in her chest, but she didn't want to push too much, too fast, so she eased back slightly and let out a shaky breath.

"Wow," she whispered.

"Yeah, there's definitely still something here." Kirby's forehead was resting against hers, and they were breathing the same air.

Quinn didn't want this moment to end. She brought her lips back to Kirby's for a quick kiss and then asked, "Do you want to stay and watch the rest of this movie with me and Fred?"

"Well, Fred seems to have made himself at home here with me, so I don't think I can go yet anyway." She gestured to Fred snuggled up in a ball on her lap. As if on cue, he hunkered down farther and pushed his face more into Kirby's hip.

"Yeah, he gets pretty cranky when he's woken up and shuffled about. He can be vicious. It's probably safer if you stay for a while."

"I like that idea." Kirby's smile made her face glow.

"Are you hungry? We could order some food. I haven't eaten much today."

"The graveyard of carryout containers sitting on your coffee table when I arrived would tell a different story." Kirby smirked. "But I'd love to."

Quinn was ecstatic the whole afternoon. They shared Indian food on the couch, binge-watched the first season of *Dear White People*, and snuggled. Everything with Kirby was so comfortable. When the last episode ended, Kirby adjusted Fred off her lap, and he rewarded her with a grumble before snuggling into the side of her thigh.

Kirby smiled at Fred as she said, "I should probably go home."

"Yeah, it's getting late, isn't it?" Quinn didn't feel tired at all, but a yawn tumbled out anyway.

"Yeah."

Yet neither of them made a move to stand. Quinn's focus was transfixed by Kirby's face. A face she never thought she'd be able to gaze at this this closely again, and yet, here she was. The air between them sizzled with anticipation.

Kirby's eyes were a stormy blue.

"I..." Quinn started but wasn't sure what she was going to say.

Kirby reached up and ran a thumb along her jaw. "I've missed your face, your lips, your eyes. I know I shouldn't. I know we should go slowly, but I can't help but do this." She pulled Quinn into her and kissed her with the passion of their first night together all those years ago. Quinn was intoxicated. Their kiss quickly heated up, and Quinn pulled Kirby up and onto her lap. Fred huffed in protest, but the feel of Kirby's body pressing her into the couch was unreal.

Quinn pulled back slightly. "I...are you sure?"

She could feel Kirby's unsteady breath against her face as Kirby nodded. "I've never been able to resist you." Then Kirby leaned back, pulled her shirt over her head and pressed into Quinn, and Quinn's brain shut off altogether.

CHAPTER SIXTEEN

The world around Kirby felt surreal as she kissed Quinn again. There was a part of her that hoped this was where the evening would go when she'd come downstairs to talk to Quinn today. She knew they should be taking it slowly, but the burn between them was as strong as it had ever been, and there was no denying it anymore. Like that night in Monterey when they'd first met. It was a cliché, but from the second their eyes met across the bar, Kirby had known where the evening would lead, just like this evening.

As Quinn begin to kiss a path from her mouth down her jawline, Quinn's hands zeroed in on the back of her bra. Before she released it, however, Quinn pulled back again.

"What's wrong?" Kirby asked.

"Nothing," Quinn said, but Kirby could see something play across her face that didn't seem like nothing, so she waited.

"It's okay if you want to wait." Kirby didn't want to push. Knowing this was where they were eventually heading, she could be patient. She knew she should be patient.

"No. Nothing like that. There is nothing sexier than you sitting on my lap like this, but I can't help but wonder if you might like to shower with me."

"Oh my God, do I smell?" Horrified, Kirby leaned over to sniff herself.

"No, no, no." Quinn said quickly and emphatically. "I'm afraid I smell. I've been in a mood since Friday. All I've done is lie on the couch like a slug. I'm sure you noticed I freshened up a bit when you first got here, but before we...you know, I'd like to actually shower. And nothing sounds better than having a little company."

Kirby stood and held out a hand to pull her off the couch. "You know I always like dirty sex, but clean sex is fun too." As she turned and ran for the bathroom, she looked over her shoulder and said, "Last one there has to wash the other's back."

Quinn caught her hips from behind as she was about to open the bathroom door, halting her progress. She whispered, "I caught you because I don't like to lose. Not because I don't want to wash your back. For the record, I'm quite happy to wash every inch of you."

As Quinn kissed the back of her neck, she released the clasp on Kirby's bra, allowing her breasts to tumble out as she slid the straps down her arms. They didn't stay bare for long, however, as Quinn reached around, cradling her breasts as though they were precious gems. Kirby groaned and pressed back as Quinn gently rolled her nipples between two fingers.

Quinn pressed a kiss to the side of her neck and whispered, "Let me start the water."

When Quinn released her, the cold air made goose bumps erupt across her chest, and her nipples hardened painfully, so Kirby wrapped her arms around Quinn for warmth. "It was chilly without you keeping me warm."

"Should we get you out of the rest of these clothes so you can get in and warm up?"

Kirby thought that was the best idea she'd heard all day, so she nodded, and Quinn quickly flipped the button at her waist and slid her pants and underwear down. Kirby felt a flash of self-consciousness. After all, she wasn't twenty-five anymore. She'd tried to stay in shape but knew she was a little saggy, a little rounder than she once had been.

But when Quinn whispered, "You are simply stunning. More beautiful than even in my most cherished memories," the self-doubt in Kirby's mind quieted, and she kissed Quinn again.

"You next," Kirby breathed, already reaching under the bottom of Quinn's T-shirt and pulling it up over her head.

"Oh God, please ignore this." Quinn exclaimed as she whipped her bra off before Kirby could even see it.

"What was that?" Kirby laughed.

"It's my laundry day-lounging bra, not fit for your eyes this evening. I wish I was wearing my sexiest lingerie for you."

"It doesn't matter what you're wearing. You're still the most magnificent woman I've ever seen." It might have sounded like flattery, but the sight of Quinn still took her breath away. "Now, let's get these ancient pants off you." Kirby barely had to press down on the waistband, and Quinn's Navy sweatpants slipped from her trim hips and fell into a heap at her feet. "Well, this is a nice surprise," she said commenting on Quinn's lack of underwear. "If I had known you were going commando all afternoon, I might have had a harder time keeping my hands off you."

Quinn grabbed her hand and pulled her into the large walk-in shower. Standing under the rain showerhead, Kirby pulled Quinn's mouth down. She nipped Quinn's bottom lip before gently sucking it into her mouth. "God, I've missed this mouth. These lips."

Quinn quickly deepened their kiss and pressed her against the glass wall of the shower. The heat from the water hadn't warmed it up yet, and Kirby gasped at the cold, but before she had a moment to realize what was happening, Quinn dropped to her knees and took Kirby into her mouth. She ran her tongue from the top of Kirby's clit down to her opening, dipping inside and reached up to massage Kirby's breast. Kirby's head fell back against the steam-covered glass and groaned. She threaded her fingers into Quinn's hair as Quinn began to increase her pace.

"Oh my God. Sweet baby Jesus." Kirby didn't think she would be able to stay standing as Quinn continued her ministrations, but when her knees went weak, Quinn wrapped an arm around her waist and held her up, allowing Kirby to truly let go. When her orgasm roared through her moments later, Quinn stood and wrapped her body around Kirby to more fully support her.

As Kirby continued to shudder with aftershocks, Quinn began to wash her. Kirby couldn't pry her eyes open to watch but appreciated the silky feel of Quinn's fingers running all over her body. When Quinn asked her to turn so she could wash her back, Kirby happily obliged.

"I hoped you'd keep your promise," she muttered.

"Of course." Quinn massaged her shoulders, down her back, her butt. When Kirby thought she was finished, Quinn pressed against her from behind and lathered her own front by sliding back and forth against Kirby. The pucker of Quinn's nipples and the soft give of her breasts as they slipped along Kirby's back was divine and made her whole body tingle in anticipation.

"Let me get your back too," Kirby offered, but when Quinn backed away, rather than get more soap, Kirby stepped behind and used her body to lather Quinn's back as well, the sensation of Quinn's cheeks slipping across her hips surprisingly erotic. Quinn reached behind her and grabbed Kirby by the hips, pulling her in closer and groaned.

Kirby needed more, so she pushed Quinn against the shower wall. Quinn caught herself on the foggy glass as Kirby reached to slide her fingers between Quinn's legs. She was so wet that Kirby let out a long moan in delight. She quickly found Quinn's pace, circling her clit as she reached between her legs from behind and slipped two fingers into Quinn's wet heat.

"Oh God, oh God." Quinn panted as she moved her hips against Kirby's fingers with more ferocity and finally let out one long shudder as she came, sandwiched between Kirby's body and the shower wall.

Quinn slowly turned and pulled Kirby into her arms. Lost in the sensation of Quinn's body and the water still washing over them until not a molecule of soap remained, Kirby had no idea how much time had passed when Quinn finally said, "Best shower ever. Thank you."

"Me too. Shall we be environmentally friendly and move this to your bed?"

"I like the way you think, Ms. Davis." Quinn turned off the water that was starting to go tepid and grabbed two fluffy blue towels from a stand outside.

"That's why they pay me the big bucks." Kirby winked as she dried herself off and ran the towel over her hair.

Quinn wrapped her towel around both of them and kissed Kirby on the nose. "Last one to the bed has to make it," she said before leaving Kirby standing in the shower with a towel around her shoulders.

Several orgasms later, Kirby lay on her side, her face against Quinn's shoulder, and breathed in the scent of her. She still smelled exactly as she used to, and Kirby sighed. Quinn's breath had slowed into the measured rhythm of sleep a few minutes before, but Kirby's mind wasn't quite ready to turn off. After having fought this for so long, she had thought that she would feel more conflicted, more worried that she'd made the wrong choice. And not only had they slept together, but she had asked Quinn on a date, so she couldn't even construe this as being a one-time dalliance. But although those fears were present, they weren't overwhelming.

More dominant was the overall contentedness she felt from her head down to her toenails. The best sex she'd had in a decade contributed, but spending time with Quinn was so...easy. The entire evening had been amazing, not just the sex piece. The thought of the future was scary, but she chose to be present in the moment rather than think of what would or could come. When sleep finally washed over Kirby that night, she felt more at peace than she'd felt in years.

❖

"Good morning, beautiful," Quinn whispered in Kirby's ear as a hint of sun started to creep over the horizon. Her condo faced north, but she could still see light trickling through her sheer curtains. She rarely woke up first, but the excitement of being with Kirby again had her ready to take on the day.

"Good morning," Kirby rasped and snuggled farther into Quinn's neck. They hadn't gotten much sleep, and they both deserved to sleep in, but it was Monday. Quinn ran a hand up and down Kirby's back in an attempt to rouse her, but Kirby buried deeper. "No, no, it's Sunday morning. Sleepy snuggle time. Shh."

"I hate to break it to you, but it's Monday morning," she whispered. "Do you want to get up and go for a run?"

"No, Sunday rest day. Also, already worked out. Shh. Sleepy time still here." Kirby was adorably still half-asleep but wrapped her leg tighter around Quinn's hip. Quinn recognized it as Kirby's old MO to try to convince her to go back to sleep.

"How about another round of working out of a different variety?" Quinn whispered. She changed the pressure and rhythm of her fingers from soothing to stimulating and began to graze the side of Kirby's breast with every pass.

Kirby still wasn't admitting that she was awake, but her hips started to press against Quinn. Quinn took that as a sign of consent to flip Kirby onto her back to allow for better access.

She enveloped Kirby's nipple with her lips as she found the wetness that was still ample between Kirby's thighs with her fingers. Kirby's nipple tightened between Quinn's teeth, drawing a groan out of Quinn as she felt a fresh surge of wetness between her own legs. Quinn slipped two fingers easily into Kirby and settled into a rhythm with her thumb on Kirby's clit.

Although her eyes were still closed, Kirby seemed to finally awaken and slid her fingers into Quinn's hair and pulled her more firmly on her nipple as she thrust her hips up to meet Quinn's fingers. Quinn could feel her own orgasm building as she rode Kirby's thigh. Kirby's hips quickened, and her cry as she came brought Quinn to the precipice herself. Less than a breath later, the feel of Kirby pressing Quinn's fingers deeper into herself and milking every shudder of pleasure out of them shoved Quinn right over the edge behind her.

When Quinn was able to lift her mouth, she looked up and smiled. "Good morning. Again."

"A good morning it is indeed. For real this time." Kirby pulled Quinn's face to her own for a kiss as she blinked her eyes open for what Quinn thought was the first time that morning. "You are a sight for sore eyes."

"Mmm. Are you hungry?"

"Maybe. What are you thinking?"

"Toast?"

"Culinary skills haven't improved in the last ten years, eh?"

Quinn pressed the fingers still seated inside Kirby hard enough that Kirby gasped and thrust her hips back into Quinn's hand.

"Was that supposed to make me regretful? If so, it didn't work."

"I always loved how easy your second orgasm was," Quinn said softly as she slowly began thrusting again, using her palm to provide indirect pressure on Kirby's oversensitive clit. "I wonder if your body will still respond as it used to. But to answer your question, no. No better culinary skills. But I have mad food ordering skills. Which we don't have time for because it is, unfortunately, Monday. Thus, toast. I have rye. And butter. Or hummus."

Kirby opened her mouth but apparently wasn't able to get any words out as her second orgasm bloomed, and she cried out before sinking her teeth into Quinn's shoulder.

Quinn lightly kissed her neck and throat until she finally began to regain awareness. "Hey, you," she rasped.

"Hey, again." Quinn placed kisses all along Kirby's face, ending with a light but lingering kiss on her mouth. "So I'm hungry—"

"Clearly, yes, you are." Kirby's grin was infectious.

"Yes, I am. And though I would love to stay in bed with you all day, it's getting late, and I think we both have to work today. So. About breakfast, how do you feel about rye toast?"

"Mmm...sounds passable, given the present company. However, I have a small amount of business to take care of before you get to toasting."

"Oh yeah, and what is that?"

Rather than speaking, Kirby used the strength in her legs to reverse her and Quinn's positions. "I have a two-orgasm deficit that I need to dig out of."

"Technically only one, but who's counting?" Quinn said before she quickly forgot how to count altogether.

❖

Sometime later, Kirby finally let her escape to the kitchen to make breakfast. She wasn't sure if Kirby was ever going to agree to let her out of bed, but she reminded Kirby that she hadn't been at her new job nearly long enough to call in sick, and Kirby finally relented.

As they ate their rye toast in surprisingly comfortable silence, Quinn debated asking how Kirby was. She wanted to check in, given everything between them, but at the same time, didn't want to be too needy. She also didn't want Kirby to panic and run again. "So…"

"What?"

"How are you doing?"

"I'm fine. I've had six—or was it seven—orgasms in the last twelve hours. But what do you mean?"

"I just mean, all of this is a lot. I've been trying not to hope so I don't get too disappointed, but I know you've struggled with everything, and last night happened so quickly…I want to make sure you're okay." She knew she was rambling but couldn't get her thoughts together. "Sorry, that wasn't articulate, but are you okay? Like really okay?"

Kirby ran a hand through her very mussed hair. "It's…I don't know. Weird. And scary. But somehow, it feels right. When I'm with you, it feels…right. I don't know how else to describe it. We've been dancing around this for a while now, but it seemed almost inevitable. I am not promising anything right now. I'm still afraid, but one day at a time seems manageable?" Her voice lifted questioningly.

Quinn smiled and placed a hand on her forearm. "I like spending time with you. At whatever speed you're ready for."

"I like spending time with you too. Even when I didn't want to. Even when I thought about jumping in the lake and turning my workout into a swim rather than a run. There was something that kept me running with you."

Quinn's heart fluttered at Kirby's words. "And you call me a charmer." She couldn't believe Kirby admitted to enjoying the time they'd been spending together and was truly going to give them a chance, however tentative it was.

There was something unbelievably sexy about Kirby sitting in her kitchen in her T-shirt, eating toast with one of her bare feet tucked under her thigh. "Do you want to shower here before you head back upstairs to get ready for work?"

"Although I would love to, as you have pointed out several times, it is, unfortunately, Monday, which I will agree is correct now that I am awake and out of denial."

"Yeah, and we slept through our run."

"I wouldn't say slept. I would say worked out in another manner." Kirby took a last bite of toast but adorably left a few crumbs on the side of her mouth.

Quinn brushed the crumbs away with her thumb before saying, "Good point. Best workout I've had in a while. I wouldn't take it back."

"Me either." Kirby's smirk quickened Quinn's breath.

"Not to be too forward—"

"You? Never."

Quinn smiled and wondered at how quickly things could go from dark to hopeful.

"So?" Kirby asked.

"Oh, yeah, so not to be too forward, but can I see you again? Soonish? Maybe today but no pressure."

"The way we're going, I'm sure we'll run into each other soon."

Wait, what? Quinn's heart skipped a beat. Did last night mean nothing? Were they still just barely friends?

Kirby's laugh and the hand she placed on Quinn's thigh pulled her out of her downward spiral. "Oh God, I'm sorry, Quinn. I'm not sure why I said that." She waited until Quinn looked at her again before she continued, "I want to see you again too. Soon."

Quinn let out a huge sigh of relief, much to her embarrassment. She couldn't even play off her shock as a joke.

"Let me check my calendar. It's not good that it's Monday, and I have no clue what my week looks like. Hmm. Normally, prepping for my week, which includes checking my calendar, is a Sunday task. I wonder whose fault it is that I missed that?" Kirby raised her eyebrows in a way that probably shouldn't have been alluring but drew Quinn in like a tractor beam. "Now, where the hell is my phone?" Kirby patted her legs where she would have had pockets if she'd been wearing pants and turned her head, looking all around the kitchen.

"Do you really think your phone is in invisible pants?"

Kirby looked at her hands and then up. "Habit?" She shrugged. "Where do you think it might be?" God, she was adorable.

"Maybe on the coffee table?"

Kirby hopped up, and Quinn unabashedly stared at the perfect cheeks subtly peeking out from below the hem of the shirt. Definitely a perfect loaner shirt selection. Kirby found her phone and jumped back around quicker than Quinn expected, catching her red-handed in her lascivious stare. Oops. Yet, she wasn't even slightly ashamed.

"See something you like, sailor?" Kirby had a mischievous glint in her eye.

"You bet I do," Quinn said on a shaky breath.

"You want to do something about it?"

"Do I ever, but it's very late." She clutched the edge of the table with a death grip to keep from taking Kirby up on her offer.

"Oh shit," Kirby said when she finally looked at the time. "I'm going to go get my pants and check my calendar. From the other side of the room. Far on the other side or neither of us are ever getting to work."

Quinn adjusted in her seat appreciating the pull of several long-ignored muscles in her glutes while waiting for Kirby to return.

"Unfortunately, this week is a real shit show," Kirby said as she walked back into the room, buttoning her pants. A pity she covered those legs up, though Quinn knew it was a necessity. "I've got a lunch meeting today and a Women in Commercial Lending networking event tonight. Tomorrow, I've got a company luncheon and a client in town that I need to take to dinner. Should we plan to run tomorrow and compare notes? Maybe my client's flight will get canceled. I can only hope."

"Me too. Sounds good. Five fifteen tomorrow morning in the lobby?"

"Perfect." Kirby ran her fingers along the hem of the T-shirt. "Can I borrow this?"

"Of course." Quinn wanted to give her a kiss good-bye but was afraid that neither she nor Kirby could be trusted to keep it at only a kiss, and she urgently needed to get Fred downstairs to the pet run and shower in short order, or she wouldn't have a chance of making it to work on time. It seemed like Kirby had the same fear as she was slowly backing toward the front door.

"I'll text you later." Kirby licked her lips, and it took everything in Quinn to keep her ass rooted in the chair.

"I'll be waiting." Jesus. Did she really just say that? "I mean. I don't know what I mean, probably exactly what I said. Never mind." She shook her head at her ridiculousness.

Kirby laughed, but the way she bit her lip rather than running for the door sent a pleasant warmth through Quinn's chest.

"I hope you have a nice day at work and don't feel too off your game after our missed run."

"I feel reasonably centered after our alternate workout." Kirby searched behind her for the doorknob. "I would kiss you good-bye, but I've got twenty-two minutes before I need to be out the door for work, and I don't trust us."

"Neither do I."

"Okay. Well, then, I'll see you soon." And then she was gone.

That night, Quinn had only been lying in bed for a few minutes, reading, when her thoughts drifted to Kirby. Again. She was willing to admit that although she and Kirby exchanged several texts throughout the day and early evening, she'd been hoping Kirby would get out of her event early enough to come by. As if her thoughts had manifested Kirby's attention, Quinn's phone chirped on the nightstand, signaling a new text:

Finally in a car heading home. Hadn't meant to stay so late, but I have an open position and was wooing a few people for it. Ugh. Exhausted.

Quinn thought about asking if she wanted to come over, but that felt too much like a booty call since it was almost eleven. That wasn't what she wanted from Kirby and didn't want them to slip into that sort of arrangement, particularly given Kirby's affinity for it in the past. So despite how much her hormones wanted her to invite Kirby over, she was going to be strong and replied:

Whew! I'm sure ur exhausted. We didn't get much sleep last night. Just falling asleep while reading a book myself.

Anything interesting? Smutty?

Quinn laughed out loud. Kirby apparently still remembered her guilty pleasures. *Wouldn't you like to know?*

Kirby responded with the panting face emoji, eliciting another laugh. However, Quinn didn't want to get too flirty. At least, she was pretty sure she wanted to be strong. Most likely.

She texted, *Ur funny. I'd love to keep chatting, but I can barely keep my eyes open. We still on for tomorrow a.m.?*

I'm going to regret that last glass of wine this evening, but yes. Sleep well, and I'll see you in 6 hours.

Good night, sleeping beauty.

Kirby's final kissing emoji warmed Quinn, and she closed her eyes and drifted off to sleep.

CHAPTER SEVENTEEN

It had been a busy week, and though Kirby and Quinn had run together every morning, they hadn't shared anything more than a quick post-run kiss since Monday. Kirby knew quick was a mild understatement, but they had been in the elevator, so they stayed pretty PG. However, it was now Friday night, and Kirby was hopeful that kissing-drought was about to change. She was getting out of work in approximately five minutes—only an hour late—and was going to meet Quinn at a cute little Italian restaurant in River North.

The initial plan had been to meet at home and then walk to dinner, but Kirby got pulled into a last-minute request from her boss on their year-to-date loan metrics, so she had to adjust. She was wrapping up now and was still leaving early enough that she could walk rather than take a cab.

She was shocked at how quickly things had changed with Quinn but wasn't feeling the panic she'd been expecting. For nearly a decade, she'd been pushing all thoughts of Quinn out of her mind, and for the last few months, she'd been trying to deny that any feelings still lingered.

Despite how hard she fought it, they still had the same explosive attraction, maybe even more. They had fallen into an easy cadence that week where they ran together every morning, texted as much during the day as their schedules allowed, and always texted or called to say good night, but she was looking forward to seeing her, touching her, tonight.

As Kirby entered the last block before the restaurant, she saw Quinn turn the corner and knew their faces had matching grins. "Fancy meeting you here, sailor."

"They do say timing is everything."

Kirby put her hands on Quinn's hips. "Hi," she said, her voice shy to her own ears.

"Hi, yourself."

Trying to keep the PDA to a minimum, Kirby gave Quinn a chaste kiss as she leaned in to hug her. The familiar scent filled Kirby's senses, and she enjoyed the moment, holding Quinn in her arms. They might have held on for a beat longer than decorum would dictate, but she didn't care.

"Shall we head in?" Quinn asked, breaking their physical connection.

Kirby nodded. "I'm starving. I worked through lunch to make sure I would get out on time and only ended up having a granola bar from the office pantry. Not that it helped me get out on time, but still. How is Fred this evening?"

Quinn opened the door. "After you. He's good. He was bummed you weren't able to join us on our evening walk but hopes he gets to see you later."

"That's a relief because I was definitely hoping to get some Fred snuggles too."

"I am very confident that could be arranged. Is Fred the only one you want to snuggle?" she said with a wink as they were shown to their table.

"Certainly not." The light press of Quinn's hand against her lower back sent familiar shockwaves through her. It was going to be a long night in the best way possible.

She was in the mood to celebrate the end of a long week and the beginning of a hopefully wonderful night with Quinn, so she ordered a bottle of Brunello that the server recommended.

"Celebrating?" Quinn asked.

"Absolutely. I closed a big loan that had a lot of challenges for one of my largest clients yesterday, I've got interviews with both the women I was trying to poach for my team next week, and even more than that…" She paused for a moment, feeling a little self-conscious about being so smitten but decided to push ahead anyway. "I want our first date to be special. What says special more than a 2012 Brunello di Montalcino?"

"Being here with you without a glare in your eye is very special, but a 2012 Brunello is a close second."

"Charmer." Kirby took a long drink of water.

"It's a gift. Or you inspire me. Maybe both."

Kirby's heart fluttered, though who was she kidding? Her heart had been fluttering nonstop since she saw Quinn looking gorgeous in her navy blue pinstripe suit with the pale pink collared shirt and a cocky smile on her face.

They split the Brunello over a full dinner and dessert, laughing and talking for nearly two hours before they slowly walked hand in hand back to their condo building. Kirby sighed. "I'm so full, but I think that gnocchi was the best I have ever tasted in my entire life. And I did spend time in Italy, if you remember."

"It was amazing. They melt in your mouth, but the vodka sauce was perfect as well. Creamy with a little tang. Thank you for sharing a few bites when I couldn't stop at one."

"My pleasure." Kirby pressed a kiss right below Quinn's ear as they stopped to wait for a walk signal. "Your eggplant parmesan was tasty too." She loved Quinn's scent in that exact spot. She could smell her shampoo and the subtle scent of her perfume and closed her eyes as she took one more breath.

"But not as good as your gnocchi."

"What can I say? I know how to pick them," Kirby mumbled.

"That you do."

When they got the walk signal, Kirby went to step off the curb but stepped wrong and would have fallen had Quinn not been there to catch her in a strong embrace.

"Whoa there. Are you okay?"

Kirby grumbled, "I'm fine. As klutzy as I've ever been. Thanks for the assist."

"*My* pleasure."

"I feel like it's time you tell me: how the hell do you walk so gracefully in heels that high? Mine are more than an inch and a half shorter, and I'm falling off curbs while you stay on your feet and catch me."

"You're a klutz, which makes me seem graceful by comparison," Quinn teased as she gave Kirby a brief kiss.

"I don't deny my clumsiness, but we both know that's not all of it. Any normal person walking around in those heels would have gotten knocked over when I fell into her. Instead, you caught me, and we both were able to keep walking."

Quinn looked away, and Kirby wondered at her reluctance to

answer since they were talking about high-heeled shoes and not anything substantial, so she waited her out.

"I've been wearing high heels for a long time. Since I was a grade-school kid, in fact. I'm not entirely sure why, but it was very important to my mom that I look the part of a perfect little lady who was also the pastor's daughter. You would think that, given their religiousness, my mother would have preferred I dress conservatively, limit my makeup, and wear kitten heels, but she took the path of my looks being a gift from God and as such, should be shown off. Not that she forced me to wear racy clothes or anything, but I always had to be in perfect fashion, perfect makeup, and high heels to show off. God forbid I stumble in church and embarrass her, so I practiced every single night." She shook her head sadly.

"How did you never tell me that about your mom before?" Kirby could picture quiet, shy Quinn as a preteen, walking around her bedroom at night in high heels, and it broke her heart.

"I prefer not to talk about them. You aren't missing anything, I promise."

"I'm sorry." Kirby squeezed her hand tighter and pulled her closer. "We definitely don't have to talk about them now."

"Thank you," Quinn said as she squeezed back. "Though these days, since I'm not twenty-five anymore, I also spend more time doing squats and lunges at different angles to work the muscles in my calves and hamstrings, as well as yoga to help with ankle strength and balance and to keep my Achilles loose. My mother did make me a little vain, after all. I do like how my legs look in these shoes."

"I knew your calves looked even better than I remembered on that day I ran into you in the food hall and you were wearing that pencil skirt." Kirby chortled, though it was an entirely true statement. Quinn's body had been made for the lines of a pencil skirt.

Quinn smugly chuckled. "I knew you were checking me out. It's why I had to stop and turn. I could feel your eyes on my back, though I had assumed you were checking out my ass."

"What wasn't I checking out? That skirt fit you like a glove, and your legs…Well, what can I say about your perfect legs other than Tina Turner in her prime didn't have anything on you. In fact, the first thing I'm going to do when we get upstairs is show your legs exactly how much I appreciate them." She was certain Renaissance women would have written odes to Quinn's legs.

"I was going to ask if I could interest you in a nightcap, but it sounds like a foregone conclusion," Quinn said, a self-satisfied glint in her eye.

"Unless you don't want to. I've been dreaming of you all week. I was wondering if you might like to come to my place instead." She lightly pinched Quinn's side before saying, "I have much better options for breakfast."

"Ha," Quinn squawked.

"We could stop and pick up Fred. I've only got a betta fish named Frank the Tank, and I'm sure he and Fred will get along famously."

"Famously? Between that and the allure of a homecooked breakfast in the morning, how can I refuse?" Quinn kissed her as they walked, and she felt truly optimistic for the first time in a decade.

❖

As they walked into Kirby's condo, Quinn stopped abruptly as she flipped on the entry light. "Wait."

Puzzled, Kirby looked over. "What's wrong?"

"Turn the light back off." Kirby did, wondering if Quinn had lost it. "Come here." Quinn set Fred on the floor and grabbed her hand. Fred sniffed in a semicircle before plopping onto his belly, clearly not feeling the need to explore the new space yet. "Doesn't this view take your breath away?"

Kirby looked out the wall of glass in front of them, back at Quinn, and then back out at the horizon, feeling like she was seeing it for the first time in a long time. An old friend that she hadn't realized she'd been missing.

It was near-dark, the sun having set while they were walking home, but there was a hint of pink still lingering at the horizon to the east, dividing the deep blue-gray of the lake from the almost sapphire blue sky, so deep in color it would be full dark soon. Between them and the horizon were the soft lights of other condo buildings, the glow from the Michigan Avenue retailers, the brighter lights of the medical center, and a few twinkles from pleasure cruises braving the October air for a few last evenings on the lake before it became too cold or too frozen.

"I..." Kirby trailed off. It had been a long time since she remembered to notice the beauty in that view. She was so used to going a hundred miles per hour during every waking minute from a need to be the best, the fastest, the most successful, that she had forgotten what it was like to appreciate the small beauties in life. She'd been running from her past for so long in an attempt to grasp a future of professional success—to the detriment of everything else—that she was missing the present.

She reached around Quinn's hips, pulling her close and leaning up on her toes until her chin was against the back of Quinn's shoulder, her view unobstructed. "Not in a longer time than I would care to admit." She was awash in…sensation. The silky feel of the bottom of Quinn's suit jacket, the press of her hips, the scent of her skin, the view in front of them. Kirby was having a hard time catching her breath. "Thank you."

"For what?"

"For reminding me that life isn't always about sprinting to the finish."

"What do you mean?"

Kirby chuckled to herself. "I forgot that, in many ways, you don't really know who I've become. When you knew me, I was a carefree soldier. Sort of. I wanted to get good grades and learn Chinese so I would be proficient at my job, but I didn't have much ambition otherwise. I didn't care if I was at the top of my class. I just wanted to have a good time and, once we met, spend time with you."

"That is the Kirby I remember from Monterey." She ran her hands along Kirby's forearms, pulling them tighter against her and interlacing their fingers.

"But that carefree girl doesn't exist in the same way anymore."

"Of course she doesn't. We grow and change, and it's been nearly a decade. No one is the same person they were a decade ago. Generally speaking, that's a good thing, Kirbs."

"Yeah, but since you and I, and even more so after the Army, I have become so focused on my profession. I'm the youngest female senior vice president at my company, and that was after a six-year detour between college and the real world. The real world for me, I mean, not for lifers like you. Regardless, that doesn't happen by working nine to five. It's a lot of hours in the office, a lot of hours networking, a lot of hours wining and dining clients. I was willing to put the job first when a lot of my colleagues weren't. They were starting families and spending time with their friends. It's a sad commentary on corporate America, but you do get rewarded for not having a personal life and channeling all your effort into the job. All my friends are in the industry. It's how I know my core group of friends, honestly."

"There's nothing wrong with wanting to excel in your career." Quinn pulled Kirby's hands firmly into her chest.

"True, but I've eschewed deeper human connections. I haven't dated anyone since you other than hookups. The last time I went to visit my parents was Christmas. Yes, they came to visit me in May, but I used to visit them several times a year. I do still talk to them most every weekend, but I've truly forgotten how to slow down. It's taken you running with me these past few weeks for me to remember why I love it. Why I love being awake before the rest of the city and getting to watch the sun rise over the lake." This realization made her sadder than she would have expected, given she thought that she'd been happy before. She'd believed she had everything she could want, but Quinn was making her see that there was a lot she'd been missing.

She was also now terrified that she was spilling too much too soon. After all, they'd only slept together again less than a week ago, and she wasn't even willing to commit to anything other than taking it day by day. But at the same time, they had been reconnecting slowly but surely over the past few months. Quinn had always been the easiest person for her to talk to about anything and everything.

"And now you've reminded me why I paid so much for this damn condo. I used to love that view. In the summer, when I would occasionally get home before sunset, I would sit out there with a glass of bourbon and relax. Now I flip the light on the second I walk in the door, and I can't even remember the last time I watched a sunrise. If you think this view is stunning, wait until you see the sun come up over the lake."

"Kirby," Quinn said as she turned. "You are—"

But Kirby pulled her down, silencing her with an impassioned kiss. Kirby reached by instinct to the single button on the front of Quinn's jacket and unbuttoned it. She groaned at the feel of Quinn's muscled torso below the silk blouse as she ran her fingers to Quinn's lower back. She pulled her closer, quickly finding her way under the shirt.

Quinn surprised her by lifting her, and Kirby wrapped her legs around Quinn's waist. The surge of wetness between her now very spread legs pressed against Quinn's abs was unsurprising, given Quinn's show of strength. She had always been strong, but this was next level, and Kirby was in.

"She-Ra move. It's a new trick. I'm digging it."

Between kisses, Quinn said, "Oh God, I always envisioned She-Ra as a lesbian when I was kid. I think I got a little wetter."

"Well, this maneuver got me wetter too, so we're even. Bedroom is that way, by the way, stud. My layout is a little different than yours."

Kirby leaned down toward Quinn's face as she continued to hold her. Kirby moved her hips from side to side to find some friction against Quinn's stomach and relieve the burning in her clit.

"*Fuck.*" Kirby wasn't sure if that was her or Quinn or maybe both of them.

"Don't ruin this She-Ra moment by making my knees go weak, Kirby," Quinn said and started to walk them down the hall.

"Sorry," Kirby whispered, not feeling sorry at all as she again found Quinn's neck with her lips and began a slow journey from the bottom of her earlobe, nipping to where Quinn's neck met her shoulder, as low as she could reach in their current position.

"Jesus, Kirby," Quinn said as she laid them both on Kirby's bed. "It's like you're trying to kill me. Or kill us both."

"Oops." Kirby smirked as she pulled Quinn's button-down over her head.

Their lovemaking took on a different tone. On Sunday night, they had both been frantic. It was a race to the finish every single time, but that night, they took their time. Quinn teased Kirby almost mercilessly but allowed her to come right before she lost her mind. Kirby enthusiastically reciprocated. But she felt different. There was more eye contact, more hand holding. She felt a shift from sex being about finding the destination as quickly as possible to enjoying the journey for the first time in almost ten years. And what a beautiful journey it was.

As Kirby lay tucked into Quinn's big spoon with their hips flush, Quinn's breasts pressing into her back, she sleepily asked, "Did you think our connection would still be this potent?"

"Honestly? Yeah." Quinn used the arm around Kirby's hips to pull her infinitesimally closer, but it somehow was more comfortable that way.

"Really?"

"Yeah. Since you, I've casually dated but nothing serious. No real sparks. I've always suspected you're the only person I could ever feel this way with. I didn't think—I still don't think—I deserve to find happiness. I devastated the only person who ever accepted me for who I am. I have too much to make up for." Her voice was small.

"Oh my God, Quinn," Kirby said, more awake than a moment before. "Is that really how you've felt for the last decade?" When she didn't answer, Kirby turned and pushed her onto her back. "That's what you truly think?" Kirby demanded as she stared.

"I…" Quinn closed her eyes and took a deep breath. When she opened her eyes again, Kirby smoothed a thumb along Quinn's furrowed brow but didn't say anything, waiting for Quinn to be ready. "I don't want you to think I'm pathetic or was irrevocably depressed. I've lived. But I've never thought I would ever find this connection again."

"Oh Quinn. Quinn." Kirby grabbed her face and wouldn't let her turn away. When Quinn finally acquiesced and looked at her, she said, "Yes, you broke my heart. Yes, I became a different person than I otherwise would have. But I've been happy. And people make mistakes. I'm not religious, but I do believe that everything happens for a reason. Truly. Life isn't a straight line from point A to point B. As you said earlier, we strive, we grow, we try to become the best version of ourselves. You aren't responsible for my choices and neither am I for yours. Are you listening to me?"

Kirby squeezed her shoulders slightly until she made eye contact again. "I need you to stop feeling so guilty. You make me feel like I'm showing you pity, which I'm not. I'm here in front of you, figuring things out as we go. We both are. But nothing here is from pity. Do you understand that I have been happy? I've been a workaholic, but I've been successful and happy. I don't regret any of it. Was I angry when you reappeared in my life? Yes. But am I happy now? Yes. You aren't a bad person. You're a person who made a bad decision. You picked the Navy over me on that one day. Or several days leading up to it. But it isn't who you are. I know you regret it. I know you aren't as cold as I wanted to believe for so long. And no one's life is defined by one moment of bad decisions. We are where we're supposed to be. I truly believe that."

"I…I…" Quinn stammered. "I've really missed you, Kirby. Truly."

"I've missed you too. Now can we please go to sleep? I'm exhausted. I know you are too, but please let go of some of your guilt. I don't want you to feel like you're destined for misery, but it's not fair to me to have to assuage you of your guilt. You have to forgive yourself and accept that you do deserve happiness."

"I'm sorry, Kir—"

"For fuck's sake, Quinn."

"I'm just kidding. I mean I *am* sorry. No, please listen." Quinn pressed a finger to Kirby's lips when she tried to interrupt, "But I'm also sorry for the position I put you in. Well, not this physical position. I'm happy about this particular position. I always love it when you're on top. I also like this position," Quinn said as she used her legs to flip them around. "I won't try to keep putting my guilt on you."

"No, you have to let it go. Seriously, don't hide it from me. *Please*, let it go."

"I'll try. And in the interim, what if I do this to distract you?" Two of her fingers slid easily into Kirby as she blazed a path of fire down Kirby's torso with her tongue. Moments after Quinn took her into her mouth, lights flashed behind Kirby's eyes as her orgasm overtook her.

Once Kirby's awareness returned, she pulled Quinn onto her chest. Enjoying using Quinn as her personal blanket and entirely satiated, she said, "I l...like you here on top of me."

"Me too," Quinn whispered.

CHAPTER EIGHTEEN

The next morning, Kirby woke before Quinn and tiptoed into the bathroom to freshen up. Fred was snoring softly, curled up in a blanket on top of his bed in the corner of Kirby's room. His little snaggletooth was sticking out, and Kirby was captivated for a moment watching his tiny cheek puffing up and down around it as he breathed. She managed to resist going over and giving him kisses all over his little head. He was such a homely yet adorable baby, she couldn't help but love him.

Ugh. Speaking of love, Kirby was slightly horrified at herself for almost slipping the L-bomb last night as she was drifting off to sleep. She and Quinn had only been seeing each other for six days, and there was no way she was going to be *that* U-Haul lesbian.

Admittedly, she had…strong…feelings for Quinn. But that had to be echoes of what they used to share, not real feelings. Was that even a thing? Not real feelings? Kirby wasn't sure, but she was positive that she wasn't ready for any feelings other than lust.

With her feelings put back into a box where they belonged, Kirby crept back over to the bed in time to see the light on her screen go dark. She picked up her phone and saw that she'd missed a call from her mother. She took her phone to the balcony to call her back, making a quick stop for coffee along the way.

Kirby popped her earbuds in and dialed her mom's number. "Good morning, Mom. Sorry I missed your call."

"No worries, dear. Did I wake you?"

"No, I was actually in the bathroom."

"TMI, sweetheart."

"Don't be preposterous, Mom."

Kirby loved the sound of her mom's laugh. It was one of her top five favorite sounds in the world. "You're right. I don't know why I'm being weird."

"What's going on?"

"I'm a little worried about your father. He's been tired lately and has had to take some breaks at work and go sit down. It's probably nothing, but I want him to go see the doctor."

"What does he say when you ask him?"

"He says he's completely fine, and there's nothing some damn doctor is going to be able to tell him about being a little tired. He just needs more sleep. But last night, he had to sit down for almost a half hour at the bar. Luckily, it was slow, but I hate it. There's something wrong. I know it."

"Why don't you make an appointment for him on a day when you both aren't working and drag him there kicking and screaming?"

"He would be so mad. And I don't actually know if I could get him to go. I'd have to trick him, and then he'd really be mad."

"I know, but a quick trip to the doctor could allay all our fears." Kirby didn't understand why people were reluctant to get checked out. It wasn't like not knowing there was an issue kept it from existing. If he knew, he could do something about it.

"You know your father. He's a hardhead. He did say that if he isn't feeling better, he will go after Thanksgiving. Speaking of, you are still coming home, right?"

"I've got my tickets, and I've already taken the full week off work."

"Wonderful! So anyway, I didn't call to dump my worries on you. How are you doing? What are you up to this weekend?"

Kirby paused while she tried to decide how much to tell. It seemed too soon to talk about Quinn, but her mother was channeling her psychic powers that morning.

"What are you trying to decide if you should tell me or not?"

Kirby rubbed the back of her neck and attempted to buy herself a little time. "What do you mean?"

"You took too long of a pause. I've said it's one of your tells, but you still do it."

"Oh, for frick's sake." Kirby tipped her head against the glass wall behind her.

"So..."

"Fine, psychic lady. Quinn is here. She's still sleeping."

Her mom gasped, but Kirby wasn't sure if it was a good gasp or a bad one. "Come again?"

"I said, Quinn is here," Kirby whispered, though she wasn't sure why.

"She spent the night? In your bed?"

"So knowing I use the bathroom upon waking like everyone else in the universe is TMI, but knowing a woman spent the night in my bed isn't?"

Her mom laughed. "Stop deflecting and answer my question."

"Yes, Mother, Quinn spent the night. In my bed. Naked. Does that make you happy?"

Her mother giggled—actually giggled—before asking, "How are you feeling about it?"

"Should I assume you mean physical sensation in this new era of nothing being too much information between us?" She was hoping she could embarrass her.

"Don't be silly, Kirby." Apparently not. "How is your heart feeling? Is your head on board?"

"I'm okay. We aren't making any promises, and are taking it slo—"

"Clearly not *that* slow." Her mom laughed so hard at her own joke that she was wheezing trying to catch her breath.

Kirby rolled her eyes, not finding her mom nearly as funny and disbelieving that she was actually having this conversation with her. "Whatever. Anyway, we still have this crazy pull between us, and I finally realized pushing her away wasn't helping anyway." Kirby still wasn't entirely comfortable with giving Quinn another chance, but it hurt less spending time with her than it did pushing her away, so she was trying to go with it despite the niggling fear still in the back of her mind.

"I'm proud of you, Kirby."

"What? Why?" What on Earth could her mother be proud of her for?

"Because you've been so closed off since you two broke up. You've been missing out on so much, so I'm proud that you're brave enough to put your heart out there."

"Whoa, whoa, Mom. No one said anything about my heart."

Her mom snickered. "Keep telling yourself that. Regardless, I'm not at all surprised that Quinn is the woman who pulled you back into the world of the living."

Quinn chose that moment to slide open the patio door and stick her head out. "There you are. I thought I lost you."

The sight of her, sleepy-eyed, blond hair tousled, and wrapped in a blanket, made Kirby smile. "Speak of the devil, here's Quinn," she said to her mom.

Quinn's eyes got big as she mouthed, "Sorry."

"You might as well come out." Kirby sighed, pulling out her earbuds and clicking the speaker button on her phone.

"Who?" she whispered.

"Who else do I talk to on Saturday mornings? My mother, of course," Kirby said.

"Good morning, Mrs. Davis." Quinn blushed endearingly, and Kirby blew her a kiss.

"Good morning, Quinn. It's so nice to hear your voice. How are you?"

"Better than expected, quite frankly." Quinn touched the tip of her tongue to the corner of her mouth.

"I'm so glad to hear that. Well, I don't want to keep you two from your day. Kirby, thanks for calling me back. I feel better after talking to you. Quinn, honey, don't be a stranger."

"Yes, ma'am," Quinn answered.

"Love you, Mom. Talk to you next week, but call me if you need me before that, okay?"

"Love you too. Talk soon."

Kirby hung up. "Sorry, I had no intention of talking to her about us, but I swear, she's clairvoyant."

"I was surprised she knew I was here. Yet not that surprised. You've always been close."

"Yeah. I can't imagine not having her." Even as Kirby approached forty, her mom was still her best friend.

Quinn grabbed her hand. "What did you mean when you said to call if she needs you?"

"She's worried about my father. He's been tired, and she's trying to get him to go to the doctor, but he's resisting. I bet she'll wear him down. I hope."

Quinn released her and placed a palm on her forearm, radiating warmth. "I'm so sorry. I'm sure your mom will get through to him."

"Thank you. Hopefully, it's nothing, but we'll feel so much better if we know for sure." She shook her head, then looked to the wall behind them as Fred started scratching on the glass.

"Time to take him for a walk," Quinn said. "Care to join me?"

"Sure." She loaned Quinn a pair of track pants and a Georgetown hoodie, and they headed out with a mildly excited Fred walking next to them.

They walked hand in hand around two blocks while Fred told all the other dogs that this was his hood by peeing on every vertical surface in sight.

"He's a goof," Kirby said as he lifted his leg on the side of a concrete planter and let one tiny drop out. "Does he realize he has nothing left in the tank after peeing on everything? I don't think that even hit the planter."

"I think it's a male dog thing. He's definitely weird, though. I never would have thought he'd be so lazy. He was quite hyper at the shelter. He seemed to scare off all potential adopters with his slightly homely looks and crazy disposition, jumping off the walls. I was volunteering late one night, and I heard two vet techs saying that he was so crazy, they weren't sure if he'd get adopted at all."

"Oh no! Poor Fred."

"I couldn't let that happen, so I started spending time with him and decided that my lifestyle was stable enough to take on a slightly crazy dog. I took him into the yard and played fetch. He was so happy to get attention that I fell in love. Within a week of coming home, he turned into the happy lazy boy who stares like I've betrayed him if I throw a toy to go fetch."

"I get it. Why take a nearby toy and throw it far away?"

"Apparently, it's pretty common for dogs in shelters to not show their true personalities while under stress, but I love my little Freddy-boy." He looked up at the sound of his name, and Quinn gave him a treat. "Watch. When we get about half a block from our building, he'll lie down and make me carry him."

They continued walking in comfortable silence when, like clockwork, Fred stopped to sniff at a planter about half a block from home, "peed" on it, and then lay on the sidewalk. "Waiting for his servant to carry him. See?"

Kirby laughed, and without warning, Quinn kissed her as she stood with Fred in her arms.

"What was that for?"

"You're beautiful even when you laugh at me. I couldn't help myself."

Kirby rolled her eyes. "Stop, you old charmer." And yet, Kirby leaned in for another kiss when the rumble of Quinn's stomach had both of them laughing again.

"It's rude to call someone old, you know. I'm barely older than you. Now, the more important topic, according to my stomach, is someone promised me breakfast this morning, and I have yet to see any food."

"Funny. Grab your liege and let's go, or I'm making you toast when we get upstairs."

❖

After satiating multiple appetites, first with a delicious veggie frittata with extra sharp cheddar and then afterward on Kirby's couch, Kirby and Quinn cuddled with Kirby's head nestled on Quinn's chest. Quinn never wanted to move again as she tightened the throw blanket around them.

Much to her frustration, however, Jillian had texted her again last night while they were at dinner, asking about her thoughts on the damn condo files that Quinn hadn't started reviewing yet.

"I really don't want to move, but I promised Jillian I would look at the condo files this weekend. Any chance I can convince you to join me?"

Kirby lifted her head and smirked. "I could possibly be convinced. What's in it for me?"

"Renegotiation, huh? You know you *already* agreed to help." Quinn didn't mind, but when Kirby just stared so smugly, she decided to play too. She shifted her hips and used her thigh to apply slight pressure between Kirby's legs. "I'm confident we can come up with a payment that would be mutually agreeable."

Kirby half smiled as she shimmied her hips. "Well, when you put it that way."

"But I'm going to need you to work before you get paid. I don't think that's unreasonable, do you?"

Kirby's laugh echoed around her living room. "Don't you think we should get another workout in first? We didn't run this morning. Again."

"We didn't sleep at all last night. Plus, you are unappeasable, so if we don't take a break now, we might not come up for air until tomorrow." Quinn giggled. "I'm holding out until we at least talk about the situation with the condo."

"Fine, taskmaster."

"If it makes you feel better, we can talk in this exact position before we head downstairs to look through what we've got."

"Why didn't you say so? I am very content here."

"Me too." Quinn sighed and ran her fingers up and down Kirby's back. "I'm not sure what exactly perked Jillian's radar about the financials, but she's pretty sure there is something amiss with the condo manager and a couple board members. The manager and staff are employees of a professional management company hired by the association to run the building, but the board members are residents and have a stake in how well the building is run, which is why it's strange that they'd be in cahoots."

"Assessments went up a crazy amount this year. It pinged my antennae as well, but I didn't want to go through the hassle of doing anything about it except bitching to my fellow owners. What did Jillian give you?"

"The last three years' worth of financial reports. I've also got a summary of all contracts from the last two years and copies of the contracts for the last year. I can get anything else we want from Jillian if needed."

"What about an analysis of the capital reserve account? They should have an annual reconciliation statement showing how much they put into the reserve, annual withdraws, etc.? Something fishy might stick out there more than in the standard income statement or balance sheet."

"I'll text Jillian. Anything else?"

"No, let's start with those, and then we can identify any other gaps once we have that rec statement. Now that's settled, back to playtime?"

The mischievous glint in her eye shot heat straight through Quinn. "You are ravenous, but I love it. Give me two minutes to text Jillian, and I'm all yours."

"I like the sound of that."

❖

As she stood in front of her single-serve coffee maker Saturday morning waiting for her first cup of the day, Kirby thought back over the last few weeks and let out a sigh of contentment. She still had work obligations several nights a week, which prevented them from spending every night together, but they ran together most mornings and often met up for lunch on days when Kirby wasn't going to be home in the evening.

The nights they did spend together were incendiary. Kirby's pulse quickened at the thought of the craving they still had for each other and the fervor with which they made love, almost as though each night might be their last. Kirby remembered things being intense between them before, but the hunger they had this time around was like nothing she'd ever dreamed.

The click-clack of little nails across her walnut floor drew her out of her head, and her attention shifted to Fred walking into the kitchen. "Good morning, Mr. Fred," she whispered as she picked him up, mindful of Quinn still sleeping a few feet away down the hall. "Do you want to snuggle with me while I call my mom?"

She was certain Fred's sigh against her cheek was an affirmation, so she toted him, her coffee, and a throw blanket out onto her balcony. She wore an oversized sweatshirt, and the November air was unseasonably warm, but that meant it was still only fifty degrees outside, so Kirby snuggled Fred on her lap and tucked the blanket around them.

Soon it was going to be too cold to sit out there for long, but fall mornings were her favorite time to be outside. The air smelled clean and fresh, and she could almost taste the apple cider doughnuts she and Quinn were going to eat that afternoon at the pumpkin farm.

"Good morning, sweetheart," her mom said as she answered.

"What's new in the mile-high, Mom?"

"Oh, you know, same old, same old. Your father seems a little better, but I'm still nagging him to go to the doctor. I even told him we could have joint check-ups together, but he's still dragging his feet."

Kirby's jaw clenched at the thought of her father's health. "He said he'd go after Thanksgiving, right?"

"Yes, but now he's saying maybe after New Year's because things are so busy at the bar between Christmas and then. But enough about that. How's work? Did you close the loan on that office tower in Portland?" A slight hitch in her voice gave away her distress over Kirby's father, but Kirby understood that she needed to talk about something else for a while.

"I did. A couple of guys on my team also closed deals in Indianapolis and here in the suburbs, so it was a good week for us."

They chatted for a while before her mom finally brought up the one topic Kirby knew she'd been dying to ask about. "How's Quinn?"

"I'm surprised you waited"—Kirby pulled the phone away from

her ear to check the time—"forty-six minutes to bring her up. I know you were dying to ask." She found herself chuckling along with her mom.

"I was trying to let you bring her up on your own, but I've only got another ten or fifteen minutes before I have to run to meet your sister for breakfast, so I don't have time to wait you out."

"Aha." Kirby enjoyed teasing her. This had become a weekly game between the two of them; it was silly, but part of her still didn't want to talk about Quinn too much. It was too soon, and she didn't want to jinx anything. But frustrating her mom was also fun.

"Stop playing and tell me how Quinn is, or I won't make your favorite mac and cheese for Thanksgiving."

"That's playing dirty, Mom. Sacrilegious, even."

"Maybe, but I'm not making it unless you come clean. Or maybe I will make it, but I won't let you eat any. You can watch as your father, Kelly, Kaleb, and I devour the entire pan."

"Fine, but I'm doing this under duress. She's good. We've seen each other a few times this week. We ate lunch together at that deli downtown that you like."

"*And?*"

"And what?"

When her mom didn't respond and she feared for her Thanksgiving, Kirby continued, "And her little dog Fred is snuggled up on my lap right now under a blanket. Do you want to see a picture?" Fred licked her hand three times before snuggling into the crook of her elbow. "He's such a sweetheart."

"She's still there this morning?"

"Yes, Mom. Sleeping butt-naked in my bed. Is that what you wanted to hear?" The gorgeous line of Quinn's exposed back, with the navy blue comforter tucked around her hips and one perfect leg wrapped on top, was an image that she would cherish forever.

Her mom hooted as she said, "If you're trying to embarrass me, it's not going to work, my dear."

"After almost forty years on this planet, Mom. I'm still not sure what on Earth will embarrass you." However, having this conversation with her mother had heat rushing through Kirby's body and sweat popping out on her palms. "You're so pushy."

"Speaking of, have you asked her to come for Thanksgiving yet?"

Kirby ground her teeth. "I've been thinking about it." Honestly, she had, almost nonstop since their chat last weekend, but she wasn't ready to commit. She and Quinn had only been seeing each other for a few weeks, and she wasn't certain it was time to reintroduce her to the family. Or what that might signal about their relationship. So far, she'd convinced herself that it wasn't serious and that they were taking things day by day—no commitment—but if Quinn came home with her, that was another story.

"Thinking isn't doing, my dear."

"I am aware of that." Kirby huffed. She was tired of being pushed. Her mother had been texting her every damn day about it. But she took a deep breath to calm herself as, despite her annoyance, she knew her mom's heart was in the right place. "I'm just not sure if we're there yet, okay?"

"You and Quinn have always been there." Her patient voice both annoyed and soothed Kirby, and she wasn't sure which effect was stronger. "Also, she's new in town, so she probably doesn't have anyone to spend the holiday with, and I'm sure she isn't going back to spend it with that wretched family of hers."

Kirby still wasn't ready to commit, but her mom's rationale was valid. And yet. "She was stationed here for a few years. She's not new in town. Anyway, bringing someone home to meet your family is huge."

"It's not that huge because we already know and like her. Just ask. If you don't, I might text her myself." Her voice was light, but Kirby couldn't be sure she was kidding.

"You wouldn't."

"Do you want to find out?"

"Fine," Kirby said. "I will bring it up in the most general terms, and if I get a green light from her, I'll actually ask." How her mother could be so loving and sweet and yet so irritatingly persistent, Kirby wasn't sure.

"That's all I ask. Keep me posted."

❖

Kirby slammed the top of the folder closed. She had finished reading through another project's construction agreement from two years ago, and it seemed legitimate. In fact, everything they'd reviewed so far seemed legitimate, and it was beginning to wear on her.

"Everything all right?" Quinn asked.

"Any word on when Jillian is going to get you that additional capital information?" Kirby rubbed at her clenched jaw, trying to alleviate the tension. "It's a little hard to see the forest for the trees without a better look at the capital reserve itself. The summary looks fine, the contracts themselves look fine, but something definitely is off here. I just can't put my finger on it. I feel like I'm spinning my wheels but not getting anywhere."

"I feel the same way. I haven't heard back from her which is weird. I'll text her again." Quinn walked into the kitchen to grab her phone.

Kirby didn't say it, but she was also still wrestling with Thanksgiving, and that wasn't helping her frustration with the condo situation. She didn't want to be away from Quinn for an entire week, which was scary and made her want to invite and not invite her at the same time. She knew her mom was right; Quinn was probably planning to spend the holiday alone, which, even as a friend, made inviting her the right thing to do. But what if Quinn didn't think they were serious enough? Maybe *she* was the one having a good time, which was too scary of a thought. Kirby rolled her head to one ear and the other, attempting to relieve the tension that had taken root at the base of her neck.

"Do you want to take a break? We've been poring over these files for hours. I could give you a neck rub, and we could watch a movie or something." Quinn's eyebrows were drawn together in concern.

"That sounds great."

Once they were snuggled on Quinn's couch with a romantic comedy and Quinn had released years of stress with a head and neck massage, she asked, "Is there anything you want to talk about? You seem a little more uptight than what the condo files would give rise to."

Kirby's relaxed brain answered, "Yes," before she thought about it. "No." Another pause. "I don't know." She sighed.

Quinn chuckled. "Those are all answers, but they are slightly conflicting, don't you think?"

Her magical fingers continued to rub small circles into Kirby's scalp, and she was having a hard time remembering why she was reluctant to invite Quinn to Thanksgiving. She opened her eyes to find Quinn looking down at her lovingly. Quinn's thumbs moved to her temples, eliciting an unexpected moan. "Your fingers are heavenly. This is exactly what I needed. Thank you."

"Not the first time I've heard my fingers are heavenly from you, but it is a new context."

Kirby felt a flash of heat between her thighs at the idea of Quinn's fingers in a different context.

"But if you want to talk, I'm here. Or if you want me to keep rubbing while we watch this movie, I'm happy to." She placed a soft kiss to Kirby's temple and turned her gaze back to the TV as her fingers continued to work their magic.

Kirby lay there, still not sure what to do. Quinn didn't act or talk like this was casual. They hadn't spoken about their relationship, how serious it was, or if they were going to stop seeing other people, but Quinn was so sweet and gentle and passionate. The lack of definition was Kirby's doing, so was she ready for serious? Meeting the family serious? Her mom had made a good point: it wasn't like they were meeting Quinn for the first time. With Thanksgiving less than two weeks away, she didn't have time left to decide.

And yet still she let it marinate. Quinn's fingers continued to rub, but the pressure lightened from a massage into a caress, and Kirby's eyes drifted shut again.

She didn't realize she'd drifted off to sleep until she awoke to Quinn's lips pressed to her forehead. "Hey, sleepyhead. You missed the movie."

"Oops. I didn't mean to fall asleep, but your fingers were so... soothing."

Quinn's cheeks were aglow. "Are you feeling a little better?"

"I am." As Kirby looked up, she knew her mother was right. "What are you doing for Thanksgiving?" Her voice was quiet, uncertain even to her own ears.

"I'm not going home. One of my colleagues asked me to celebrate with her and her boyfriend and his family, but that feels weird. I've only known her a few months. I might curl up with a few books and catch up on my reading. Holidays only have the meaning we give them, so this is basically just a four-day weekend for me."

"Several days of reading does sound nice." Kirby hesitated. "But it *is* a holiday. And you should be with family, people who care about you."

Quinn scoffed. "My family isn't exactly the 'caring about you' type."

Kirby tapped her belly as though playing the piano. "Actually, I was wondering if you might want to come home with me." Kirby halted her dancing fingers and tried to slow her speech to make it less apparent that she was a bundle of nerves. She didn't know if she wanted Quinn to accept or decline and was terrified about what her conflicting desires meant. "I know we haven't been seeing each other again for long, and my family can be a little overwhelming, but my mom suggested you should come. She's always had a soft spot for you. She told me she might text and invite you if I didn't." She laughed, then realized her mistake.

Quinn's shoulders dropped. "Oh, it's only your mom who wants me there?"

"No. No!" Kirby said more forcefully. She hadn't meant to hurt Quinn and wanted to fix it as quickly as possible. "I also want you there. I don't want to go a week without seeing you." Shit. Did she actually say that? Somehow, her heart hadn't gotten the memo that they were playing it cool. However, seeing Quinn's relieved smile quieted her internal monologue.

"I would love to."

She tried to suppress her sigh of relief, but for all Kirby's internal conflict, Quinn's acceptance made it impossible for her to deny that was what she'd been secretly hoping for. Despite her best efforts to keep things casual, she was quickly falling for Quinn again. It was frightening but also exhilarating to know that this thing between them wasn't casual to either of them.

CHAPTER NINETEEN

Quinn looked out the window at the picturesque, snowcapped mountains as the plane began its final approach into Denver International Airport. She'd had two glasses of wine during the flight in an attempt to quell her nerves, but it wasn't working. Her fingers trembled around the e-reader that she definitely wasn't reading, and that slight movement had nothing on the trembling going on in her stomach.

Kirby had taken vacation for the full week, so she planned to meet Quinn at the airport in about half an hour. It had been four long days since she'd dropped Kirby off at the airport on Saturday afternoon. She'd quickly grown accustomed to seeing Kirby at least once every day, so not having her around made the week feel off-kilter. It didn't help that things were slow at the office, and Nylah had taken the week off to host Thanksgiving for Nate's family, who were flying in from Texas.

Her chest vibrated at the thought of seeing Kirby while her stomach churned at the thought of seeing her family. A decade ago, Kirby's relatives had felt more like family than her own parents ever did—but that was before she'd broken their baby's heart. Kirby was the youngest, and they were a little protective, so Quinn feared their reactions now.

Kirby promised that they were fine and excited to see her. After all, Sherry was the one who'd invited Quinn to spend the holiday with them. And yet, when she'd first met him, Kaleb had subtly threatened her about what would happen if she broke his sister's heart, so, yeah, that was still hanging out there. Maybe Kirby's family wanted her to come out so they could kill her and dispose of her body at that animal sanctuary Kaleb worked at.

Well, that was a dark rabbit hole. *Pull yourself together, woman. You are going to be fine.* Quinn again tried to focus on the romance novel in her hands, but the story of Diana and Lane wasn't pulling her in as quickly as it normally would, so to quiet her racing mind, she tried to focus on Kirby instead.

They had spoken every evening after Kirby's parents went to bed, and her heart quickened remembering their dirty encounter last night. The mere thought of watching Kirby's face while she was pleasuring herself had Quinn squirming in her seat.

Kirby's face had been slightly blotchy when Quinn FaceTimed her.

"Hey, you. Did you just get back from a run or something?" Quinn had asked.

"No, when you didn't answer my call before, I got to wondering what you were doing."

"I see, and what were you picturing?"

"I had this vision of you lying in the middle of your bed, naked and writhing, while you had one hand on your clit and the other on your pink dildo, slowly sliding it into you. In and out. In and out. Your hair was spread across the pillow, and my desire to be there was too strong to resist."

Quinn had actually been walking Fred and had forgotten her phone upstairs, but Kirby's fantasy was much better than reality, so Quinn damn sure wasn't going to correct her. "Oh, really? What did you decide to do about it?" Her voice was barely a whisper as she went from zero to completely turned on in two-point-five seconds.

"I started by grazing one fingernail across my left nipple. Back." Kirby took in a sharp breath, and Quinn felt herself begin to come undone. "And forth. And back and forth. It started to swell beneath my fingertip, so I pinched it, tugged it. That felt so good that I switched to my right and gave it the same treatment." Kirby's breathless description had wetness pooling in Quinn's sex. Kirby let out a little moan as Quinn's fingers traced a path to her nipple mirroring Kirby's description.

"And then what?" Quinn prompted.

"My clit was pounding so hard that I had to reach down there. I was so wet. I dipped my finger inside for a moment to gather some wetness but couldn't help slipping that finger and its friend in and out a few times, keeping pace with the picture of you moving that dildo ever so slowly." Her eyes widened slightly as she moaned.

"Oh my God, Kirby. You might be the death of me." Quinn found her own wetness and made tiny circles right above her clit.

Kirby bit her lip and let out the sexiest sigh. "Then the phone rang, and it was you. I had to stop playing with my nipple in order to answer it, but it was worth it to be able to see your face and hear you while I touch myself and wish you were here with me. Tell me what you're doing to yourself," Kirby whispered with an unfocused look in her eyes. When her tongue flicked out of her mouth along her top lip, Quinn's phone slipped from her fingers, hitting her on the chin before landing on her chest.

Recovering it, Quinn said, "I'm slowly running two fingers along both sides of my clit as I trace my tongue along the outside of your ear." Kirby's eyes slowly closed as she listened. "Listening to your voice as you touch yourself has made me so turned on and so wet that with the tiniest bit of pressure, I could make myself come, but I'm trying to draw it out."

Kirby blinked her eyes back open and made eye contact, ratcheting up her arousal even further. "Will you come with me? I am so close. I want to hear you and feel you as I come." Kirby's voice was like warm water running down her body, and Quinn knew she would oblige. She wouldn't even have a choice.

The jolt of the back wheels connecting with the tarmac and the squeal of the breaks shook Quinn back into the present as the force of the deceleration pushed her forward in her seat. With relief, she looked down and was clutching her book and the armrest and not tracing herself over her jeans as she feared she might be.

The plane slowly taxied to the gate, and Quinn could feel her clit sliding between her drenched lips as she was held captive in her seat. She tried to shift to find a position that provided less pressure on her sex, but that seemed to make things worse. She needed a cold shower before meeting Kirby's family to put out those flames, but she would have to settle for freshening up in a bathroom stall and splashing her face with cold water.

When Quinn stepped into the terminal, the busyness of the airport bombarded all her senses. It had been crowded at Midway as well, but since she'd left in the middle of the afternoon, it wasn't quite crazed yet. However, in Denver, people milled around every gate, and she could barely get around the line of pre-boarders as she exited the Jetway and stepped into the terminal.

Her mouth watered at the smell of cinnamon rolls emanating from that annoying shop she was pretty sure was in every airport in every city. While they smelled amazing, the taste never quite lived up to the smell. Such a disappointment. And yet, maybe she would grab one to share with Kirby. It never hurt to check again and see if they were better. Yes, she was a stress eater. She wasn't ashamed.

She scanned the terminal as she tried to figure out which way to baggage claim. She almost missed the familiar face in the sea of people, but when her brain registered what her eyes had seen, she turned back. There, leaning against a column, was Kirby, looking radiant. And delicious. And not only because she was already horny after her mile-high flashback.

Kirby's pixie cut was mussed perfectly on top, and she was wearing jeans with knee-high chocolate-colored boots and a deep maroon sweater cut low enough to show a hint of cleavage. The look was completed by a leather jacket that, combined with her relaxed posture and crossed arms, gave Kirby a hint of badass that enflamed the arousal Quinn was already trying to suppress.

Quinn felt her smile grow with her excitement as she walked straight toward Kirby. "Hey sailor, looking for a good time?" Kirby asked as she approached.

"Always," Quinn said as she crushed her mouth to Kirby's for a brief but intense kiss. "But don't tell my girlfriend, she's got a jealous streak," Quinn responded with her old phrase before she even thought about it. Shit. Her eyes widened as she realized what she'd said. Given Kirby's skittishness, Quinn hadn't meant to mention the "G" word anytime soon.

Kirby's eyes got wide in what appeared to be horror until she laughed and squeezed Quinn's hip. "I'm only kidding. We're taking things slow, but we've spent time together almost every day for the last month and a half. And you are here spending Thanksgiving with my family. I think we can use the word girlfriend, okay?"

Quinn forcefully pushed out a breath and let the relief wash over her. "Okay. You look…" She searched for the right word, but it was a struggle. "Just, damn."

"I look 'just, damn'? That doesn't exactly sound like a compliment." Kirby snickered.

"Sorry, it definitely was a compliment. I was tongue-tied because you look so perfect. I don't often see you in sexy casual mode. Normally, it's work mode or chill mode, but this"—she gestured at Kirby's body—"takes my breath away. Then again, you always do."

"Thank you," Kirby shyly said. She was so adorable that Quinn pulled her close for a chaste kiss. As Quinn reluctantly released her, she looked up and saw something that had her lightly rethinking her "freshen up" plans.

She pulled Kirby to the side of the concourse and quietly said into her ear, "I have a tiny confession to make."

"Do you?" Kirby drew out a simple two syllable phrase into about seven. "I like the sound of that."

"I was feeling a little stressed on the plane about meeting your family. I couldn't focus on my book, I had a couple of drinks, but I was still feeling a little panicked." Quinn hoped her ears weren't turning red at the embarrassment of her thoughts and what she was about to suggest.

"What did you do to calm yourself down?" Kirby ran her index finger along Quinn's collarbone.

"Well, I focused on something else. Something from last night. A particular vision. The problem is, now I'm a little uncomfortable." Quinn shifted her hips. "I had been planning to freshen up before I saw you, but now that you're here, I have a different plan."

"Oh?" Kirby's interest was clearly piqued.

Rather than answering, Quinn looked at the vacant family restroom they were standing next to and then back at Kirby. She lifted her eyebrows.

"Abso-fucking-lutely." Had they been standing outside, Kirby's smile could have been seen from outer space as she pulled Quinn the couple of steps to the restroom.

❖

Quinn had been feeling calmer, but now that they were in Kirby's borrowed car, she felt her anxiety ramping back up. As if psychic, Kirby placed a hand on Quinn's knee and said, "I promise, it is going to be okay. My mom is on cloud nine she's so excited to see you."

"I note that you didn't mention your dad or siblings."

Kirby shook her head and laughed. "Don't worry about them. No one is going to be home when we get there, so you're going to have a little time to get settled in. Mom wanted me to bring you directly from the airport to the bar, but I told her you needed to have a little time."

"Thank you." Quinn laughed as she exhaled her relief. "I love your mom, but she's a little overzealous."

"Mom, Dad, and Kelly are all working tonight, and weirdly, the night before Thanksgiving is almost always insanely busy, so the bar is going to be hopping. I told Mom we *might* come by after dinner, but I wasn't sure."

"Sounds good."

"And the rest of them? They're a little protective, but they're happy that I'm happy. They aren't going to grill you or anything. Mom will kill them if they make you feel unwelcome, so, please, relax." She pulled Quinn's hand to her mouth and kissed each of her knuckles.

They ended up at the bar after Kirby took Quinn to her favorite pizza joint for dinner. It only took a minor pep talk, but Quinn had been won over. She hadn't gotten to see the bar the last time they'd visited Quinn's family and was curious about the scene of so many of Kirby's memories.

Although she was pretty sure Kelly glared at her whenever she wasn't watching, she was relatively certain none of them spit in her drink. Tomorrow would be the true test, with Kaleb and his wife and kids coming over in addition to Kelly, Sherry, and Kirby's father, Seth, but Quinn was feeling optimistic as she held Kirby in her arms that night and drifted off to sleep.

❖

Thanksgiving went as well as Quinn expected. She tried to only be alone with Kirby or Sherry as much as possible, but Seth, Kaleb, and Kelly all managed to corner her before the feast. Seth was the first to get her alone that morning, when she'd run outside to grab the ice melt from the garage so she could spread it along the walks; they were forecasting four to six inches of snow that evening.

Fortunately, Seth's confrontation was the funniest of the bunch. He'd stealthily followed her into the garage, and when she noticed him standing right inside the doorway, he was shifting his weight from foot to foot.

"Hey, Seth. Something I can help you with?" All the while praying he was going to ask her to hand him the snow shovel.

"Look." He paused and glanced at his feet before continuing. "You really hurt Kirby. Like, really hurt her, which hurt me and Sherry."

"I know. I am so incredibly sorry for everything that transpired back then. It was my fault, and I was a coward, and I ran because I feared for my career. I am so grateful that the Fates have crossed our paths again, and I promise you, I will not repeat the same mistakes." She hoped he could see the earnestness in her and understand that she would never do anything to hurt Kirby again.

"I know all that. Sherry told me." He wrung his hands. "Kirby is the happiest I've seen her since you two split. It sounds like she's working a little less, and I can't tell you the last time she came home for a full week. All of that has to be your doing."

"I don't know about all that, sir, but she makes me happy, and I'm doing everything in my power to keep her happy as well." The last six or so weeks had been heaven for Quinn as she was rediscovering something with Kirby that she thought she'd lost forever, and there was nothing Quinn wasn't willing to do for or with her to protect it.

"Yes, right, well, that brings me to the point. What exactly are your intentions? Are you planning on having a little fun with her and moving on?"

"Absolutely not, sir. I'm in—" Quinn cut herself off when she realized what she was going to say.

"In what?"

"Oh hell." She decided she might as well leave her internal censor at the door if she wanted to get back into everyone's good graces. "I'm in love with her. I have been every day since the moment I met her eleven years ago. I thought I'd lost my chance and resigned myself to be alone. And then I ran into her, and I kept running into her, and slowly, her icy wall started to melt. I think your wife had a lot to do with that, and I am so grateful. Since we've started seeing each other again, I realized how much I've always loved her. I thought I'd pushed away all my feelings years ago, but as it turns out, I'd only hidden them. Now my heart is so full, I feel like it might explode. But I can't tell her yet, so please"—she stressed the word and squeezed Seth's forearm—"don't say anything to her. She's so skittish, I'm afraid if she knows I love her, she might run. I don't think I can handle losing her again."

He smiled, and she relaxed, knowing the truth had won him over. "I can't tell you how happy I am to hear that, Quinn." He patted her shoulder a few times. She thought they were finished until he squeezed a little harder. "However, if you hurt her again, I swear, I will find you, and I know where to bury your body so you'll never be found." He smiled and patted her once more on the same shoulder before giving her a gentle push out the door.

"Um, okay," Quinn managed to get out despite being blindsided by the death threat from the least violent man she'd ever met. "Good to know, but it won't be necessary."

"Good, good. Now that I've gotten that little papa bear chat out of the way, how about a drink?"

His whipsaw change of mood and tone made her chuckle. "Ten minutes ago, I would have told you it's too early, but after our chat, I think I'm ready."

"Excellent. Let's go." He put his arm around her shoulders and pointed her back to the house.

"What about the ice melt?"

"Don't be silly. I did that an hour ago. I wanted an excuse to get you into the garage where all the saws and tools are. So you would understand I mean business."

He was definitely a man of many surprises, and a deep laugh rumbled out of her belly. "Message received, sir."

"Please don't call me 'sir.' It was fine while I was dressing you down, but Jesus, I'm not that old."

She popped to attention and gave him a salute. "Aye, aye, Captain."

"That's more like it. I always liked you, Quinn. Much more than any of those yahoos Kelly likes to bring around. I think she's bringing her tatted-up boyfriend, Greg, this afternoon, God help us. I'm always afraid he's going to get his beard hair into the serving dishes. What she sees in him is beyond me." His humor was the opposite of her own father. She loved it.

"He can't be that bad, can he?"

"Oh, wait till you meet him. And cover your drink when you're standing next to him. I swear, he sheds like a puppy during season change. And he looks like ZZ Top. Well, a young ZZ Top. At least he's not an old guy. She dated a guy a couple of years ago who had to be within a year or two of me."

"I've missed you. You're the dad I always wished I had." She shoulder bumped him as they walked onto the porch.

"You're too kind, kid. And a bit of a suck-up, but I can't hold that against you."

She put a hand on his arm to get him to stop. "I may be a suck-up, but I sincerely mean that. My father isn't a nice man. Not to his kids, not to his wife, not unless someone from the congregation is watching. But you, you are a genuinely kind human. I used to wonder who I would be if I'd had a supportive father like you growing up. I will never know, but I am happy to have you back in my life."

Seth pulled her into a tight hug, which was surprising because he had never been much of a hugger before. As quick as it started, though he released her and turned. "Cocktails are waiting," he called as he pulled the back door open. She thought she saw him wipe at the corner of his eye but knew that had to have been a figment of her imagination.

Her conversations with Kelly and Kaleb went in a similar manner. Though slightly less emotional, with no L-words dropped by Quinn and a little more banter. However, both said almost the same thing: if she hurt Kirby again, they knew where to dispose of her body. Creepy that they all went that way, but she didn't plan to hurt Kirby, so it was moot.

"Where'd you go?" Kirby nudged Quinn back into the present that evening with a gentle poke in her side.

"Be careful there. I ate a lot of food."

"I poked your side, not your stomach. I think you'll be fine."

"You're probably right, but let's not find out. Unless it's a different kind of poking, if you know what I mean." She wiggled her eyebrows a few times for emphasis. She pulled Kirby more fully against her side on the loveseat while the whole family sat around the TV watching their beloved Broncos take on Dallas.

"Okay, silly. But anyway, where did your mind go?"

"I was thinking about your family. How lucky you are and how much they all love you."

"Uh-oh, what happened when I wasn't around?"

Quinn chuckled at how transparent she was and spoke softly enough so only Kirby could hear. "I had interesting conversations with your dad and siblings today. All three grilled me on my intentions and happened to mention that if I hurt you again, they know where to dispose of a body so it will never be found."

Kirby took a sharp inhale before she said in horror, "They did not."

"They did, but it was okay. I won them over with my charm, and how happy you seem now didn't hurt either. And I'm pretty sure they meant disposing of me at Kaleb's animal sanctuary, so if I have to go, there are worse ways. At least that way, I can be a part of the circle of life."

Kirby laughed so boisterously, everyone in the living room looked over. "Sorry. All good over here," she said loudly. When her family looked back to the TV, she whispered, "Good to know that when you die, you want to be food for exotic cats."

"It's probably cheaper than a real funeral," Quinn said flatly.

"Morbid but okay," Kirby said and sighed contentedly. "So today wasn't as bad as you'd feared?"

"Definitely not." She was relieved at how well it went. She fit back in with Kirby's family as if no time had passed.

"Well, as a reward for being such a brave sailor today, I'm going to steal you for a few hours tomorrow so we can go hiking over at Red Rocks, just the two of us. We can do a little hashtag OptOutside-ing before we go hang out at the bar in the afternoon with everyone."

"Sounds perfect." Quinn was surprised at how much she meant that. She'd feared this weekend would be awkward, and she would feel like an interloper, but it actually felt like she'd fit back into Kirby's family seamlessly. She wasn't even anxious about going to the bar the next afternoon. Also, several hours alone with Kirby hiking sounded pretty wonderful. She hoped with her whole heart that things could stay this perfect forever.

Chapter Twenty

Quinn had always found February to be the least pleasant month in Chicago. The holidays were long past, and she had no long weekends until the end of May. All the snow that once glistened white was black by February, and the holiday boughs and decorations that were full and green in planters, spreading holiday cheer in November and December, were wilted and brown and depressing by February. The change of season was still nearly two months off, and the short days wore on Quinn, making even minor frustrations seem nearly insurmountable. This year, February felt equally dismal—if not worse.

That Christmas had been the best of her life. Kirby's parents and sister came to town for the holiday and stayed in Kirby's apartment while Kirby stayed with Quinn for the full week. Waking every day with Kirby in her arms and Fred snoring on the floor gave Quinn a spring in her step as they spent every day seeing the best tourist sights and every night lighting up her sheets. But when her family went home, Kirby went back to staying in her own apartment, many nights alone, and it had Quinn feeling off her game. Things at work seemed to go crazy for Kirby, but Quinn missed her and their growing closeness that had suddenly developed a rift.

She couldn't think of anything in particular that would have been the catalyst for this distance that started growing at the end of the holiday season when Kirby's family left. Kelly had been a little standoffish, as always, while in town, but Quinn felt like she'd really reestablished her bond with Sherry and Seth, which she thought would have made Kirby happy too. Nothing made sense, so with the lack of a better scapegoat, Quinn tried to blame Kirby's detachment on the weather.

As the days dragged on, Quinn had hoped to lighten the February doldrums with a romantic Valentine's Day, but Kirby had taken a last-minute business trip to Memphis. Their "romantic" evening ended up being a thirty-minute FaceTime while Kirby ate room service in her hotel.

Maybe she should suggest a quick trip to someplace warm and sandy for a few days. They could get away from the cold and the pressures of work and reconnect. Was it too soon? After only four months, it didn't seem like they should need to reconnect. Their physical connection was as hot and satisfying as ever, but Quinn felt like something was going on.

When Quinn looked up from the contract she was reading at the table, Kirby's brows were furrowed, and her jaw was tight as she glared at the document in her hands.

"What's got you scowling that much?" Quinn asked. They were reviewing the condo files again. Over the past few weeks, they'd made some additional requests from Jillian, but they still hadn't found any obvious signs of wrongdoing.

When Kirby looked up, she paused, almost as if she couldn't decide what to say. "I'm starting to think that the people who have been running this damn building are fucking morons. You excluded, of course." Her facial expression almost looked like she was in pain. "I'm frankly disgusted that I voted for any of them."

Quinn was perplexed as Kirby continued. "I'm looking back at the ten-year capital plans for the last five years and watching how it changed. The point of the plan is so assessments can be adjusted to reserve funds for any major capital projects without having to significantly increase assessments in that given year. It helps to reduce assessment volatility."

Quinn nodded. She had never thought of it prior to being a condo owner and a board member but had learned a lot in the last few months. "Right. From a unit value perspective, a condo building with unpredictable assessments will reduce the overall value of each condo."

"Exactly. And not every owner is going to have the funds sitting around to pay triple or quadruple assessments from the year prior."

Quinn sighed, thinking back to her leaner financial days. "I can only imagine what it would be like to have saved in order to buy a condo in a nice building, have assessments triple overnight, and not be able to pay them. That person would either have to sell or the association would be forced to lien the owner and could move to evict. It would be terrible, but the association wouldn't have a choice because of their fiduciary duties to the other condo owners."

"Which is what the condo leadership is going to be faced with given their piss-poor fiscal management. The first two years I looked at are fine, but starting three years ago, the amount they spent on some projects wildly exceeded the estimates in the capital plan in place. For example, this lobby renovation ended up costing nearly two hundred thousand dollars over what was included in the capital plan. Either the person who made the plan was incompetent, they expanded the scope without anyone realizing how much more it was going to cost, or something more nefarious is going on. But I don't have any proof of which one. Shouldn't there have been audits every year?" Kirby pushed the folder away in disgust.

"I would have thought so, but if several board members and the independent condo manager are both in on whatever may be going on, they could have worked together to keep it hidden. Jillian has only been the president for a year, and she seems to be the first person to raise a red flag."

Kirby yawned, and Quinn noticed how tired her eyes looked. "I didn't realize how late it had gotten," Kirby said as she looked at her watch.

"Sorry to have kept you up so late looking at this. We can keep digging another night. Do you want to stay? Since you're so tired and all? It would save you having to traverse the wilds to get back home." She gave Kirby her best flirty smile.

It apparently wasn't enough, and Quinn's heart sank as she watched Kirby's chest heave on a long sigh. "I wish I could, but I'm so tired, and I've got an early flight tomorrow."

"An early flight?" Quinn didn't remember her mentioning anything about a trip this week.

"I have to fly to Nashville tomorrow. We have an office down there, and I have a small contingent of my team based there. Unfortunately, we're terminating an employee tomorrow. I need to be there to reassure the team and meet a few candidates to replace him."

"That sounds exhausting. When do you come back?"

"Tomorrow night, but I don't get back until late. It's going to be an exhausting day. I feel fatigued just thinking about it."

Quinn placed a hand on Kirby's forearm, her skin warm beneath Quinn's fingers. "I understand if you want to sleep in your own bed, but if you want to stay here, I promise I won't keep you up. We'll only sleep. Scout's honor."

Kirby smiled sadly. "I appreciate the offer, babe, but I've got a six a.m. flight, and I still need to pick out my suit, make sure all my files are in order, and you shouldn't have to get up at two thirty in the morning because I haven't gotten myself together." She leaned in for a kiss. "I will probably fall right into bed tomorrow night, but do you want to do breakfast on Saturday?"

"Sure." Saturday? In the absence of an early morning wakeup call, couldn't Kirby fall into Quinn's bed tomorrow night? She tried to hide the disappointment by turning away and standing up to walk Kirby to the door. "Have a safe flight tomorrow, okay? I'll be home tomorrow night if you want to come by."

Kirby looked at her with sleepy eyes. "I'll try. Good night, sweetheart." She gave her a quick kiss and left.

After Kirby left, Quinn went right to bed, but sleep eluded her for what felt like an eternity. She couldn't help but wonder what was going on between them. Kirby seemed so distant. Maybe it wasn't the weather at all. Maybe Kirby had realized she didn't love Quinn like she used to and was trying to figure out how to tell her. Quinn wasn't sure what time she finally fell asleep, but the last time she looked at the clock, it was already three a.m., and her mind was still mired in the fears of what could be wrong between her and Kirby.

❖

Kirby stood in line waiting to board her flight home from Nashville and battled the sheer enervation from the day weighing on her. She had promised herself at least two glasses of shitty airplane wine since she didn't have a chance to grab a civilized bite to eat and a decent drink at the airport before her flight. After having been up for seventeen hours, she deserved it. It was a good outcome on the day—the team was back in a good place, and she liked all of the candidates that she interviewed—but days like today took their emotional toll.

Without all of the stress of the day ahead of her, Kirby's mind went back to Quinn's apartment last night, and her heart hurt as she remembered the look on Quinn's face when she'd declined to stay the night. She had wanted to. Desperately. But something Quinn had said over Christmas about not coming out to her family really bothered her, and she still wasn't quite sure what to make of it. The longer it sat with Kirby, the worse she felt, and the more distance she allowed to open between them. She wasn't sure why she hadn't simply asked about it.

Five months ago, Kirby couldn't have imagined seeing a future with Quinn again after everything, but now...now it was all she could think about. But if Quinn wasn't serious about her—if she was still planning to only be half-in—Kirby had to hit the eject button now. Before her heart got more involved than it already was.

Work had taken a crazy turn in the new year, which did keep her busy and traveling more than normal, but she also felt herself pulling back from Quinn. If Quinn insisted on staying in the closet to her parents, how could she be all-in? And if she wasn't, how could they have a future?

Admittedly, Quinn not being out to her parents probably wouldn't affect their day-to-day lives that much. They lived on the other side of the country, and Quinn had said they'd never visited her anywhere she'd ever lived. But if she wasn't out to her parents and siblings, who else might she not be out to? Who might she try to hide Kirby from?

Quinn had refused to stand up for them ten years ago, and if she was still too afraid to come out now, what would happen if she reconciled with her family? Would she actively hide Kirby? Would she decide that their relationship wasn't worth the relationship she could have with her family after all these years? Could Kirby trust that Quinn would even be honest with her? Kirby acknowledged that she probably still had a little PTSD about this, but it didn't make her wrong, and if Quinn wasn't ready to fully commit, if she wasn't ready to be fully out, Kirby *had* to protect her heart. And yet she didn't want to. She wanted to open up to Quinn completely, but the big what-if still hung out there and clouded their every interaction.

She needed to talk to Quinn before she herself was the reason that her heart got broken again. But she was entirely too tired to do that tonight.

When her taxi pulled up in front of her building a few hours later, all she wanted to do was fall into bed, but she couldn't deny she wanted to be in Quinn's arms when she did. The pull was so strong, it wasn't a surprise to find herself knocking on Quinn's door rather than heading upstairs to her own.

Quinn pulled open the door wearing low-slung sweatpants and a US Navy sweatshirt with her hair pulled back into a messy ponytail. God, she even made casual look amazing. "Hey, Kirby." Her face lit up. "I wasn't expecting to see you until tomorrow."

"I hope it's not a bad time. I…I wanted to see you." Her eyes had drifted closed of their own accord in the elevator ride up, but seeing Quinn gave her energy.

"No, come in. It's a very good surprise." Quinn pulled her into the apartment by her hands and thoroughly kissed her. "It's very good to see you. I was hoping you would come by."

It felt so good to be held. Kirby felt the stress of her day slipping away in Quinn's embrace. "It was such a long day. I couldn't bear the thought of not seeing you, not sleeping in your arms, tonight." Kirby knew they still needed to talk, but tonight she just wanted to be enveloped in Quinn's warm presence.

"I'm glad. Being with you is the best part of my day. Every day. I've missed you." Quinn ran the pad of her thumb over Kirby's lower lip and she kissed it. "Let's go to bed."

Kirby swooned all the way into Quinn's bedroom and out of her clothes.

CHAPTER TWENTY-ONE

Quinn woke the next morning wrapped around warmth, her head on Kirby's shoulder, and smiled. Waking up holding Kirby was her absolute favorite way to start a day, and she'd missed it. Her smile grew larger when she realized that Fred was on Kirby's other side, snuggled with his head on her hip.

"Good morning, beautiful," Kirby murmured, pulling her focus away from her phone.

"Good morning. Are you feeling better this morning?" Quinn hoped that a night of solid sleep, complete with full spooning action, helped with all the stress.

"I am. Thank you for being my soft place to land last night." Kirby pulled her closer and kissed the top of her head. "Everything ended well yesterday in Nashville, but it was an emotionally taxing day. Despite how deserved a termination is, it's always hard, especially if they have a family. All I wanted to do when I got back was snuggle with you."

"I'm glad to hear that. Are you hungry? I could make us—"

"Toast?" Kirby interrupted with a laugh.

"Well, yeah. Or oatmeal. I might also have some coconut milk yogurt." Quinn tried to look chagrined, but Kirby had to know what she was getting into when she stayed over. Quinn's kitchen was never well-stocked; her idea of a home-cooked meal generally involved grabbing carry-out rather than delivery.

"As appetizing as those sound, why don't you take this little guy out?" Kirby ruffled Fred's ears. "And then come meet me upstairs? I'll whip up a frittata. I did invite you to brunch today, after all."

Kirby slid away and adjusted a much-put-out Fred to climb out of bed. Quinn wasn't ashamed to enjoy the view as Kirby padded naked across her bedroom. "Do you mind if I borrow sweats and a T-shirt? I don't want to put that suit back on. Feels too much like a walk of shame on a Saturday morning."

"Of course, babe." Quinn handed her a pair, exchanging them for a kiss.

"Thank you. I'll see you upstairs. And bring Fred-O. He doesn't like to be alone, and I'm not sure when I'm going to be willing to let you go."

"Aye, aye, Captain."

Once she got Fred ready to go, Quinn's thoughts drifted back to the distance she had been feeling with Kirby of late. Kirby seemed fine that morning, but Quinn had resolved to talk to her before any more distance opened between them. She had to believe that whatever was going on was something she could fix, provided she knew where things had gone astray.

Thirty minutes later, after taking Fred down and having a quick shower to freshen up, Quinn knocked on Kirby's door. She heard "Come in" yelled from within, so she opened the door and walked in to see Kirby sliding the frittata into the oven.

Kirby smiled when she stood. "Hi." A hint of uncertainty flashed across her face, and Quinn knew that whatever was going on was still sitting between them. Quinn took a modicum of comfort from the fact that Kirby had come to her the night before when she needed their connection but couldn't ward off the wariness that something bad was coming.

"Hi. How long until breakfast is ready?"

"Twenty minutes or so. Do you want coffee?"

"Please." She needed some fortification if she was going to get through the discussion she knew was coming. Should she wait until Kirby brought it up, or should she push the issue? Yesterday, she had decided to push it, but in the light of day, continuing to tiptoe around seemed the better idea. It was certainly less scary. What if it was something Quinn *couldn't* fix? After finally reconnecting with Kirby, the thought of losing her again was too much to bear.

"Thank you," she said as she took the cup. Their fingers grazed on the handoff, sending a pleasant surge through Quinn's chest. But, no, they needed to clear the air. Better to rip the bandage off and try to fix whatever lay beneath than to pretend everything was fine when it wasn't. "Do you want to talk about it?"

"Talk about what?" But Kirby's expression didn't look puzzled. It didn't look baffled. It looked resigned, so Quinn waited. It felt like the longest pause she'd ever experienced, and she was preparing to break the silence when Kirby spoke first.

"You said something. When my parents were here. It was sweet: you were telling them how much they mean to you. But you also said that you could never tell your parents that you're gay."

Quinn wasn't sure what to say. Kirby was right. She did say that, and she'd meant it. "They are...not good people. Not supportive."

"So you meant it. You never plan to tell them?"

The look of devastation on Kirby's face had her questioning all her choices, but if she told her parents or her family who she was, they would never talk to her again. They weren't close, but they were still her family. The only family she had. Making that conscious decision, that decision that would cut her off from them forever, felt like too much. "They don't need to know. They don't need to know who I love."

"How can you say that?" Kirby squeaked and then pressed her lips into a thin line.

"I see them once a year max...in a bad year. They don't know me, and they don't need to," Quinn said, trying to remain calm. Trying to quell the panic.

"So what? They're never going to know I exist? What if we decide to have kids? I don't know for sure if I want them or if you do, but if we decide to, do they get to know their grandparents?" Kirby was almost yelling.

Quinn had a difficult time swallowing in the face of Kirby's fury. "If we have kids, they're better off without them. Trust me. They bring nothing but hate and self-loathing."

"If they're that bad, why do you want them in your life at all?"

"They're my family. How do you make a conscious decision to remove them from your life?" Quinn didn't like her family, but other than Kirby, they were all she had. They loved her in their own way. Contemplating life as an orphan was terrifying. If wasn't like she had a family of choice she'd assembled as an adult to rely on. She had her family and Kirby.

"What if there was an accident, or you got sick? They could, and I'm sure they would, deny me seeing you since they have no idea who I am. They'd meet me at the hospital." Kirby picked up the knife from the cutting board and hit the handle on the counter as if to emphasize her every point.

"They'd deny you access anyway. They'd say our lives aren't God's way and wouldn't let you see me even if they knew who you were. *Especially* if they knew who you were." Her voice had also ratcheted up to a near yell, and she felt tears of frustration build in her eyes.

"And that's okay with you?" Kirby yelled back. "It's okay if they get to decide that?"

"We'd sign a power of attorney. They wouldn't. I swear."

"And that's supposed to make me feel better? You're going to lie to them about me, and then if you're in an accident, they'll still find out about me at the hospital. But don't worry, I can still make your medical decisions? I hate to break it to you, but that doesn't—"

The kitchen timer went off, breaking the tension. Kirby walked calmly to the oven, took the frittata out, and placed it on the stovetop. Quinn didn't understand how she could be so calm. It seemed like they'd been discussing the weather with how collected Kirby looked. Her only tell was a quiver when she set the pan down.

When she turned back, her expression was composed despite the tears sliding down her face. She used her fingertips to wipe them away as if they didn't matter and turned her head from side to side. "So once a year, you are going to leave your real life behind, go home, and pretend to be the perfect but weird spinster daughter and aunt? This isn't 1970. Lesbians, gays, queers, trans people, we don't have to hide anymore! What are you going to say if they ask if you're dating?"

"They aren't going to ask." Quinn knew they would never ask for fear of what her answer would be, and they would also have to actually give a shit, which she didn't think they did. But even as she said it, Quinn knew that answer would never satisfy Kirby. It wouldn't satisfy her if their situations were reversed, and Quinn knew, given the circumstances of their original breakup, Kirby had to be panicking at the parallels. She just didn't know what else to do or say to allay her fears.

Kirby let out a scathing laugh that sounded more like a jeer as she said, "That sounds an awful lot like Don't Ask, Don't Tell, doesn't it? It didn't work out so well for us last time." She slammed the knife back onto the cutting board and stormed out of the kitchen.

Quinn jumped up to follow her. "This isn't like last time. I swear, you come first. Always. I will always choose you." Quinn tried to reach for Kirby's hand, looking for something, anything to reestablish a connection between them.

"You aren't choosing me. Again. And I can't trust you to. How can we have a life together if you're living a lie? You're almost forty years old, for fuck's sake." Kirby yanked her hand out of reach and paced around the living room.

"It's not a lie, Kirby. You are not a lie. We are not a lie." Quinn didn't care that she was starting to sound hysterical. She couldn't lose Kirby. Not like this. Not again.

"I think you should go. I need time to think."

"Kirby, please. Please don't do this." But Quinn could hear the same words from so long ago echoing in her ears, and this time around, they were no more effective than the last time. She stared into Kirby's tear-stricken yet blank face. She had completely shut down. Shut her out.

Kirby picked Fred up, nuzzled the top of his head, and handed him to Quinn. "Please. Just go."

Quinn took him and walked to the door hunched over, gutted. As she reached for the doorknob, she turned back in a last effort: "Can we talk next week?"

"I don't know. Maybe. I'll text you." Her voice was flat. Lifeless.

Quinn wondered how she could shut down like this. She felt like her heart was fracturing into a million pieces, and Kirby was showing as much emotion as a Vulcan. Quinn knew it served her right. She had treated Kirby the same way when their positions had been reversed ten years ago. Fuck. She opened the door and walked out, praying it wouldn't be the last time.

CHAPTER TWENTY-TWO

It had been almost a week since their breakup, and Kirby still felt dreadful. Part of her wanted to run back to Quinn and apologize, tell her she was sorry for being so judgmental, but the other part of her knew her inevitable heartbreak would only be worse when Quinn's family got their claws back into her. She would start to second-guess whether it was worth it: the lies to her family, the hiding, and decide it was too hard. Just like with the Navy.

After Quinn left, Kirby threw away the frittata and went back to bed. She sent her mom to voice mail, which she never did, and texted, asking if they could talk later because it wasn't a good time. Her mom had been gracious, telling Kirby to call whenever was convenient. Kirby still had guilt over not calling her back; it was already Friday.

She'd make it up to her tomorrow when they spoke, though she still wasn't ready to tell her that she'd broken up with Quinn. She knew her mom would support her but would still be incredibly disappointed. Had they actually broken up? Kirby didn't see another way around it, but she supposed she hadn't said "I don't want to see you anymore" or anything of the like. Still, her mom would ask about Quinn, and what could she say?

The only bright spot all week, as she intentionally avoided Quinn and tried not to think too deeply about the rest of her shitshow, was that Allie was going to be in town that weekend. She was passing through Chicago on her drive from Maryland back to Monterey to become an instructor at the place that had shaped them all and was going to stay with Kirby for the weekend. She'd been so lost in her own inner conflict about whether to confront Quinn or not and then the breakup— or was it impending breakup?—that she'd completely forgotten Allie was coming until Allie had texted to confirm.

They'd stayed in contact, though it had been years since they'd last met in person. Now, seeing Allie was going to be a welcome distraction. Her wife had already driven out to Monterey, taking their two kids and dog a month ago so the kids would be there for the start of school, but Allie's official change of station was next week, so she was only heading out now. Kirby loved Allie's family but was happy, given her present emotional turmoil, that it would be just the two of them this weekend.

Allie had been the one to take leave and help Kirby pick up the pieces after Quinn had broken her heart before, so it felt like fate that she was here now, a decade later, with the situation reversed. She'd want to do it again, right? In case she was being a bad friend, which she probably was, Kirby picked up two bottles of disgusting coconut rum that Allie still loved, one to drink that night and one for Allie to take with her. She hadn't even told Allie about Quinn coming back into her life, no less about the Breakup: Round Two. Regardless, Kirby was eager to see her old friend and catch up. She promised herself that she wouldn't actually monopolize their days together moaning about her love life, despite her present heartbreak.

When Kirby opened her door that evening to see Allie standing on the other side, she pulled her into a close hug and said, "It's so good to see you. Gosh, how many years has it been?"

"You're squeezing the life out of me, but I think three. When Marie and I came out with the kids for a visit. They were so small. But why is it that I seem to always be the one coming to you?"

Kirby didn't want to admit her recent revelation that she hadn't been a great friend to anyone of late, so she laughed and joked to divert their attention. "I'm irresistible. Though now that you're going back to Monterey, try keeping me away." Kirby pulled her into the apartment. "God, it's good to see you. Let's get a drink. After the past week, I definitely deserve it, and I want to hear how Marie and the kids are settling into Monterey."

Kirby started making their drinks: coconut rum and pineapple for Allie—she cringed at the smell as she opened the rum—and an old-fashioned for herself.

"It isn't that bad. It tastes like vacation," Allie said.

"It smells like suntan lotion." Kirby suppressed a gag.

"As if that rubbing alcohol you drink smells any better," Allie said. "So tell me, what's wrong with you? You're"—she swirled a finger at Kirby—"weird."

"I will tell you, but let's talk about you first." Kirby did want to talk about it all but wanted to try to be a good friend first.

After talking about how excited Allie was to go back to Monterey, how the kids were loving it, and how she had a romantic getaway planned for Marie in Napa in a few weeks, Allie circled back to Kirby. "Okay, now that I've given you my whole life in a nutshell, what is going on with you? You seem like that string quartet in *Titanic*. Smiling and playing an upbeat tune as the whole ship is going down around you."

Kirby laughed at how accurate that image felt. "I'm going to apologize in advance because once I get going, I might talk for hours, but if you can believe it, after ten years, I ran into Quinn again." Kirby ached even saying her name.

"Quinn Prescott? As in, the breaker of hearts, Quinn Prescott?"

"That's the one."

"Holy serendipity, Kirby."

"If you can believe this, we'd even started dating. But we broke up last weekend." Kirby felt the tears starting, but she tried to shove them back in. She was afraid if she started crying, she might never stop.

"I can't believe that bitch broke your heart again." Allie looked like she was ready to go hunt Quinn down that second.

"I know, except it didn't go down like you're probably picturing." Kirby told her every sordid detail, from the moment they ran into one another through last weekend, when she'd found out that Quinn never planned to come out to her family, keeping her entire personal life a secret from them, and thus why she had to break up with her.

"Shut the front door." Allie hit her in the shoulder in what Kirby assumed was a friendly manner but still kind of hurt. "You *did not* actually break up with her because she isn't out to her shitty family, did you?"

"You make it sound like I was in the wrong. How can we try to build something together if she's lying about everything? She's too afraid to be herself, and I can't do it. I can't wait for that shoe to drop. So I did the only logical thing. I broke our hearts first. Before either of us gets even more invested."

"This comes only from a place of love, sweetie." Allie placed a hand on Kirby's knee and squeezed. "But seriously, what the fuck?"

"What?" Kirby couldn't believe Allie wasn't on her side. She'd been a mess after Quinn left her the first time, not leaving her apartment for almost a week. She'd already taken the time off, so she didn't even have to go to sick call to stay home. She didn't shower for that whole week and had been a sobbing mess. Allie was the only reason she'd survived and was able to find some sense of normalcy. She should know why Kirby couldn't risk her heart.

"You. And Quinn. Are soulmates. All of us were envious of you and your connection when you first met. We missed you hanging out with us all the time, but we were so jealous. Anyone within a two-mile radius could feel your connection. You were like 'hashtag relationship goals' for the rest of us. I was almost as heartbroken for love as an institution when you broke up. You guys made me believe in soulmates, and I was devastated along with you."

Kirby had no idea everyone else could see or feel their connection. Or that everyone envied them. She'd been happy in her love cocoon with Quinn and had almost forgotten about the outside world, though she and Quinn had tried to see their friends occasionally.

"So after a decade, you serendipitously run into one another, revisiting the whole 'soulmates' thing, and because there's one tiny thing that you aren't comfortable with, you cut and run? Did you even try to talk to her about it?"

"Not exactly," Kirby muttered.

"No, huh? I hate to break it to you, babe, but you were looking for an excuse." Allie cocked her head as if trying to say, challenge me on this.

Kirby shook her head vehemently. "Not at all. It's not a little thing, and how can you trust a liar?" Lying to her parents could easily spiral into lying whenever her sexuality wasn't convenient, which could spiral into lying to Kirby herself about lying to others about it. Although she wasn't aware of Quinn having lied to her since they'd reconnected, one white lie was like a gateway drug. Kirby couldn't do it.

"What did she lie about?"

"She's lying to her family about who she is." Kirby knew she still had a little PTSD about her partner not being completely out after how Quinn had behaved the last time around, but it didn't make her wrong. Quinn didn't stand up for them, didn't even try to make things work in the face of a little adversity last time. Why would things be any different this time?

"Is she?" Allie sounded patronizing, but she didn't know what it was like to be with someone so far in the closet they wouldn't fight for you. The dread sat in Kirby's stomach like a medicine ball.

"It's a lie by omission. It counts."

"She hasn't come out to them, but they haven't asked her. She hasn't taken anyone home, but she hasn't made anyone up for them either, has she?"

"It's exactly like before in the military." It had to be the same. Quinn wasn't comfortable with who she was then, and that clearly hadn't changed, so it was only a matter of time until she did the same thing. As long as Quinn continued to be ashamed of who she loved, Kirby knew she would eventually be thrown to the side when it got too hard or when she got tired of lying to her family. Just like the last time. Kirby was being sensible and ending it when it would hurt less and before Quinn had a chance. This way she was in control and wouldn't be blindsided again.

"I only knew her a fraction as well as you did, but I have to disagree. Her family sucks. She isn't going to choose them over you. From what you told me, she's in love with you. And your family. And you think she'd choose hers because they're blood?" Allie had a sad smile.

Oh God. A decade ago, Quinn didn't know what she could do with her life without the Navy. Her life before was completely intertwined with it, but now she barely even spoke to her family. Kirby hadn't ever heard Quinn speak to them on the phone and never talked about them unless Kirby asked specific questions that Quinn couldn't dodge. They really didn't matter, which, Kirby had to admit, she already knew in her heart. But did one lie spin into more and more? Quinn had never lied to Kirby before, and when they first met, they were both lying every day about who they were to their respective commands. If that level of lying hadn't impaired her relationship with the truth, nothing probably would. Kirby felt like she'd swallowed a huge meatball, and it was lodged in her throat. What if she'd thrown away her soulmate from baseless fears? She felt sick. That medicine ball of dread in her stomach doubled in weight. "Shit."

Allie simply nodded.

Kirby's head was spinning, but the fact remained that Quinn hadn't stuck up for them before. Could she now if she had to? Would she?

"Did you try listening to her side when you brought up your concerns? Or did you just toss her out?"

Kirby stared into her amber drink. "The second one," she mumbled. She took too large of a sip of her old-fashioned and told herself the tears in her eyes were from the burn in her throat from that sip and not the burn of remorse.

"I know you haven't had a lot of relationships in the last decade, but talking about problems will work wonders."

"You don't have to be an ass, O Wise Relationship Oracle." Kirby smiled to take the edge off her remark.

"I know, but it's fun to be the wise one sometimes." Allie smirked.

Would talking to Quinn really help? Could she trust her? Had she simply been looking for something, anything, as an excuse to protect her heart even as she was falling for Quinn all over again? Did it mean that much to her to be the one who decided it was over? "Fuck."

Her phone rang and caused her to jump six inches off the couch. "Who the hell...it's my mom. That's weird. We normally talk on Saturday mornings. Sorry, Allie, give me a sec." Kirby swiped to answer. "Hey, Mom. What's up?"

"Kirby?" Her father's voice.

"Dad? Why are you calling on Mom's phone?"

"I'm sorry, sweetheart. You need to come home."

Kirby's heart leapt so high into her throat, it seemed like it might leap out of her mouth. "What's going on?"

"It's your mother." His voice cracked, and Kirby knew it was going to be bad. Really bad.

"Oh God, Dad. What's going on?" Tears sprang to her eyes as her chest constricted.

"She collapsed in the kitchen. I think she had a heart attack. Kelly did CPR, but we don't know how long she'd been out. She's in the ambulance right now, and Kelly and I are following. We don't know anything. Please, just come."

"I'll get the next flight out. I'll text the info. Please call me as soon as you know something. What hospital?"

"Adventist. I love you, Kirby. I'll see you in a few hours."

"I love you, Dad. Kiss Mom for me when you see her."

"I will."

As Kirby hung up, a sob escaped her. Allie had moved next to her on the couch and wrapped an arm around her, and Kirby sank into her shoulder.

"How is she?"

"They don't know. She's in the ambulance. They think it was a heart attack. I have to get there." Her brain had been a little foggy after a couple drinks, but she felt completely sober now. "I have to find a flight."

"Go pack a bag and give me your phone. I'll find a flight."

"Okay. Thanks." Kirby raced into her bedroom to pack. She felt like a robot as she pulled out her carry-on and started throwing clothes into it. She wasn't even sure what she was pulling out. The thought of losing her mom was overwhelming, so she tried to focus on the task at hand. She threw whatever would fit into her suitcase. She was sure there'd be something to wear, and in a hospital, what did it matter anyway?

Allie walked into the bedroom. "There's one flight out tonight in an hour and a half. Can you make that? Do you want me to call a Lyft? Are you ready to go? Should I buy it with the credit card in your profile?"

"Yes, yes, close enough, and yes. I need to get a few things from the bathroom, and I'll be ready." She ran, grabbed her "go bag" of bathroom products and toothbrush, and threw it into her suitcase.

"Okay, Joey will be here in six minutes."

"Perfect." Back into the closet. More clothes. God only knew which ones; she just kept stuffing until the suitcase was full. She thought she'd grabbed underwear.

"What's the closest hotel to here?"

"What? Why?" Why that would matter?

"I need to find somewhere else to stay."

"Don't be foolish, stay here. It's not like you're going to make off with my TV or my fish or something. Here's a spare key. Keep it. Feed Frank the Tank before you leave, okay?"

"Who?"

"Frank. My fish. On the bookshelf. I'll show you. And thank you. Feel free to stay as long as you want. Enjoy your bachelorette-hood for another couple of days."

"What the hell are you talking about?"

"Just never mind. Thank you. I…"

"I know. Take care of your parents. Call me when you know more."

Kirby pulled her into a tight hug. "I will. Drive safe when you leave, and I'll talk to you soon. And thank you." Kirby couldn't express her gratitude enough, so she tried to communicate how much she loved her through the hug.

"Okay, your car arrives in one minute. Get out of here."

❖

Quinn had given Kirby a full week. A full fucking week of silence. More than. Quinn managed not to text despite thinking of her every minute since Kirby had thrown her out. But she couldn't wait anymore. It was Saturday afternoon, and it had been a week of Quinn creepily stalking the lobby as much as she could without actually looking creepy. Still nothing.

So now she stood outside Kirby's door, wiping her sweaty hands on her jeans and trying to untie the knots in her stomach. She lifted her fist to knock at least three times before she finally found the courage to bring her knuckles to the door.

She gave it a beat or two and thought she heard someone shuffling inside, but no one came to the door, so she had raised her hand to knock again when the door opened. Quinn was a bit shocked to see a slightly older version of a familiar face. "Allie?"

"Quinn Prescott. Wow. You look exactly the same. Except maybe hotter."

"Wh…what?" Why was Allie standing in Kirby's entryway in pajamas, and where was Kirby?

"Come in. She's not here, but she told me about you."

Quinn followed reluctantly. With as angry as Kirby was, Quinn didn't feel right being in her space. "Where is she?"

Allie yawned before she said, "Denver."

"Why, and what are you doing here? Not to be rude." Though she probably was.

"I'm heading back to Monterey to take an instructor position and am passing through. Kirby and I were having a few drinks and reconnecting last night when she got the call."

"Reconnecting?" Quinn mumbled. How exactly?

She didn't think her emotions were that obvious, but her jealousy must have been because Allie said, "Not like that. We've never connected in the biblical sense. You know, if the Bible had gays. Anyway, she knows my wife and kids." There was a clear emphasis on the "wife" part as Allie wiggled her left hand, showing a wedding ring, and Quinn let loose a sigh of relief. "She told me about what happened with you two."

"I'm not sure if her talking about me is good or not, but why is she in Denver? What's wrong?"

"She's at the hospital."

Quinn's stomach lurched. "Oh no, is her dad going to be okay?"

"Okay, I think, all things considered." Allie's brows wrinkled.

"He's been abnormally tired lately, and her mom has been worried."

"He's not the one in the hospital. I mean, I'm sure he's at the hospital too, but it's her mom. She had a heart attack."

"What? Sherry? No." Quinn's knees buckled, and she stumbled back until her legs hit the couch and she sank down. Sherry was the glue of Kirby's family. She had to be fine. "Is she okay?" Quinn finally managed.

"I don't know. Kirby texted me when she landed last night, but I don't have any updates yet."

"Do you know what hospital?" Her mind was racing as she formulated a plan.

"I think she said Adventist."

"Thank you. How long are you staying?"

"Only until tomorrow. It's embarrassing, but I'm so freaking tired, I'm going to take an extra night of sleep before getting back to the real world."

"I won't judge. Or tell your wife, whom I don't know. I promise. Thank you for the intel. I have a flight to book after I talk to my boss, but I hope we can catch up sometime. I would love to hear about your family. Or even better, meet them."

Allie surprised Quinn when she said, "Me too." She smiled. "It's probably a friend violation, but I can't help it. I love love. Kirby needs support right now more than anything, but she loves you, even if she isn't ready to admit it, and I think she'll come around. She's just scared."

"I was being an ass, and I've tried to fix it, but it's good to know she doesn't hate me. Thank you. Truly."

"Will you text me? Keep me updated?" Allie asked.

"Of course."

"God, I hope her mom is all right. I know Kirby is close to her."

"Me too." Quinn squeezed Allie's hand. "Thank you for everything, and I promise I'll keep you posted on all fronts."

Chapter Twenty-Three

When Quinn landed, she didn't know what to do, so she hopped in a cab and asked them to take her to Adventist Hospital. She hoped there was only one Adventist in the city and was embarrassed for not spending the time to google that before she landed. She lamented the fact that the last time she'd flown to Denver, it was full of so much hope and anticipation for seeing Kirby's family again for Thanksgiving, while this time, she was praying Sherry was going to be okay.

Quinn approached the check-in desk at the hospital with a confidence that she didn't feel as she asked for Sherry Davis. She was running on caffeine, a cheese sandwich, and nerves, and even if the very nice volunteer told her where to find Sherry, did she have the nerve to go up?

The odds were seemingly in her favor as the attendant told her Shery was in the ICU and how to get there, which left Quinn with a dilemma. She wanted to be there for Kirby, and she wanted to support Seth and Sherry, but she didn't want to overstep. She didn't want to make an already terrible situation worse or make things harder for Kirby, but she also couldn't imagine being anywhere else.

Which was how Quinn found herself sitting off the elevator lobby on the ICU floor with her roller bag standing next to her. She was afraid to go down the hall, but she couldn't leave either. So she remained rooted in the lobby, looking around and biting the inside of her cheek, mired in indecision.

"Quinn?" Kelly walked toward her looking drained. Her eyes were tired, and her hair lacked its normal styling.

But she spoke to Quinn. That had to be a good sign. "Hey, Kelly. How's your mom?"

"She's...okay. So far. She's still sedated while they assess the damage to her heart. We're taking turns sitting with her while we pray. Does Kirby know you're here?"

"Not exactly."

"What does that mean?" The look on her face had Quinn again second-guessing whether she should have come.

"We had a fight before she left. A week ago, actually. It's why I'm standing here in the elevator lobby alone like a stranger, but when I heard, I couldn't imagine being anywhere else. I love your mom. And I love your dad. And I love your sister. So here I am. Unsure what to do."

Kelly sighed. "I've always wanted to not like you, Quinn."

She wasn't sure what to do with that.

"But it's hard. You're quiet but sincere, loving but not sickly sweet. When you broke up with Kirby, I thought I'd been right about you all along. But Kirby has better fucking taste than I do." Kelly let out a self-deprecating chuckle. "I don't want to admit it, but you're a good person. It's quite annoying. But I love my sister, and I know you love her too. And our parents."

"I'm...sorry?" Quinn didn't know what the right response was but felt she needed to say something.

"Ugh. See? So likeable." Kelly shook her head. "She went back to the house a little while ago to get a shower, take a nap, and bring us dinner. If you don't dawdle, you can probably catch her. Then come back. I know Dad will be happy to have you here and so will Mom. When she wakes up." Kelly sniffled, and Quinn noticed how red Kelly's eyes were.

"I'm sure she's going to be fine. Your mom is a fighter." She squeezed Kelly's forearm. "Thank you for your help."

"I hope I see you later." At Quinn's puzzled look, she said, "I really mean that. You're one of the good ones." She pulled her into a very unexpected hug, and Quinn went with it, but it felt weird. Kelly had never been more than standoffishly polite, but it was an emotionally charged time.

She squeezed Kelly's shoulders. "Thank you. No matter what happens with Kirby, if you or your parents need anything, I'm here."

❖

Kirby was bone weary. She'd been at the hospital for nearly forty-eight hours, napping occasionally in the uncomfortable plastic chairs in the ICU waiting room. Neither she nor Kelly nor Kaleb wanted to leave their father—or mother—there alone, but Kirby had pushed everyone else to rotate, to take a break from hospital food, to sleep in their own beds, and to get a shower. Somehow, she'd managed to rotate herself to stay at the hospital each time for two days before someone noticed. She couldn't imagine being more than a few feet away from her mom while she was fighting for her life. She had coded twice during those forty-eight hours, and Kirby had never been more afraid. She'd spent too many hours working rather than with her family and hated herself for all of the missed time.

It was Kaleb who finally realized that she'd never left and ganged up with their dad and Kelly to force her out a few hours ago. She obliged to humor them, knowing she'd never be able to rest. She pretended to be excited to get to sleep in a real bed when they confronted her but the dread about leaving had Kirby so weighed down, she didn't know how she was still upright. Still, she put on a brave face and drove away while Kaleb watched. He apparently didn't trust her to leave unless he observed her exiting the parking lot.

Kirby had dutifully driven away despite the seizing in her throat as she pretended to smile and wave. But the weight of going to her parents' home while her mom was fighting to survive became heavier and heavier every tenth of a mile she drove. There was a vise around her esophagus that was pushing tears into her eyes. Yet she continued, convincing herself that the pressure would dissipate the farther that she got from the hospital. As the wishful thought passed through her mind, she knew it was a lie even her subconscious wouldn't be sold on.

And yet she still believed she could make it. Until Meghan Trainor's "Mom" came on the radio, and the pressure in her chest built to the point of agony. Her vision tunneled, and she pulled to the side of the road before she hit something. She barely had time to steer to the curb before full sobs overtook her, and she doubled over in the driver's seat, face against the steering wheel. She was overwhelmed by the fear of losing her mom, losing her sense of identity, and sobbed alone. She lost track of time as tears poured straight from her soul and dropped onto her lap.

Her mom, larger than life, looked so small in that huge hospital bed, with lines running everywhere, connecting her to every medical machine, all seemingly beeping at different intervals. The hardest part had been seeing her intubated, her mouth, always so animated, slack open, with a tube coming out of it taped to her face. Her mom was the strong one. She was the one who held everyone together, but now she was lying there so weak. Kirby and her dad and siblings had to take turns holding each other together.

As her sobs began to subside, Kirby became aware of the feel of the steering wheel against her forehead. The scent of sandalwood air freshener permeated her nose. Kirby tried to pull herself together so she could get back to the house, but as she looked up, she saw a Sprouts grocery store, and a minor plan on how to spend the next few hours began to form in her mind.

She had always found cooking therapeutic and decided to pick up two pot roasts to cook, one for her family and one for the hospital workers caring for her mother. She slipped into a trance at the kitchen counter, cutting the potatoes, carrots, and onions and then lightly sautéing them, and browning the roasts before transferring it all to the roasting pan and placing it in the oven. Her mom had taught her how to make a pot roast when she was younger, always calling it better than chicken soup for the soul. She had stood right next to her in this kitchen, her mom showing her the tricks to making the perfect roast. Kirby didn't realize she was crying until a tear landed on the back of the hand wielding the chef's knife.

Her mom couldn't die. She was too young. Kirby still had too many things for them to do together, too many things for them to talk about. She promised God that if her mom pulled through, she would be a better daughter. She would visit more often and never miss a Saturday chat. She'd take her parents on the European adventure they'd always talked about but never had the money for.

Her thoughts drifted back to Thanksgiving, when she and Quinn had been here together. Her mom had been so happy for them to be back together. Her dad had been weirdly aloof at first, but after the first eighteen hours, he seemed to warm back up, whereas her mom had been almost giddy from the moment they'd walked into the bar together. On several occasions, her mom had evicted her from this kitchen to have private chats with Quinn, the topics of which Kirby still didn't know.

Thinking of Quinn, the hollowness in her chest grew even more cavernous. Sitting vigil at her mom's bedside with nothing to do but think, Quinn monopolized the thoughts not centered on her mom. Kirby finally realized she had used the first sign of trouble as an excuse to run away from the love of her life because she was afraid. She wished Quinn were there to hold her and tell her everything was going to be okay. Being with Quinn made everything feel better. Less scary.

After putting the roasts in the oven and setting the timer on her phone for four hours, Kirby lay down on the couch. She didn't have much hope of sleep, so she flipped on her childhood feel-good movie, *Oliver and Company*, and tried to lose herself in the antics of Oliver and Dodger.

❖

Kirby jerked awake with a start, her heart racing. She wasn't sure what had yanked her out of her nightmare about a funeral, but she felt grateful to be pulled into the real world as she wiped the tears off her cheeks. She panicked at the thought of her nightmare being a premonition, so she texted Kelly and Kaleb to get an update.

As Kirby set her phone back down, heart still pounding, she heard the doorbell. She had no idea who it might be but padded to the front door to see in case it was a neighbor checking in.

She saw Quinn standing on the other side with an uncertain expression on her face but otherwise looking as gorgeous as ever with the wind blowing her hair from beneath a black knit beanie. "Quinn. How did you...What are you...How are you...here?" Kirby finally formed a complete question, her brain foggy.

"I hope it's okay that I came. I went to see you, and Allie was in your apartment. She told me about your mom. I am so sorry, Kirby. I couldn't stay away knowing she was in the hospital, and you were in pain." Her eyes were watery, and that did Kirby in.

She pulled Quinn into her arms and let out a light sob. "Of course it's okay. I'm so glad to see you."

The feel of Quinn's arms around her, her hands lightly rubbing her back made Kirby feel like things might be okay. "I'm sorry. You were right. It's why I went to your apartment yesterday afternoon. I have so much I want to tell you, but it can wait. How's your mom?"

"I just got a text update. No change. She's still sleeping, but she's not out of the woods. She coded twice in the past forty-eight hours, but the ICU team was able to revive her." Quinn pulled her in more tightly as Kirby's tears began to flow again. "I'm so scared."

"I know. She's going to be fine, Kirby. I know it. She's a fighter and has too much life left in her."

They stood like that for a long time in the foyer, Quinn holding Kirby and soothing her with gentle motions along her neck and back while Kirby cried, face buried in Quinn's shoulder. All of the fear and tension of the last two days poured out of her into Quinn's safe arms.

As Kirby's tears began to subside, Quinn whispered, "Why don't we go sit on the couch?"

Kirby nodded, realizing that her legs were struggling to hold her up and Quinn was bearing a lot of her weight.

Quinn held her close as they moved to the couch and pulled her tightly against her side once they sat down. "*Oliver and Company*, huh?"

Kirby noticed that the movie had started over again while she slept. "When I was sick as a kid, this was the movie my mom would put on to make me feel better. Oliver was such an adorable kitten, and Dodger would never let anything bad happen to him. I needed a little comfort today."

Quinn pulled her more fully into her chest and lightly kissed her temple. "Are you cooking something? It smells amazing."

The press of Quinn's fingertips rubbing her scalp were so calming that Kirby had a hard time forming sentences. "Pot roast. Mom's favorite," she mumbled and fell asleep.

❖

Quinn hadn't known what to expect when she'd knocked on Sherry and Seth's door, but it hadn't been to be holding Kirby as she slept an hour later. She knew Kirby wouldn't want to sleep for too long, but she clearly needed the rest since she was out like a light as soon as they'd gotten settled. Quinn had shifted so that her head rested in Quinn's lap rather than against her chest, allowing her to stretch out on the couch.

Kirby was always beautiful, but as she lay there, her face relaxed and snoring softly, Quinn had never seen anyone more lovely. She continued to run her fingers through Kirby's short hair, brushing her bangs off her forehead and savoring the soft feel between her fingers. Her heart broke for all of the Davis clan, but at the same time, her heart felt so full of love for Kirby. And gratitude that Kirby took her back with no explanations. She didn't know what the future held for them, but she prayed it wasn't only because Kirby was in an emotional place. That Quinn wasn't just a convenient shoulder. She would be whatever Kirby needed but didn't know how she'd survive if Kirby didn't want her back.

Kirby's phone began to chime, so Quinn picked it up and silenced it. She hated to wake Kirby but was sure she wanted to get back to the hospital.

She began to press a little more firmly, running her fingers through Kirby's hair and quietly saying her name. After a few repetitions, Kirby's eyes fluttered open. Her tender smile when she made eye contact with Quinn was everything.

"Hey, sleepyhead."

"Hey, yourself. What time is it?" Kirby's voice was endearingly gravelly as she spoke.

"It's about four. Your alarm went off a minute ago. I didn't want to wake you, but I was sure you would want to get back."

"Yeah. I need to check the roasts."

"Why don't I do that while you take a shower?"

Kirby chuckled, smelling her shirt. "Do I smell that bad?"

"No, silly, but your sister mentioned that you had come home to take a shower and get some sleep in a real bed. You didn't quite make it to a real bed, but you were snoring at least."

"You talked to Kelly?" Kirby's eyebrows drew together in confusion, as though she couldn't quite work out a puzzle.

"Yeah, I ran into her at the hospital. She told me where to find you."

"Huh? She really is coming around."

"She was surprisingly candid and said as much. Truthfully, it might also have been the longest conversation I've ever had with her. It was...bizarre but not bad."

Kirby smiled before she pushed off Quinn's lap. "Thank you," she whispered before she ghosted a kiss across Quinn's lips.

"For what?" Quinn asked, tucking a wayward strand of hair behind Kirby's ear.

"For everything. For coming here. For holding me. For helping me sleep. I..." She trailed off and bit her lip as she looked down. "It means a lot."

"Always," Quinn breathed. She grazed her fingers across Kirby's cheek. "Now, off with you. I'll go check the roast. Oh wait, how do I know if it's ready?" She knew Kirby found her lack of culinary skills funny, so she hoped that would lighten the moment.

"You're cute," Kirby smiled, her tone patronizing. Exactly the response Quinn had angled for. "Stick a fork in it and see if meat comes off the roast easily. If it does, pull it out. If not, give it a little more time."

"Aye. Aye." Quinn gave her a mock salute.

"Oh, will you turn on the burner under the pot with water? We need to cook the egg noodles too."

"Now *that* I can handle." They both laughed, but rather than getting up, Kirby continued to stare. "What?" Quinn asked, afraid of what she might be thinking.

"Nothing. You just…I just…Nothing." Kirby visibly swallowed before she kissed Quinn sweetly and said, "I'm just grateful you're here. Thank you. Let's get ready and head back." Kirby went upstairs while Quinn checked on the roasts and cooked the noodles as instructed.

When Quinn pulled into the parking lot of the hospital, she saw Kirby breathing heavily out of the corner of her eye. She interlaced their fingers. "Hey, it's going to be okay, okay?"

Kirby's temple twitched as she flexed her jaw. Her nostrils flared as she took a deep breath. "I know. I hope. But I'm nervous. When I'm here with her, I see her every hour. Not much changes. Now I've been away for a few hours, and it's a lot scarier. What if she looks worse? What if she is worse? I know it's silly, but while I'm keeping watch, it feels like nothing bad can happen. Without me being here, protecting her, what if something bad happened?"

"If something bad happened, someone would have called you. And she's going to be okay. Let's just go see her, okay?" Quinn squeezed her hand and tried to communicate all the love that she had for Kirby, for her family, through that connection. She prayed that she was right and that Sherry was going to be okay. She felt in her bones that she was.

❖

After three days in the hospital, Kirby was starting to go a little crazy. Her mom's heart still wasn't pumping enough blood through her body, and the doctors didn't know if it was going to be temporary or if her heart wasn't going to heal. They'd taken her off the ventilator and stopped the medication to keep her in a coma, but she hadn't woken up yet. Her dad was trying to remain stoic, but Kirby knew he was a mess inside.

So she had taken to pacing. She paced around the ICU waiting area like a caged tiger until her father finally threw her out, saying that if she was going to release that much nervous energy, she needed to do it outside. So she paced the corridor between the waiting room and the elevator. When she started getting dirty looks from the nurses, she started pacing on different floors. She was terrified of getting too far from the ICU, however, in case her mom did start to wake up.

While pacing, she thought about her parents and how much love they had between them after so many years of marriage. She thought of the last time her mom called her and how she'd dodged the call because she'd broken up with Quinn and didn't want to admit it. She thought about Quinn and how she'd taken a week off work to be there at the hospital while they sat vigil. She realized how lucky she was that Quinn had fallen back into her life after Kirby had literally fallen into her at Pride.

She'd been Kirby's rock in the last twenty-four hours. Holding her hand so Kirby didn't feel alone. Going and grabbing food for everyone so none of them had to leave the hospital or eat the vile cafeteria food. Sometimes, Quinn would pace with Kirby, but often, when Kirby felt the need, Quinn would stay in the waiting area and talk to her father. When Kirby had left this last time, they were talking about a new bourbon that her dad had recently found and wanted to add to the bar.

After a quick tour around the first floor, Kirby's heart fell to her knees when she walked into the waiting room and saw her dad, Kelly, Kaleb, and Quinn standing. She quickly asked, "What's wrong?"

Kelly turned to her and smiled, "Mom squeezed my hand when I was in there and mumbled a little bit. She's not awake yet, but she's starting to come out of it." Kelly had tears streaming down her face, but they were good tears. Kirby ran over and grabbed them all in a group hug.

CHAPTER TWENTY-FOUR

I don't know why everyone is making such a fuss." Kirby's mom said. "I'm fine. I practically have a clean bill of health."

"Mom, you know that isn't true," Kelly said, clearly exasperated. Their mother was not exactly the best patient. "Mom, you need to take it easy. What the doctor said was, this was a wake-up call. You need to reduce your hours at work, start trying to work out a bit, and eat healthier," Kirby said, backing her sister up.

Her mom scoffed. "He said I need to reduce my stress. The only reason I was stressed was because I thought your father was about to have a heart attack. I'm a healthy weight, but my cholesterol *might* be a tick high. That's it. I'm going to be fine."

"Mother." Kirby intentionally used that rather than Mom, the equivalent of her mom using Kirby's first and middle names when she was in trouble. "She said your cholesterol and triglycerides were through the roof *despite* you being a healthy weight and that you needed to make some serious dietary changes."

"Exactly. She *didn't* say I need to reduce my hours or start exercising. Nor did she say I need my daughters to hover over me like I'm a toddler. My heart is fine, no permanent damage. I'm eating healthier already. I read that vegan book and am ninety percent on board. But if you keep making me stay in this *fucking* bed, *girls*, I'm going to have a heart attack out of frustration. I'm not trying to go back to work yet, but holy hell, kids. I'm a grown adult. *And* your mother. Not the other way around."

Her mom had been out of the hospital for a week, and Kirby was close to heading back home. She had a lot of vacation time saved up and was working remotely as much as she could, but she had some clients who were in need of her attention. Since her mom was doing better, Kirby needed to get back, though she promised to visit again soon.

Quinn had gone home five days ago, and for Kirby, the loss was palpable. They video called each other every night, but Kirby wanted to hold her again. And talk. She wanted to set things right with Quinn, but they hadn't talked about the short breakup the whole time she was there. She was pretty sure Quinn still wanted to be with her, even after she had been so horrible, as evidenced by Quinn's coming to Denver and taking care of the whole family. She'd held Kirby every night as they went to sleep, but they hadn't cleared the air, and it was weighing on Kirby's mind.

"How did you almost mess things up with Quinn?" Kelly asked.

Kirby wanted to strangle her for asking that in front of their mom.

"What?" their mom asked. "You tried to ruin things with Quinn? Is that why she went home?" Her voice raised three octaves.

Kirby shot daggers at Kelly, but Kelly gave her a look that seemed to say, you wanted to change the subject too. Which was true, but she *really* didn't want to get into things between her and Quinn. "No. She had to get back to work because she was out of vacation days. Everything went down a few weeks ago. Before you got sick. But Kelly is right. I fucked up. I…" She paused to gather her thoughts, make herself not sound like the villain she was. "I got scared and used the fact that she isn't out to her family to break up with her. I was an idiot. I was afraid. But she surprised me when she showed up. She held my hand. She kept Dad company when I needed to pace the length of fifty football fields. She made sure we all ate. She was—"

"Exactly what we all needed," Kelly interrupted.

"What?" Kirby asked. Disbelief raced hot through her veins. "I thought you didn't like her?"

"Ugh. It wasn't that I didn't like her per se. She was always just so fucking perfect. She worshiped you, she loved Mom and Dad, they loved her. It was really fucking annoying." She made a gagging sound and a silly face, and Kirby punched her in the shoulder. Kelly exaggeratedly rubbed her arm. "Ouch!"

"Don't you 'pouty lip' me. Were you jealous?" Kirby knew the singsong tone of her voice was a little shitty but was compelled to give Kelly a hard time.

"Shut up." Kelly rolled her eyes. "The answer is 'maybe,' but it's clear that woman still loves you. And us. For some unknown reason."

"Don't be catty." Their mom threw an envelope at Kelly like a frisbee and hit her square in the chest. "Just because Kirby is attracted to non-biker studs doesn't mean anything. There's a sweet, tattooed, bearded Harley rider who is going to worship you and love us waiting for you too. It's impossible to imagine someone not loving us." All three women laughed at that image. "And you, Kirby. Don't fuck this up."

"What?" Kirby said, caught off guard yet again.

"You heard me. Don't fuck this up because you're afraid. That girl had a terrible upbringing with her abusive, pious parents and traitorous siblings."

"What?" Kirby repeated again. Evidently, she only had a one-word vocabulary now. But abusive? Traitorous?

"Is that the only word in your word bank anymore?" Her mom asked with a smile. "Go home. Set things right with your woman. And for fuck's sake, stop messing them up."

Kirby only half heard when Kelly replied, "You dropped more f-bombs in the last sixty seconds than I've heard you say in a year, Mom."

Kirby was speechless. She knew Quinn hadn't had the best childhood, but Quinn had never gotten that deep into it. Quinn always changed the subject. How did her mom know so much? Why would Quinn have shared details of her past with her mom but not with Kirby?

"Kirby, stop looking so perplexed. I cornered Quinn at Thanksgiving and wouldn't let her leave until I'd grilled her thoroughly."

"I can't believe she told you details I don't even know." Kirby rubbed her forehead, trying to stop the spinning inside.

"I didn't exactly give her a choice, sweetheart. Talk to her when you get home. I know *you* know how I can get. Irresistible."

Irresistible was not the word that Kirby would use, but there was truth there. When her mom got it into her mind to get to the bottom of something, she was like a terrier chasing a rodent.

"You are something else, Mother."

"I know. Now hand me that pile of mail. I saw something with the hospital logo on it, and I think they screwed up the dates of my stay. I want to make sure I get it resolved before the insurance pays for a service I never received."

Kirby felt a tumbler fall into place in her mind. *Paying for services never received.* Maybe that was why everything was always so over budget at the condo building.

❖

When Kirby landed at Midway, she was expecting to take a taxi home and catch up with Quinn later that evening, so she was pleasantly surprised to see Quinn standing outside of security holding Fred in one hand and a sign with Kirby's name printed on it in rainbow colors in the other. Kirby managed to restrain herself from running to Quinn and simply quickened her pace until she wrapped Quinn in her arms.

"I didn't realize how much I missed you until I had you right here in front of me," Kirby said, face buried in Quinn's hair.

Poor Fred grunted, sandwiched between their chests and winter coats as Quinn pulled her closer. "How can you smell so good after a three-hour flight?" Quinn leaned back. The look in her eyes sent a spark through Kirby. The searing kiss that followed turned that spark into full-blown fireworks.

Quinn's kiss was strong and demanding. Her tongue didn't ask for access to Kirby's mouth; it took it. Kirby melted into her chest, forgetting that they were in public, at the airport, and that Fred was between them until Quinn began to soften their kiss, dialing the intensity back. "I've missed you," she said when she finally pulled away, her thumb still skimming Kirby's jaw.

"Let's go home." They had so much to talk about, but tonight, all she wanted was to lie with her skin against Quinn's and feel their breathing sync as they slipped off to sleep. Maybe a few other horizontal activities too. She was willing to keep their options open.

"My thoughts exactly." Quinn pulled her briskly to the exit, her red roller board suitcase trailing behind them.

The interior of Quinn's car was as spotless as always and smelled masculine but not overly so. Maybe it was that Midsummer Night fragrance or something. Whatever it was, it was unbelievably sexy and even more so when Quinn slid into the car and pulled Kirby in for another searing kiss. "Will you hold Fred-O while I drive?"

Fred looked at Kirby with pure love in his eyes. "Of course. I've missed my main man." He snuggled his scruffy head against her chin, and Kirby tried to swallow an unexpected lump. Quinn, her golden hair like a halo around her face in the parking lot lights, looked so beautiful, and Kirby was struck with how much love she had for Quinn and Fred. How lucky she was that Quinn had dropped everything to be there for her and her family.

"What?" Quinn asked.

"Nothing," Kirby said quickly but didn't look away. As they approached a stoplight, Quinn turned and stared back. Kirby's heart jumped. "I…" she started but didn't want to confess her love in the car. The moment didn't feel right, even though her heart was screaming with the need to let the words out. "I'm just grateful for you. It was a fantastic surprise to see you waiting for me at security."

Quinn's cheeks flushed, though Kirby could barely see in the darkness of the car. "I didn't want to wait any longer to see you. Also Fred was incredibly demanding. He kept asking all day what time you got in tonight. Wouldn't leave me alone about it."

"You really do love me, don't you, boy?" Kirby made kissy sounds at him and was rewarded with a little kiss on the chin.

"He does." Quinn looked over again for a beat longer than was probably safe while driving. "He definitely does." That look felt like it meant a lot more, but it was dark and late, and Kirby wasn't sure.

Ready to break the tension, Kirby switched focus to the condo quandary. "I forgot to tell you, yesterday my mom said something about the hospital charging her for services she didn't receive. It got me thinking, what if that is what the condo manager and a few of the board members are doing? What if the condo was paying for services that it never received, and that's why every job went over budget?"

"Interesting. How do we figure that out?"

"We do a little digging into each project. Review the budget and the actual invoices and see if anything jumps out. Check to see that all companies are actual companies and not fronts. Might not be it, but it is worth exploring."

"You're a smart one."

"You got that right." Kirby poked her in the ribs. "Do you want to come up to my place?" she asked as they got out of the car.

"I thought you'd never ask." Quinn reached for her hand as they walked while Fred's little nails, a tiny pitter-patter on the concrete deck, serenaded them. Kirby had missed this easy camaraderie. And with Fred as their trusty sidekick, of course.

When they got into Kirby's condo, she was tempted to drag Quinn down the hall to her bedroom, but she also wanted to clear the air. When Quinn had shown up in Denver, it had felt like they'd made unspoken promises about the future, but that left a lot of room for misinterpretation. After so much time in the hospital with nothing to do but think and the subsequent realization that she'd been a fool, Kirby knew there were words she needed to say; she needed to make things right.

"Can we talk for a few minutes? Maybe have a glass of wine?" A look of disappointment flashed across Quinn's face as her eyes darted almost imperceptibly down the hallway toward the bedroom.

"I thought we'd..." Quinn took the corner of her bottom lip between her teeth, and Kirby's resolve to talk first faltered.

"Trust me, I want that too. But there is so much I need to say to you. While we were in Denver together wasn't the right time, nor was it during our video chats." Kirby moved into the kitchen via muscle memory, grabbed two wineglasses from the pantry and a bottle out of her rack, not even paying attention to what type or vintage it was. "But we haven't been great at saying what we mean, what we need, what's in our hearts. And I want that to stop. I want to tell you everything that was in my heart when I saw you in Denver. Everything I'm feeling now." She paused as she turned the corkscrew and look directly at Quinn. "Everything I've always felt." The squeak of the cork when Kirby began turning the corkscrew again was nearly deafening in the quiet condo.

Quinn nodded, but Kirby saw her hand tremble slightly when she handed her a glass.

Once they were settled on the loveseat, knees angled together and touching, Kirby said, "Before I got the call about Mom, Allie was in town. She..." Kirby trailed off, chuckling as she remembered Allie's diatribe. "She didn't pull her punches, and—"

Quinn shook her head and tried to interrupt. "You were right, though."

Kirby tucked a piece of hair behind Quinn's ear, lingering for a beat. "I wasn't. I was so busy trying to protect my heart that I broke it myself...before you could. I was looking for an excuse, and I found it. And then I got the worst news of my life."

Quinn grabbed her hand, squeezing it while rubbing a thumb over the back.

"We didn't know if she was going to pull through. I felt so alone. More alone than I've ever felt. Since before birth, my mom has been my rock. She was always my confidant, my co-conspirator. And there was nothing I could do. She looked so small on the ventilator." Her throat felt thick with unshed tears. "The only other person I've ever been close to like that is you. And I messed it up. Short of Mom waking up, all I wanted was for you to be there. To hold my hand, to hold me and tell me everything was going to be okay. And then you were there, and you did all of those things. Without me asking. Without asking anything in return."

Kirby finally looked up. Quinn, who never cried, had tears threatening. "I love you," she whispered. "How could I stay away when you were going through that?"

"I love you too. And I can't believe you beat me to saying it. It's been on the tip of my tongue since you got to Denver."

"It's been on the tip of my tongue since the moment you stomped on my foot at Pride, so I've been repressing it a little longer. You were right about my family. I have no idea why I even pretended to have a relationship with them, and I was being a coward by living a lie to maintain the semblance of a relationship that never existed. I wanted to be normal and have a normal mom and dad, but pretending doesn't make it so."

Quinn scoffed, and Kirby squeezed her hand, encouraging her to continue.

"Both my parents were perfect to the outside world. Pastor, trophy wife, perfect kids, but they weren't good people. They were abusive during my childhood. My siblings and I walked around on eggshells, trying to do whatever it took to avoid attention. My most egregious offense was stumbling in the outlandishly high heels Mom wanted us to wear. That's why I used to practice every single night and why I can wear heels almost twenty-four seven. Well, that was the most frequent offense until I was seventeen and met a girl."

Quinn cleared her throat, and Kirby hated to see her struggling. "We don't have to talk about this tonight if you don't want."

Quinn shook her head. "No, I want you to know. No more secrets. I know I shouldn't have any shame, and I am working on it." She met Kirby's gaze. "I was a senior in high school, and her name was Cynthia. She had the most lustrous, long brown hair. We were in the same trigonometry class and started studying together. It wasn't my best subject, and she had taken it at her last school. Cynthia and I flirted for a few weeks, though I didn't understand that was what it was at the time. I didn't have crushes on any of the boys at school, but liking girls that way wasn't on my radar. It was on Cynthia's, though. She was from San Francisco and was much more worldly than I. One afternoon, we were at her house studying, and she kissed me. It was the first life-altering moment of my young life, even though it was a very chaste,

G-rated kiss that could easily have been in a Disney movie. If they had lesbian kisses on Disney." She laughed sardonically.

Kirby sat her glass down and scooted closer to Quinn, interlacing their fingers. The vision of a seventeen-year-old Quinn discovering her sexuality made her smile, but she knew the story was about to get more difficult for Quinn and wanted to be nearer. She wished she could take away, or at least lessen, her pain.

"We never did anything more than kiss, but one afternoon, Cynthia was at my house, and we were lying on my bed kissing rather than studying. My mom came in to grab my laundry without knocking and saw us. We jumped apart, but the damage had been done. Mom kicked Cynthia out and told her she wasn't welcome in our home again. Mom locked me in my room until Dad got home from the church office. I tried to deny that we'd been doing anything, that we'd ever done it before, but it didn't matter. Mom and Dad tag-teamed that night, telling me that I was unnatural and took turns trying to beat the gay out of me."

Kirby had always known she was lucky with how well her family took her coming out, even as a child. But hearing Quinn's story chilled her to the bone, despite the warmth from the wine and the heat of love coursing through her. "Quinn…"

"I didn't tell you for sympathy. I just wanted you to understand. I called my mom before I went to Denver and came out. I told her I was a lesbian, that I'd always been a lesbian, and despite her and Dad's best efforts to pound the gay out, I was still a lesbian. I wasn't going to let my baggage shame me anymore."

Kirby winced. "How did you leave it with them?"

"My mom told me I was going to hell. I told her I was sorry to hear that she felt that way, but I disagreed. I told her I hoped she could see past her hate so we could someday have an actual relationship, but I was no longer going to masochistically keep coming home for holidays while pretending to be someone that I'm not."

Kirby was disgusted that people still thought it was okay to say things like that. Especially to their own child. Kirby wasn't normally a confrontational person but would love to give Quinn's mom a piece of her mind. "I'm so sorry you had to draw that line in the sand, but I am so proud of you. And I am sorry if you have truly lost them."

"It's hard to lose something you never had." Quinn shook her head and ran her thumb along the bottom of her eye, capturing a tear before it could fall. "Interestingly," she continued, "I texted my siblings and came out, thinking I would never hear from them again. But we've actually been having a good conversation. I don't think we'll ever be besties, but I'm closer to them now than I have been since before I was seventeen. I would happily trade a relationship with the assholes who birthed me to have even a superficial relationship with my siblings. We'd been close from birth—united against our parents—until the gay incident. Then I was the outcast. They started treating me like they could catch the gay from me. My two younger brothers fought over who didn't have to sit next to me at dinner, and my older sisters who were at college stopped coming home and hanging out with me. I'd always been reserved and a bit of a loner, but after that, I pulled even more into myself. I couldn't trust anyone, and I felt even more uncomfortable in my skin. I thought anyone who saw me could see the gay in one glance."

Kirby's heart broke for seventeen-year-old Quinn, confronted with the harshness of homophobia so blatantly when she was barely more than a baby. It was no wonder she was so hopeless at almost being outed. She'd joined the Navy to get away from home and certainly couldn't go back if she'd been dishonorably discharged for "homosexual conduct," as the military termed it. Unlike Kirby, Quinn had never had a safe place to land. Kirby wished that Quinn could have trusted her to be her safe place, but Quinn hadn't had many, if any, experiences in life to show her that anyone could be trusted. Her panic made a lot more sense.

"Oh, Quinn." Kirby slid closer, pressing the length of their sides together.

Quinn looked into her glass before she took a sip. "Wait a second. Is this our wine? From our winery?" Her voice was heavy with disbelief.

"I didn't look at what I grabbed. It could be. Do you want me to go check?"

"Ha." Quinn pointed at her. "*You* told me the second time we ran into each other that you barely even remembered the winery, and you hadn't had the wine since."

Kirby half smiled and tried to look sheepish. "I'm not sure if you could tell when we first started running into each other, but I wasn't happy to see you."

"That's putting it mildly."

"I was angry—so angry—because I told myself I was over you. I'd been telling myself I was over you for years, but I clearly wasn't. I had never moved on, and every time I saw you, you took my breath away. Every time I saw you, it became more apparent that I wasn't over you—nowhere close to it—but I wasn't ready to admit it. I couldn't admit it. I was doing a lot of lying back then. Lying to myself, lying to my friends, lying to you. The wine was probably one of the least consequential lies that I came up with." Kirby looked down as she laughed.

Quinn traced little shapes on the back of her hand, making it hard to concentrate, but Kirby pressed on. "Despite how angry I was with you, you were always the one. I think that's why I was so devastated when we broke up. I could see our future all the way to us being little old biddies sitting on our front porch in a loveseat rocking chair, drinking wine, and in an instant, it was all gone. I didn't understand how there could be a future without you."

"I will never do anything to jeopardize that future again. I love you." Quinn paused and closed her eyes. "I also love how that feels rolling off my tongue again. It feels like my tongue is home."

"I love you too. Mmm. That does feel good. Though I can think of a better home for your tongue if you're willing. You know, now that we've cleared the air." Her eyes were drawn to Quinn's mouth as she drew in the side of her lip. Her pulse quickened as she waited for Quinn's response.

"I can't think of anything else I'd rather do."

EPILOGUE

I cannot believe that the condo manager and two board members embezzled over one and a half million dollars from the condo association, and no one realized what was happening," Quinn said to Jillian and Kirby as they sat around their high-top table.

Jillian shook her head. "I know. The fact that the condo manger, the chief engineer, and two board members—technically three, considering Mr. Jones before his passing—were on board with it is disgusting. Sincerely, thank you both for helping me. Figuring out that they were passing through fake invoices in legitimate projects was impressive, ladies."

"It wasn't me. You should thank Kirby." Quinn squeezed her hand and smiled. She was so proud of her.

"Don't be so bashful, Quinn. You helped too. And you roped me in to help you, showing amazing foresight."

"Yes, but you're the one who figured out the fake invoice piece of it." Quinn kissed her cheek. Sometimes, it still boggled her mind how easily they clicked together after all this time, but Quinn was no longer afraid. Kirby was the best friend she'd ever had and still owned her heart. Luckily, she now knew she owned Kirby's too.

"True. Once I reached out to a general contractor friend of mine, it made a lot more sense. There's no reason to have a company no one has ever heard of, which doesn't even have a website, perform 'wall prep' for every project, no matter the scope." Kirby shook her head, and Quinn was still in disbelief that so many people were in on this, and yet no one figured it out until Jillian raised the red flag.

"To the good news." Jillian raised her beer glass. "The management company wanted to keep this quiet, so they're fully reimbursing the association for all the money that was embezzled, we have a new manager, a new chief engineer, we're filing charges against the board members, and association dues are back where they should be. We're almost whole again, and it's all thanks to the two of you. Truly. Here's to you." Quinn and Kirby lifted their glasses and toasted a job well done. And a bright future ahead.

Later that evening, Quinn and Kirby were curled in bed, Quinn's head on Kirby's chest, and Kirby tracing a path up and down her back. Quinn let out a purr of pure satisfaction.

"What are you thinking about?" Kirby asked.

"How lucky I am." Quinn pressed up onto her elbow. "A year ago, I thought I could be happy for the rest of my life focusing on my new job, my condo, Fred. But I also thought that I'd die an old spinster, having never found love again. And yet, somehow, here you are."

"Here *we* are." Kirby pulled Quinn down and kissed her. Thoroughly. By the time Quinn pulled away, she was writhing on Kirby, their breasts rubbing together. Kirby's knee had also lifted at some point, putting the most delicious pressure directly on her sex. "But I think I'm the lucky one."

"We can both be right. Regardless, seems like we're both winners." Quinn smoothed the side of Kirby's face, ran her thumb along Kirby's bottom lip. When Kirby sunk her teeth into the pad of Quinn's thumb, she pushed her hips harder into Kirby's thigh but wasn't finished. "For the past ten years, it's like I've been carrying you with me. You were always right outside my field of vision, but I always knew you were there. There has always been something between us. Something that defied all logic and rationality. I've never stopped loving you. Never stopped longing for you. You are it for me. I love you so much. So, so much."

"I love you too. More than I would have ever believed possible. Now get back down here and show me exactly how much you love me."

Quinn spent the rest of the night, and vowed to spend the rest of her life doing exactly that.

About the Author

Krystina Rivers has been a lover of romance novels since she was probably too young to read them and developed an affinity for lesbian romance novels after she found her first lesbian romance on a shelf in a used bookstore in 2001. Despite a lifelong desire to write romances, she never had the time to write her own until the COVID-19 pandemic struck, and she no longer had to commute to the office or travel regularly for work.

Krystina grew up in Florida but, after spending six years in the military, now calls Chicago home. She works in commercial real estate and lives with her wife and their two dogs and three cats. When not working or writing, Krystina can be found reading with a glass of wine in hand, doing yoga (occasionally with a glass of wine in hand), snuggling with her fur-babies, or trying to convince herself that it is not too cold to go for a jog outside.

Books Available From Bold Strokes Books

The Business of Pleasure by Ronica Black. Editor in chief Valerie Raffield is quickly becoming smitten by Lennox, the graphic artist she's hired to work remotely. But when Lennox doesn't show for their first face-to-face meeting, Valerie's heart and her business may be in jeopardy. (978-1-63679-134-0)

Cold Blood by Genevieve McCluer. Maybe together, Kalila and Dorenia have a chance of taking down the vampires who have eluded them all these years. And maybe, in each other, they can find a love worth living for. (978-1-63679-195-1)

Greener Pastures by Aurora Rey. When city girl and CPA Audrey Adams finds herself tending her aunt's farm, will Rowan Marshall—the charming cider maker next door—turn out to be her saving grace or the bane of her existence? (978-1-63679-116-6)

Grounded by Amanda Radley. For a second chance, Olivia and Emily will need to accept their mistakes, learn to communicate properly, and with a little help from five-year-old Henry, fall madly in love all over again. Sequel to Flight SQA016. (978-1-63679-241-5)

The Hummingbird Sanctuary by Erin Zak. The Hummingbird Sanctuary, Colorado's hottest resort destination: Come for the mountains, stay for the charm, and enjoy the drama as Olive, Eleanor, and Harriet figure out the meaning of true friendship. (978-1-63679-163-0)

Journey's End by Amanda Radley. In this heartwarming conclusion to the Flight series, Olivia and Emily must finally decide what they want, what they need, and how to follow the dreams of their hearts. (978-1-63679-233-0)

Secret Agent by Michelle Larkin. CIA agent Peyton North embarks on a global chase to apprehend rogue agent Zoey Blackwood, but her commitment to the mission is tested as the sparks between them ignite and their sizzling attraction approaches a point of no return. (978-1-63555-753-4)

Something Between Us by Krystina Rivers. A decade after her heart was broken under Don't Ask, Don't Tell, Kirby runs into her first love and has to decide if what's still between them is enough to heal her broken heart. (978-1-63679-135-7)

Sugar Girl by Emma L McGeown. Having traded in traditional romance for the perks of Sugar Dating, Ciara Reilly not only enjoys the no-strings-attached arrangement, she's also a hit with her clients. That is, until she meets the beautiful entrepreneur Charlie Keller, who makes her want to go sugar-free. (978-1-63679-156-2)

With a Twist by Georgia Beers. Starting over isn't easy for Amelia Martini. When the irritatingly cheerful Kirby Dupress comes into her life, will Amelia be brave enough to go after the love she really wants? (978-1-63555-987-3)

The Witch Queen's Mate by Jennifer Karter. Barra and Silvi must overcome their ingrained hatred and prejudice to use Barra's magic and save both their peoples from not just slavery, but destruction. (978-1-63679-202-6)

Business of the Heart by Claire Forsythe. When a hopeless romantic meets a tough-as-nails cynic, they'll need to overcome the wounds of the past to discover that their hearts are the most important business of all. (978-1-63679-167-8)

Dying for You by Jenny Frame. Can Victorija Dred keep an age-old vow and fight the need to take blood from Daisy Macdougall? (978-1-63679-073-2)

Exclusive by Melissa Brayden. Skylar Ruiz lands the TV reporting job of a lifetime, but is she willing to sacrifice it all for the love of her longtime crush, anchorwoman Carolyn McNamara? (978-1-63679-112-8)

The Game by Jan Gayle. Ryan Gibbs is a talented golfer, but her guilt means she may never leave her small town, even if Katherine Reese tempts her with competition and passion. (978-1-63679-126-5)

Her Duchess to Desire by Jane Walsh. An up-and-coming interior designer seeks to create a happily ever after with an intriguing duchess, proving that love never goes out of fashion. (978-1-63679-065-7)

Take Her Down by Lauren Emily Whalen. Stakes are cutthroat, scheming is creative, and loyalty is ever-changing in this queer, female-driven YA retelling of Shakespeare's Julius Caesar. (978-1-63679-089-3)

Whereabouts Unknown by Meredith Doench. While homicide detective Theodora Madsen recovers from a potentially career-ending injury, she scrambles to solve the cases of two missing sixteen-year-old girls from Ohio. (978-1-63555-647-6)

Deadly Secrets by VK Powell. Corporate criminals want whistleblower Jana Elliott permanently silenced, but Rafe Silva will risk everything to keep the woman she loves safe. (978-1-63679-087-9)

Enchanted Autumn by Ursula Klein. When Elizabeth comes to Salem, Massachusetts, to study the witch trials, she never expects to find love—or an actual witch...and Hazel might just turn out to be both. (978-1-63679-104-3)

Escorted by Renee Roman. When fantasy meets reality, will escort Ryan Lewis be able to walk away from a chance at forever with her new client Dani? (978-1-63679-039-8)

Her Heart's Desire by Anne Shade. Two women. One choice. Will Eve and Lynette be able to overcome their doubts and fears to embrace their deepest desire? (978-1-63679-102-9)

My Secret Valentine by Julie Cannon, Erin Dutton & Anne Shade. Winning the heart of your secret Valentine? These award-winning authors agree, there is no better way to fall in love. (978-1-63679-071-8)

Perilous Obsession by Carsen Taite. When reporter Macy Moran becomes consumed with solving a cold case, will her quest for the truth bring her closer to Detective Beck Ramsey or will her obsession with finding a murderer rob her of a chance at true love? (978-1-63679-009-1)

Reading Her by Amanda Radley. Lauren and Allegra learn love and happiness are right where they least expect it. There's just one problem: Lauren has a secret she cannot tell anyone, and Allegra knows she's hiding something. (978-1-63679-075-6)

The Willing by Lyn Hemphill. Kitty Wilson doesn't know how, but she can bring people back from the dead as long as someone is willing to take their place and keep the universe in balance. (978-1-63679-083-1)

Watching Over Her by Ronica Black. As they face the snowstorm of the century, and the looming threat of a stalker, Riley and Zoey just might find love in the most unexpected of places. (978-1-63679-100-5)

Always by Kris Bryant. When a pushy American private investigator shows up demanding to meet the woman in Camila's artwork, instead of introducing her to her great-grandmother, Camila decides to lead her on a wild goose chase all over Italy. (978-1-63679-027-5)

Exes and O's by Joy Argento. Ali and Madison really only have one thing in common. The girl who broke their heart may be the only one who can put it back together. (978-1-63679-017-6)

Paris Rules by Jaime Maddox. Carly Becker has been searching for the perfect woman all her life, but no one ever seems to be just right until Paige Waterford checks all her boxes, except the most important one—she's married. (978-1-63679-077-0)

Shadow Dancers by Suzie Clarke. In this third and final book in the Moon Shadow series, Rachel must find a way to become the hunter and not the hunted, and this time she will meet Eshee Yumiko head-on. (978-1-63555-829-6)

The Kiss by C.A. Popovich. When her wife refuses their divorce and begins to stalk her, threatening her life, Kate realizes to protect her new love, Leslie, she has to let her go, even if it breaks her heart. (978-1-63679-079-4)

The Wedding Setup by Charlotte Greene. When Ryann, a big-time New York executive, goes to Colorado to help out with her best friend's wedding, she never expects to fall for the maid of honor. (978-1-63679-033-6)

Velocity by Gun Brooke. Holly and Claire work toward an uncertain future preparing for an alien space mission, and only one thing is certain—they will have to risk their lives, and their hearts, to discover the truth. (978-1-63555-983-5)